His Captive Asset

His Captive

Asset

UNA ROHR

His Captive Asset

Copyright © 2020 by Una Rohr

All rights reserved. No part of this book may be reproduced or transmitted in any form or by any means without written permission of the author.

ISBN: 979-8-9882794-9-5

Published by:
Bound & Crowned Press

CONTENT EXPECTATIONS
AND TRIGGER WARNING

This is a Slow-Burn,
Enemies-to-Lovers Romance

There is no explicit spice in Part I, and things only start to heat up in Part II. Please sit back and (I hope!) enjoy the ride.

This is a Dark Romance

When we (eventually) get spicy, we get edgy. This story is intended as a work of fiction and does not function as guide on how to safely practice kink in the real world. *His Captive Asset* features two characters operating under several muddying layers of games and desires. They aren't sure what they themselves want or what the other wants, and boundaries will be pushed. There are no safe words in espionage.

Please do not read this if kink is offensive to you. The protagonist in this story is selling herself as a sub at action, so certain dark desires are contained within.

Lastly, this is an entirely fictitious story involving non-existent branches of British and American Intelligence agencies conceived solely for the benefit of this work. Neither the departments created within, nor any events described, are real or based on real-life occurrences. Any similarity to individuals either living or dead is not intended by the author.

PART I
God's Gift to
British Intelligence

CHAPTER 1

N O ONE EVER mentioned my name in our weekly meetings, so I was stunned silent when it happened. Just like everyone else in the room.

Each sleek head around the ODX conference table turned in my direction, sending my heart racing.

To make matters worse, I'd just lifted a blueberry muffin to my face. *Of course.* Unlike the glamazon agents to my left and right–who would never dare permit carbs to pass their perfectly plump lips and settle on their subtly curved hips–I dug into our catered breakfast.

Freezing mid-bite, a crumbly chunk of fruit and bread fell from my open mouth to land noticeably on my meeting notes. Out of the corner of my eye, I saw Adriana cringe on my behalf.

"Poppy?" Riley asked the question on everyone's mind. "Poppy's not an agent. She's an assistant data admin."

Junior Process Manager, I corrected. If only in my mind.

Carter, our Division Head, held up one hand.

"I know, I know. But we've scoured the database for any agents, active or retired, as well as any sleepers to pull from the field, and no one matches the necessary physical description *but* Poppy. The girl we need to impersonate is nineteen, petite, redheaded, and fluent in Russian. Besides, she won't be an agent, more like our own… planned, planted asset."

My palms began to sweat.

Is he saying… he wants me for a mission?

"Poppy is twenty-four," Adriana pointed out, literally pointing one blood-red fingernail in my direction. She was thirty-three but decided to stop aging at twenty-seven. Her body obeyed her command, much like people did when she asserted her will.

"And she looks seventeen," Carter replied.

I frowned, resisting the urge to cross my arms over my modest chest–a deficiency highlighted by the ample sexuality oozing from every other female in the room.

"What's the mission?" Adriana asked.

Lips forming a tight circle under his graying moustache, Carter sucked in a breath.

Right there–that should have warned me. He put our team of female agents in mortal danger every day. What could possibly make *him* hesitate to deliver the specs?

"It's an immersive event for the wealthy with particular, intimate proclivities."

A guttural laugh from Marxon cut across the room. "Tell it like it is, boss. It's a fetish party where rich guys buy submissive girls at auction. The girls volunteer to be sexual playthings for the week."

Whistles, cat calls, and laughter filled the brightly-lit room. To my left, Riley slammed the table as he hooted.

My face burned and I hoped the embarrassment read as distaste and *not* any secret titillation at the word *submissive*.

Carter keyed up a picture onto his laptop, projecting the image to the room.

I shifted uncomfortably as I stared at what could be my own photograph, in a *much* more flattering light. What caught my attention most was the particular shade of red hair—not dark, auburn—but bright, coppery. Vibrant blue eyes stared at the camera. With her long, strawberry hair and soft face, the girl did bear a resemblance to me. A prettier version of me.

"Klara Volkov," Carter announced. "Born in New York City to parents who emigrated from Russia in 1991. Fluent in English and Russian. Very precocious. She's been chomping at the bit to be of age to sell herself at this party. When her father fell ill, she delayed volunteering last year."

Adriana snapped, "And how, pray tell, has this Klara girl been motivated not to attend this year?"

"Marxon was very convincing."

Marxon grinned, crossing arms as thick as honey-baked hams.

"Plus, we sweetened the deal by getting her father on an experimental drug and added a nice token of our esteem so that their family doesn't have to worry about paying the mortgage while he's in treatment."

The money and the muscle, I thought.

Carter clicked a new picture, displaying a castle so impos-ing my mouth dropped. The stone structure was a legitimate fortress, straight out of the medieval ages, straight out of a fantasy, with turrets and ramparts. If I had to guess, it easily held fifty rooms or more and made my heart flutter just to glimpse on the screen.

"Each year the event is held at Wistlock Castle in Wiltshire, England, two hours west of London. The next event is in two weeks. While most of the attendees are innocent, we have reason to believe someone involved in the planning, or participating in the bidding, is part of a sex trafficking ring. They may be soliciting females during the party and they're especially focused on targeting youthful and underage girls. We need an asset to fly to London and impersonate Klara, to take her place at auction and find out any information she can. *This is not a mission to engage.* The objective is to observe and report."

My head spun, sluggish to comprehend. I misheard Carter. We needed to slow down and start again.

"I—I do speak a little Russian," I said, finding my voice. "But I don't know anything about the current political climate, customs…"

"That's fine," Carter said. "You just need language basics in case a buyer wants to converse."

Staring at me, Adriana blinked her large, dark eyes. She sat like an elegant bird, half-perched on the credenza, having arrived late, as usual. I knew she was upset because she let her South African accent slip.

"You want Poppy to pretend to be some kind of sex slave to a bunch of rich guys for a week? In order to uncover an actual sex slave ring?"

"It's not a party for sex slaves, it's for submissives who are game to play," Riley said, waggling his eyebrows suggestively. "She only has to have sex with one guy, the guy who buys her."

Adriana's death stare clearly said, *that makes it better?* Riley raised his hands in defense but he didn't stop grinning.

It's not as if Adriana and our other female agents didn't do that sort of thing all the time. But that was their job. That was why they spent years in training.

I hadn't the skills to fight or seduce or even operate in a stealthy manner. I'd never been in the field. I hardly left my cubicle, even for lunch.

"So why *this* party?" Margot asked from across the table, tossing her silky blonde waves as she spoke.

"We're not sure," Carter hedged. "It may be that the recruiter believes a submissive girl is more likely to acclimate to her new position, once she finds herself in a foreign country with no hope of escape."

My stomach instantly soured, making me feel ill.

"As I said, if we're lucky, our asset will be approached in an attempt to recruit her, or she may observe the attempted recruitment of someone else. It would perhaps be in the form of an invitation to an exotic party further abroad. Could be Tangiers, could be Mersin. Somewhere to function as a gateway to her final destination."

I really felt like I was going to throw up the muffin I'd just eaten as Carter detailed a girl's worst nightmare. A parent's worst nightmare. Like something from that movie, only in real life there was no handsome Irish father to rescue his daughter at the end.

A feeling began crystalizing in my gut, fast and certain. I *wanted* to be assigned this mission. More than just for needing to move up in the agency, although I desperately sought that too. But most of all, I wanted to do something meaningful, to help these women.

Debate flooded the room, all at once.

About me.

"How is Poppy going to pose as a seductress? Look how she blushes just talking about it."

"Not a seductress, a submissive. It's called modesty. And some Dominant men like that shade of shame on a lady."

"What would you *know about modesty, Margot?"*

"She doesn't have much in the way of breasts."

"But she's got a nice ass."

Smacking my hand against my forehead, I avoided eye contact, waiting out the *delightful* group scrutiny of my physical failings. But it sank even further, just to complete my humiliation.

"What about Tereza, the girl from Romania? She looks like this Klara woman," Adriana volunteered.

"Tereza's hair is dark," Carter said. "We need someone with red hair on… all parts of her body."

I froze.

He couldn't mean…

"So, shave her pubic hair," Adriana shrugged.

Oh my god, we were not having this conversation in the middle of the workday.

"The men like the girls to arrive with some covering, in case they prefer it or want to remove it themselves." Carter brought his own hand to his forehead, rubbing with annoyance. "There's actually an extensive rule book to follow. Even if we dye it, Tereza's body hair is black and it's going to show somewhere. *Enough,"* Carter warned.

"We don't even know if her bush is red," Riley helpfully pointed out.

Once again, the heads of all my colleagues swung in my direction.

To hear the color of my pubic hair.

I was certain my face turned as red as the answer. My stiff, collared shirt clung to my body with newly-formed sweat. Seeming to have lost my ability to speak, I stuttered to affirm an auburn shade.

"It's—um, well, it's—"

Before I could finish, a new voice entered the conversation from behind me, brusquely interrupting. His arrogant, accented tone could not be mistaken.

"She's not an asset."

The declaration, seeming to carry a double meaning, pierced me as physically as if a screwdriver plunged into my chest and spun, painfully twirling my tendons and tightening my muscles. I longed for the earth to open up and swallow me.

Not him, I thought, grinding my teeth, face flushing deeper. Anyone but *him* in the midst of *this* discussion. What was he doing here?

"It's not about the color of the girl's nether region," he remarked, tone clipped. Sauntering through the back door, his assertion cut across the room. Shame rose within me at his easy dismissal; resentment boiled at the way he thought the world and everyone in it attended his every word.

"It's that she's entirely incapable of succeeding in this mission. She has no talent or skill in the field whatsoever."

Even if he had a point, he didn't need to make it so cruelly.

God, I hated him.

CHAPTER 2

GRAHAM *FUCKING* KELLUM.

God's gift to British Intelligence.

And to women, you'd think, by the way even the femme fatales around me bat their lashes and smiled seductively when he strode to the table, as if *they* vied for *his* attention. I could see their eyes rake over his form to take in the cut of his bespoke suit, the shine on his polished shoes, the easy manner in which he carried himself that miraculously endeared him to the men as well as the women.

Graham fucking Kellum. The man who could serve a backhanded compliment as easily as he could wield a backhanded swing on the court, courtesy of his overpriced education. Though he hardly bothered veiling any comments at me, preferring to serve disdain my way. It bothered me all the more that no one else seemed irked by his cocksure attitude; indeed, many fawned over him because of it.

In all fairness, he *could* be charming to others. But he belittled me whenever work took him this side of the pond. Which seemed frequent the past few months.

I guessed our offices were cooperating now.

Aspen, who'd been curiously silent throughout, finally spoke up.

"Graham makes a sound point. Do we really want to jeopardize something this important by placing it in the hands of an admin?"

Junior Process Manager, I mentally screamed.

"With nothing to recommend her physically? No offense of course, Poppy."

Aspen smiled one perfectly blood-boiling smile in my direction, smoothing back her long, chestnut hair.

Of course she sided with Graham. Despite my friendliness to everyone in the office, Aspen liked to pretend I didn't exist, even on the best of days. On the worst, her face seemed to twitch, scrunching her nose when I entered a conversation or walked by. My usual philosophy–*kill 'em with kindness*–oddly irritated her more, so I'd switched to an avoidance scheme. If Aspen walked into a room, I found reason to scurry out.

Opening my mouth to defend myself–without a real plan as to what to say–Margot beat me to it.

"I think she makes a good candidate," Margot remarked, her southern twang coming through. "She'd be cute at auction. With that long hair and wideset eyes and round face, she kind of looks like a doll. Or she would, if she contoured her make-up and filled in her brows and took down her hair. And if she stopped wearing those pantsuits. And wore a better bra to make it look like she's got something on top…" Margot trailed off, clearly assessing a long list of my necessary improvements in her head.

Quite helpful.

"Why can't we put a man on this job? As a buyer, instead?" Adriana asked.

"The screening process for acceptance as a woman is difficult enough. For a man, it's nearly impossible," Carter explained. "While the girls come from all over the world, the men are frequently repeat participants from an elite circle of buyers. Often they're even familiar with one another."

Adriana sneered. "Got it. So just a bunch of rich blokes getting their jollies off in friendly unison."

"She could be our little Russian doll," someone piped up. "What are those things called again? Where you open them up and another doll is hidden inside?"

"Who gave you an education in Russian?" Riley asked, cutting in. "Daddy dearest?"

Directly over my shoulder, Graham slapped a folder onto the table, making me jump—and to my mortification, *dammit*—let out a little squeal.

Was that a dossier on me?

"Her mother. Her father gave her that stubborn set to her mouth that isn't equipped to remain sufficiently shut under cover."

Graham wasn't at all malicious with his words, just matter-of-fact, which somehow made it worse. He hovered behind me, over me, forcing me to crane my neck up if I wanted to look at him. He held Carter's gaze, and the way the two men stared at one another made me feel like a silent conversation went on between them.

A frustrating lump formed in my throat. On the one hand, I felt small. Like a child unable to take part in the game the grown-ups played, a game every other woman in that room played. On the other, I felt exposed in a very adult manner, my sexuality–or lack thereof–laid bare on the conference table for all to examine its worth.

What right did Graham have to steal this opportunity from me? Because he was older and outranked me? Despite numerous appearances of late, he wasn't even employed at ODX. *He wasn't even an American citizen.*

Maybe other women jumped to satisfy his whims, but I'd be damned if he was going to order me around.

I *would* be like a Russian doll. Who knew what surprises lay beneath my surface?

In a moment of bravery, I squared my shoulders. Letting one side of my lip curl, I tilted my head down and looked up with a gaze both firm and suggestive.

"I can do it," I said.

Every head swung in my direction.

The sound of my voice–gravelly, confident–surprised even me, belying the frantic beat of my heart.

Bodies froze. Carter inhaled deeply, considering his verdict, I hoped.

From the way he crossed his arms and the tough set to his face, I couldn't tell what it might be. His well-developed mask, like everyone's in the room, was unbreachable if he willed it so.

It seemed the longest break in history as I held my breath, pulse racing. Once again, I got the feeling something silent crossed between Graham and our Division Head as the two men stared.

Finally, Carter cocked his head to the side and proclaimed, "I'm assigning Poppy to this mission. I want a team of our best girls to prep her."

Elation shot through my chest. *Take that, Graham,* I thought, relishing my victory.

Out of the corner of my eye, I watched him for a reaction. But I saw only a twitch in the muscle of his cheek, indicating he'd perhaps clenched his jaw.

"How are we going to get Poppy ready for a mission in two weeks?" Adriana asked. "No offense, Poppy, but we've been training half our lives. What can we possibly teach her in that short time that will prepare her for the multitude of scenarios she might face in the field?"

"I'm well aware, Adriana," Carter said, waving a hand. "Do the best you can. The nature of this… function… works on her behalf. She doesn't need to actively lure a mark. She just has to—"

"Sit pretty and auction herself to a man's every sexual desire for a week."

Carter shot Adriana a warning look. "Since you're the most skeptical, I'm putting you in charge of her transformation. You and Margot will see to whatever grooming she requires as well as instructing her in the basics of subterfuge, self-defense, asset protocol…"

Margot rubbed her hands together with anticipation.

"Makeover," she cooed, eyes sizing me up like I was, in fact, a doll for play.

CHAPTER 3

I WALKED THE HALL practically *floating* to the gym. ODX, Oubliette Division X, was one of several semi-rogue branches of covert intelligence in the United States. Oubliette, meaning a place to put us and forget about us. Once the government created our organization, they wanted to know little-to-nothing further about our existence.

Plausible deniability and all that.

I couldn't help but grin as I pictured myself sauntering through that stunning castle during an erotic party like *Eyes Wide Shut*. Only a lot less creepy. And without any potential for murder, I hoped.

Turning down the hall, I passed Carter's office on my way to the gym. His door was ajar.

"Poppy," he called out, catching me as I walked by.

I halted, heart skipping a beat.

"Don't worry about the mission. We've got someone else to do it."

I blinked, slow to process the sudden news. My stomach understood first—it sank. I failed to school my face before it too fell, clearly disappointed.

Some spy I made.

No, I scolded myself. *If you want something, you have to fight for it.*

Stepping into Carter's office, I pushed the door wide. "Sir, I—"

My eyes rounded. Graham sat the chair opposite Carter's desk, staring at me with an expression I couldn't read.

Oh, you bastard. You had something to do with this.

He held a cigarette in his right hand, which was odd, because I'd never seen him smoke before. And he'd had plenty of opportunities around Carter, who smoked a pack a day. Also, it was prohibited inside the building.

I wanted to say a million things. I wanted to stand up for myself. To argue for my capabilities, to fight for the mission. But at the sight of Graham, I opened my mouth and what came out wasn't any of those things.

God, it wasn't even close.

"You can't smoke in here. It's against company policy."

What?

Why had I said that?

What was wrong with me?

I sounded like a petulant child.

He smirked, that son-of-a-bitch smirked. It looked boyish, roguish, on his masculine face.

Without any urgency to reply, he took a drag on his cigarette. After he blew out a puff of smoke, he said, "Well, Ms. Greer, are you just going to stand there or are you going to report me to HR?"

My cheeks flushed.

I fucking hated him.

A devil caught my tongue as I countered, "Are you just going to sit there or are you going to tell me what you said to Carter to rip me off the mission?"

At my newfound bravado, a heavy silence filled the room, but Graham didn't seem to care. The British bastard raised his eyebrows at me and the smirk tilted upwards just a hint, almost enough to be called a grin.

Did he think I'd find it charming like all the other girls? Because I didn't.

I crossed my arms and met his stare, raising my own eyebrows in return.

Carter's gaze flicked back-and-forth between the two of us and I wondered what went on behind his stony expression.

"Graham has a colleague better suited to the role," he explained. "Agent Brooks. She's trained, she's a match for Klara, and she's already in London."

Hearing the finality of my boss's decision, my whole body deflated. It wasn't like me to get emotional at work, yet I suddenly wanted to cry.

It's just that I really wanted the opportunity.

It's just that Graham really got under my skin.

Somehow, I mustered the composure to nod and uttered, "I understand. Thank you for the consideration anyway."

I knew my voice was thin and small and I scurried away before anyone could see my quivering lip. I didn't stop my brisk pace until I reached the doors leading to the rear parking lot.

So close, I thought. *I'd been so close to actually* doing *something with my life and Graham fucking Kellum snatched it away.*

CHAPTER 4

"**D**O YOU REALLY want to be an agent?"

You've got to be kidding me.

Of all the places he could go, Graham stepped out back, to what? Smoke another cigarette?

His voice came from behind me and I didn't feel the need to give him any respect by turning to meet it. I had been standing there at least ten minutes, trying to wrangle my disappointment. Without looking over my shoulder, I spat the venom he deserved.

"What do you care? You succeeded in stopping me."

"You're sniveling from one setback and you think you'd survive in the field?"

How dare he?

"Are you deliberately being an ass or does it just come naturally to you?"

The words were out of my mouth before I could stop them. I folded my lips between my teeth, momentarily fearful that my unprofessional outburst would bring trouble.

But Graham said nothing. I could feel his eyes boring into my back, through my shirt. Margot was right, I shouldn't be wearing pantsuits. Especially not in July when the heat, in addition to today's nerves, made me sweat. I'd always covered up because I felt that wearing revealing clothing made me look foolish, like I tried (and failed) to compete with the temptresses surrounding me.

"What is it you want, Ms. Greer?" Graham's tone was oddly devoid of its usual antagonism, but I could still picture the set of his smug face.

A long silence drawled, broken only by the nearby chirping of birds. I don't know why I suddenly elaborated, but I did. My vulnerable emotional state made me want to explain and Graham was the only one there to talk to.

"I don't know," I sighed. "I just… want to do more, move up. You can't get into management here. Women, I mean. It's almost all men."

"You think it's sexist?"

I spun on my heel.

"You don't?"

Graham cocked his head at me and I studied him in return.

Altogether, his features were admittedly handsome—dark hair, white teeth, nice jawline, trim waist. But I begrudgingly acknowledged that wasn't even his charm. It was something about his easy confidence that made women react to him the way they did. Other women.

"I think it was sexist, yes, for a long time," Graham replied. "But things have changed. Unfortunately, there's a reluctance to retire and so new positions aren't opening. No one is moving anywhere and the status quo remains."

If he was trying to be kind for some reason, he failed. His little speech came out too authoritative, speaking to me as if I were a child. Skeptically, I searched Graham's face for his true meaning. His eyes were one of his most striking features—a peculiar blue-gray that twinkled with amusement or darkened with warning. At the moment, they did neither. Why was he standing there in the first place?

I bit the inside of my cheek to keep from asking him why he insisted on humbling me in front of my co-workers. If we had this conversation off-site… maybe at an office party, maybe if I were drunk, I could have summoned the courage.

But this was work, and ODX—as well as our British counterpart, EI6—had an almost militant chain of command I'd already bucked by calling him an ass. Also, I couldn't seem to form the question without sounding whiny.

Her colleagues put their lives on the line every day, but little Poppy wants to know why you're mean to her.

"We don't have the same issues at EI6," Graham remarked. "Well, not anymore. Men and women so often transfer throughout Europe that new positions in London frequently open up. Even under current regulations, we fly below the radar."

He delivered the statement as a matter-of-fact. I frowned, unable to decide if he was bragging or… hinting at an offer?

That couldn't be.

He was manipulating events again, this time to my face.

Forgetting rank, I snapped, "Don't try to placate me with your false courtesies. Don't act as if you didn't go behind my back to sabotage my career. I don't appreciate further… further trickery and I won't ever forgive this."

I caught the fingers of Graham's left hand twitch, as if he meant to flex or fist them—but the moment was there and gone. I turned away to listen to the birds again.

The sudden creaking of the back door made me start. Carter poked his head out.

"Poppy, Graham. Glad I found you together, this concerns you both. Kellum, I'm sorry. I just got in touch with your office in London. Agent Brooks has been wounded in action. She'll recover, but she won't see field work anytime soon." Carter worked his jaw, "Routine mission not twenty miles outside of the city. It was supposed to be safe."

He turned to me with an upward flick of his head. "You're in, Poppy. You begin training tomorrow."

"Thank you, sir. Thank you!" I said, grinning. "I won't let you down."

Standing across the blacktop, Graham said nothing, as usual. But I saw him slowly close his eyes at Carter's decree, as if he could close out the news, his defeat.

"Oh, and, Poppy…"

I snapped my head back in my boss's direction.

"I do need to know if you're a… natural… redhead?"

I understood Carter asked, as delicately as possible, if the hair between my legs was red. I felt my face color, all the more because Graham stood near enough to hear the answer. I didn't want to give him the satisfaction of having any intimate knowledge of my body… it felt like giving him power over me, and that was the last thing I needed.

"Uh… yes, sir. I am."

I swear that son-of-a-bitch's lips scrunched, as if to stifle another smirk.

CHAPTER 5

"NICE MOVE," MARGOT praised, after I successfully deflected her attack from behind. Every morning for the past week and a half, our self-defense lessons began at nine a.m., sharp. I met either Adriana or Margot in the basement gym that ran the length of our building. Adriana was the tougher of the two—she had six inches on me and boasted striking muscles where I carried only spindly limbs. Too much time spent lifting books to my nose instead of lifting weights.

"No point in teaching her more than the basics," Carter had ordered. *"There's no time, and I don't foresee her in any situation where she'll need hand-to-hand combat. This is just a precaution."*

Before that first day, I'd never even held a gun. By the end of the week, I'd fired a Beretta, several Glocks, and a variety of smaller, discreet weapons, custom-made by our agency. Handling the recoil and making sure I didn't shoot myself in the foot were my primary concerns. The nuances

of each trigger mechanism weren't something I spent time memorizing.

After all, the chances that I'd even see a weapon were almost non-existent. Carter reiterated that he simply couldn't, in good conscience, send someone into the field with no knowledge whatsoever.

"Thank you, Margot," I replied, slapping her hand in a high-five motion.

A new voice echoed from the door.

"Perhaps it would benefit you to try that on a partner who won't announce the type of attack before engaging?"

The hair on my neck stood on end. I hadn't seen Graham or heard his voice since the day Carter assigned me the mission. He'd immediately flown back to London. Tail-between-his-legs, I hoped.

Spinning on my heel, I turned to face him.

He stood languidly in the doorway, one foot crossed casually over the other. He wore dark gray trousers and a white, collared shirt. He'd rolled his sleeves to the elbows. I hadn't remembered seeing him so casual before. Perhaps as unkempt as would pass for a man like Graham. As if he'd come straight to ODX from Dulles Airport.

"Thanks, but we're good here."

I spun back on my heel.

Instead of hearing his footsteps recede, I heard Graham enter the room.

"Perhaps you didn't hear me—" I began.

"Actually, Poppy, I think he has a point," Margot mused.

I frowned at my so-called friend.

"And I have to use the little girl's room anyway. Can you take over for a bit, Graham?"

Don't leave me alone with him, I thought. *He's liable to injure me just so I can't board the plane.*

"Unfortunately, yes. I've been asked to provide assistance," Graham replied, clearly having other things he'd rather be doing. "Carter wants her to train against someone other than the girls."

"Great!" Margot smiled, skipping off without a care in the world, abandoning me.

Wonderful.

My current state of dishevelment further tilted the imbalance of power I always felt in Graham's presence. He had ten years on me. His position far outranked my own—especially now that he was moving into some kind of managerial role. Yet he still knew much more about physical combat than I did. And now, even in his casual attire, he looked cool, collected. Meanwhile, loose strands of hair came out of my braid, sticking to my face. My discount, beat-up, workout gear clung to my sweaty body.

I wondered if I stunk.

I chided myself for caring.

Graham moved and the way he approached seemed quietly threatening. Like he'd already switched into a predatory, attack mode. He practically stalked.

I crossed my arms.

"What do you want to teach me that Margot cannot?"

I watched his tongue slide across his teeth as he breathed out one low chuckle.

"Let's start with the basics, shall we?"

He gave me no time to prepare—I guess that was the point—when he lunged.

I was *pathetic,* putting up almost no fight to speak of before

Graham somehow pinned my arm behind my back. His hard body pressed against mine, leaving me panting and feeling more awkward than I thought possible. My stomach quivered with something like butterflies. For a moment, Graham held me like that. Then he released me so abruptly I stumbled forward.

Narrowing my eyes, I spun around and vowed to do a better job this time.

When Graham attacked, I got one punch to his shoulder and I kicked his thigh for all I was worth—though I had been aiming at buckling his knee.

I think the struggle surprised him because he couldn't immediately pin my flailing arms. Instead, he knocked me off my feet and slammed my body down onto the mat, hard enough to hurt.

Before I could blink, Graham's solid form caged mine. His torso pressed flush to my chest and his hands wrapped around my wrists to contain them on either side of my head. It took only a moment of thrashing to realize I wasn't going anywhere and with a huff, I ceased.

Goddammit.

My cheeks flamed, as usual, to have Graham hand my ass to me as he so loved to do. To demonstrate how weak and ineffectual I was. Physically, this time, just for variety's sake.

I met his blue-gray eyes and don't know why, but I gulped. Inhaling, I caught his clean, masculine scent. Feeling the strength in his muscles, I became aware of his body not just as *Graham, the British Bastard,* but as—

"Teaching you to fight is a mistake," he said.

—*a man.*

For a moment, I'd almost come to think of him as something other than a smug ass.

The only mistake was allowing you into ODX business.

I lifted my chin so that he wouldn't see how his words made me feel small. I let my voice edge with ire.

"Because I'm hopeless?"

"There's not enough time, it can only give you a false sense of security which will cause more harm than good."

"Oh, do tell me what I should be doing, Graham. That's your favorite pastime, isn't it? Bossing people around. What should I do when confronted with an enemy? Hide in a corner and cower?"

"Yes." Graham blinked. His voice deepened. "Stay alive. Live to fight another day."

Suddenly, Margot walked into the room and cooed cheerfully, "Thanks for taking over for a bit, Graham! Oh, and Aspen is looking for you."

Graham released me, rising in an effortless, elegant, manner. For a moment, I thought he might offer his hand to assist me in standing. Then I remembered who I was dealing with.

"Happy to help," he told Margot, insufferably pleased with himself. Pushing myself up, I stared at his back.

Only then did I think of a hundred things I should have said in my defense.

CHAPTER 6

REACHING AROUND, I pulled my ponytail tighter and smoothed my face. We'd set up today's practice in an interrogation room, not unlike those seen in police movies. Cold, stark, designed to intimidate even before adding the pointed torture devices the girls thoughtfully lined up on the table in front of me.

It was a change from my usual routine: cardio, weight training, agent protocol.

Throughout each day, Adriana drilled me in the basics as well as what to do in various *"what if"* scenarios. *What if you're hurt in the field? What if your cover is blown? What if you suspect there's another agent in play?*

Wistlock strictly forbade modern technology for its guests. Not only was this my first mission; I'd be going in dark. No contact with a handler.

Licking my lips, I focused on Adriana and began the practiced lie.

"Stop!" she commanded.

"What?"

Adriana shook her head. "Don't lick your lips. It looks like you're stalling or acting out of nerves."

"Oh. Right. Okay."

I took a breath and started again. "My name is Klara Volkov. I was born in New York City. My parents emigrated from Russia. I enjoy sub–"

My little speech cut off as the door opened and Graham sauntered into the room.

"Uh… I enjoy su–submissive sex."

Why was he here?

Why was that so hard to say with him *here?*

Closing my eyes, I felt the blush creep up my cheeks, the heat on the back of my neck. My lie had been a horrible effort, but it wasn't my fault.

"Carter asked me to help with her training again today," Graham said impatiently, waving one hand. Then, suddenly the pinnacle of politeness, he asked Adriana, "Would you like some assistance?"

Say no, I willed.

"Sure," she shrugged. "Can't make her any worse than she already is."

I shot Adriana a look.

"You know I love you, but you're a terrible liar, Poppy."

"Thanks," I said, flashing a sarcastic smile.

Graham leaned over and whispered something into Adriana's ear. She nodded, and I followed her with my eyes as she left the room, delaying the moment I'd have to acknowledge Graham.

Finally, I folded my arms and looked up at his towering figure.

Graham's charcoal suit clung to his lean form, as usual. His wardrobe choices seemed to be either gray or black suits, always a cut more formal than the suits the men in our office wore—if they donned one at all. A few months ago, Graham had grown a short beard and moustache, something like the rugged stubble of a day or two without shaving. It made him look even older and I begrudgingly admitted it suited him.

Graham stared at me intensely but did not speak.

Suppressing a shudder, I realized that if he'd gone to Hollywood, the sharp contours of his face and the flash in his eyes screamed *"Cast me as the villain."*

Was this a game already? I wondered. *Whoever speaks first, loses? Like a negotiation?*

Whatever.

"What did you say to Adriana?"

"I told her I could intimidate you better if we're alone."

I nearly choked.

"Excuse me?"

Graham shrugged, casually taking the chair across from me.

"Can you think of a scenario where you'd ever be questioned with your best friend cheering you on from the sidelines? As unpleasant as it may be to acknowledge, it's more threatening for you, a girl, to be alone in a room with a man. The mind races with chilling possibilities."

I could feel the heat creep up my neck again. *What was that supposed to mean?* Was this an intimidation tactic already?

"Especially if the man is a known adversary."

I blinked. So Graham didn't deny that he disliked me.

Well, good. Glad we're on the same page.

"What have they told you?" Graham asked. "Don't breathe erratically, don't touch your skin, maintain eye contact. A look to the left is lying, right is recollection." He shook his head, dismissively, and folded his hands on the table between us.

"You can find all these tips, and more, on the internet. And yes, it's the gold standard that the best lies have a kernel of truth. Not only will you remain calmer when telling it, you might be able to send your adversary on a wild goose chase sorting out fact from fiction."

He leaned back, spreading his hands. "But how about diversion?"

I'd been following him intently until then, but at that comment I furrowed my brow, giving a small shake of my head.

"Let's play a little game. I want you to pretend I'm your father."

My mouth dropped. I hated myself for it and hoped he didn't notice or read anything into it. Because it *didn't* mean anything. It was just... why, of all the scenarios to choose, had he picked *that one?*

To cover my embarrassment, I scoffed, "Why? Because you're old enough to be?"

Graham shot me a dark look. "Hardly."

Leaning back across the interrogation table, he instructed, "Let's say you need to lie. You've snuck out for the night. Said you were at your friend Olivia's house, but went to a party instead. When you return home, I'm up waiting. Maybe you're late. Maybe I'm suspicious for other reasons. You don't know. But when I ask you where you were that evening, what do you say?"

I schooled my expression and looked him dead in the eye.

"I was at Olivia's house."

"And now you've earned yourself a punishment."

I *did* choke when he said that, coughing on nothing but air.

What the fuck?

"You're trying too hard," he explained. "Try telling me something else to divert me. Or better yet, *obscure* something else. A distraction, a false lead."

I frowned. He'd lost me.

"Maybe your friend Olivia attended the same party. Maybe you found out she's dating a boy you like and it started a fight between you two. Maybe nothing of the kind occurred. But pretend it did and toss out a breadcrumb just the same."

He held my eyes, making sure I paid attention.

"When I ask, 'where were you this evening,' try this—" Graham affected a distraught expression and continued, *"I was at Olivia's and she's a bitch and I don't want to talk about it."*

I would have laughed to hear him act the moody teenager if it wasn't so utterly brilliant—if *he* wasn't so utterly brilliant as he spoke the words. It worked. I became distracted by the accusation, wondering what Olivia had done, even as I knew he purposefully misled me.

"Shall I stomp up the stairs in all my teenage drama?" I offered.

Graham smiled, raising his eyebrows in approval, amused.

"I was at Olivia's and she's a cunt and I don't want to talk about it."

I took the liberty of upping the ante by switching out the insult, partially to shock him. Feeling like I'd nailed it, I lifted my chin.

"How's that?"

"Well done. You would have fooled most dads." Then, voice a bit huskier, he added, "Though if I were your father, I'd punish you for lying and wash out your mouth for such foul language."

What the actual fuck?

My stomach flipped; my smile faltered. I gaped, stupidly.
Was this a part of the intimidation tactic? Or maybe because
I was headed to a kinky party?

I might have thought the comment playful, but his face…
there was no trace of playfulness. His eyes were harder and
darker than usual, making me squirm. I didn't like this game.
I felt suddenly embarrassed, ashamed.

"I–I…"

I didn't know what to say. Maybe to an older, proper man
like Graham, the word "cunt" sounded like a rude remark
from a foul-mouthed American girl.

It seemed a monumental task to meet those stony eyes,
so I stared at the table. Graham's hands were folded neatly
before him. I fixated on his silver ring, maybe a family crest
of some kind.

"I probably took it… that was probably too far."

When Graham said nothing, it hit me that I had spoken
only for wanting *him* to reply. To protest, to break the tension.
I was pissed that he didn't. I was pissed that he'd pushed me,
that I allowed him to intimidate me. I hadn't done anything
wrong, and yet I practically apologized. How *dare* he push me
around like that, in ODX offices, no less? This was my turf.

"What is your *problem* Graham? I'd say it's that I took
your colleague's place, but you didn't want me for this mission
from the very beginning. How incompetent do you think I
am? It's not even an operation to seduce! All I have to do is
just be… passive."

Graham's mask didn't move and for some reason, that
made me want to affect him even more. Like I just wanted
to push his fucking buttons the way he pushed mine, and I
couldn't even find them.

"I don't have to manipulate anyone or shoot a gun or jump from trains or whatever agent stunt it is you think I'll fail at," I spat, slamming a fist onto the table. "All I have to do is submit. It's *nothing* compared to a real mission. All I have to do is nothing! How can I fail at that, Graham? Am I not even nothing? Am I less than nothing?"

"Worse."

I blinked, drawing in a quick breath. His one word squeezed, like a hand around my windpipe, making it hard to speak. He did it again. Made me want to cry.

"I'm worse than nothing?" I whispered, hating the weakness in my voice.

That muscle in his cheek feathered.

I shot to my feet and stormed out of the room before he saw my lip quiver.

"Poppy."

Did I hear him half-heartedly call my name, or was that just my imagination?

CHAPTER 7

"DID YOU TAKE your pill today?" Margot asked, eyeing a pale nail polish as we began our final beauty treatments.

Each day, estheticians prepped my body in more ways than I'd ever known a body could be pampered. Deep tissue massages to ensure proper blood flow. Seaweed wraps for toning. Sugar scrubs to shine the skin from my décolletage to the soles of my feet. Facials with weird electric microcurrents that made my complexion glow like a teenager's.

Not to mention, the painful waxing. Under my arms, all over my legs, and in my bikini area. Which we tidied only according to the specifications in the rule book.

The Wistlock Rule Book wasn't an actual book, to my disappointment.

I pictured something leather-bound, embossed, carrying the deep scent of secrets with top notes of intrigue. Heavy and prized throughout the years.

What I received was an emailed document with seventy-two pages of legalese my eyes bulged to peruse, quickly disabusing me of my fantasy. There were no slick pictures of dark and opulent parties, no masked men or women in elegant attire, no pretense at all to convey anything other than the weighty significance of its missive.

The message was clear: What happens at Wistlock, stays at Wistlock. Or a team of rabid lawyers will descend upon your sorry being and eviscerate you, until there's nothing left but bones for the carrion crows.

I could barely pay attention to the final grooming as my mind was in overdrive, racing toward one place.

The auction.

What would the castle look like inside?

Which man would buy me?

What would he look like?

Could I really do… everything a stranger commanded?

And then, the harder questions came, knotting my stomach.

What if he was the sex trafficker we were looking for?

What if I didn't find out any useful information?

What if something dangerous happened?

"Poppy," Adriana snapped me out of my thoughts. "Did you take your pill?"

I nodded. Girls were required to take birth control and I'd been using the pill anyway. I thought that heaving the burden onto the female showed a lack of forward-thinking equality, but then I remembered the basis of this event might not be the best place to look for equality benchmark-setting. At least both male and female participants had to provide clean bills of health.

After my finger and toenails were painted, the girls ushered me to another chair where our hairdresser awaited.

"We'll apply a gloss for shine, add long layers, and give you a nice blowout," the elderly stylist appraised, turning my head left and right. Her own gray hair was swept into an elegant twist I imagined to be nuisance to style each morning, but did look quite beautiful.

Two hours later, the stylist sprayed a soft holding mist over my head, and the thin line of her mouth actually turned up into a grin. She prepared to turn me around when Margot cut in.

"Wait!" Margot enthused, lighting up. "Let's not let her see herself until she's *fully* done."

Adriana waved a disinterested hand in my direction, indicating the decision was up to me.

"Um. Okay."

"Poppy, you've *got* to relax," Margot said. "You're gonna have fun, you'll see. I bet there's a lot of hot men at your party, and the hottest one of all will be smitten by you. You might even find yourself enjoying it. This one time, in Estonia…"

"Don't get her hopes up," Adriana warned, glaring. "They won't all be Estonian beefcakes. That operation was an anomaly."

"Fine," Margot threw up her hands. "I'm just sayin'. You don't have to be so doom-and-gloom, Adri. Be positive, Poppy! The rule book said the men have to meet certain physical standards too. Not too old, not too fat, responsible with personal hygiene and grooming… They want a sexy party. What lure would there be for the women if the men weren't *somewhat* attractive?"

"Let's see…" Adriana drawled, "maybe they're secretly looking for a sugar daddy. Maybe Wistlock is paying them, behind the scenes. Maybe they're strung-out, looking for a fix. Or any other number of reasons. Keep in mind, Poppy isn't like you."

"Hey! What's that supposed to mean?" Margot knit her brows.

"I'm sorry," Adriana rested her hand on Margot's shoulder. "What I mean is, you think everyone is attractive."

Margot crossed her arms.

"It's a good thing," Adriana soothed. "You find the good in everyone, something to like."

And I don't?

"Poppy is… particular."

"Thanks," I said, letting my sarcasm show.

Adriana made an exasperated face. "That can be a good thing too. It's not really good or bad, it's just *you.*"

"Sounds bad in this scenario. You're saying it's unlikely I'll be attracted to the man who buys me. That I'll have to have sex with him all week, while he physically disgusts me."

"Well," Adriana sighed, her face softening. "I tried to protect you from this mission, Poppy."

I was *so* tired of everyone treating me like I hadn't the competency to do anything beyond process data. And by "everyone," I might have meant Graham. But the concern in Adriana's eyes made me reel in my frustration.

"I know you don't want to see me get hurt. But please, don't look at me like I'm some sacrificial lamb, headed for the slaughter," I said. "I *want* to do this. I want to help these women. I have to be some man's pretend sex slave for a week? These girls I might help save, they are doomed to this fate for *life,* for *real.* How can I be so self-centered as to, to… put the need for a chiseled jawline over lives I can save?"

I thought I read something proud in Adriana's face, maybe *spoken like a true agent.* But all she said was, "Let's get her to lash extensions."

I SHUFFLED INTO YET ANOTHER make-up chair, thankful I'd be spared my nightly instruction in more intimate matters. By far the most embarrassing part of my day, the one that gave me more butterflies in my stomach than self-defense, was Carter's required education in *"whatever kinky stuff they're doing over there in that castle."*

I quickly learned it was one thing to be titillated by the *idea* of kinky sex. It was another to understand the grand scope, the variety of fetishes and manifestations, the nuances of rules and play. And so, every evening I immersed in a nightly world of BDSM by viewing a stream of erotic movies and pursuing an endless parade of fiction Adriana and Margot curated.

I gave up trying not to blush after the first night. I claimed a chill and donned a sweater to hide my hardened nipples. I wore my loosest pantsuits, for fear that the wetness gathering between my legs would be visible.

Even a woman who *wasn't* turned on by dominance and submission would have had a hard time keeping her mind from wandering into some dark and dirty alleys when bombarded with that volume of porn each evening.

Finally, two nights prior, Adriana had me practice my submissiveness by obeying her commands—though not before Riley poked his head into the room, eagerly recommending his services to "make it more real."

Adriana had picked up a riding crop from the table and stalked toward him with such threat that he scampered from the room, shouting, "Just trying to help!"

But even play-acting with Adriana made my breathing erratic. I wondered how I would face a room full of men with *this* in mind.

While naked.

While one of them bid… on me.

To be his personal, sexual plaything.

CHAPTER 8

"**L**ADIES AND GENTLEMEN, *may I present Ms. Klara Volkov, ingénue, submissive, little Russian doll ready to serve at your pleasure!*"

Later, I realized Margot's use of the word "gentlemen" should have been a tip-off. But at the time, my nerves overrode any sense as she introduced me to our co-workers.

The lashes glued to my eyelids tickled every time I blinked. Only when she'd finished all my make-up did Margot turn my chair around, letting me see the transformation.

I sucked in a breath, gasping at my own reflection.

It was me, but... the best version of me. Like a highly flattering picture, capturing the right angle, the best light.

But I *kept* the angle, I took the light with me as I moved.

My eyes seemed bigger and wider than ever. A coppery shimmer swept across my lids brought out their bright blue, making them pop. It sparkled against my pale skin and seemed to match the flickers of copper in my hair. She'd filled in my sparse brows and worked a little eyeliner at the outer edges of my eyes.

"Not too much," she cautioned, when instructing me on how to repeat everything on my trip. "We're keeping you youthful."

To that end, she'd rubbed an apricot blush on my cheeks and applied a rosy-pink lipstick. Subtle highlights on my cheekbones, brow bones, and cupid's bow gave me a dewy shine. My skin glowed ethereal; my lips, pouty and plump. Two weeks of strict dieting and four hours of daily cardio flattened the nagging little pooch on my tummy. Even my muscles seemed longer, leaner, though I knew it couldn't be possible in that short time. Could it?

The crowning achievement was my hair. The stylist made good on her promise of shine—it radiated a fiery gold when I tossed my head. The blow-out gave it body, a smooth bounce. Falling in loose waves halfway down my back, I felt like a goddess. A tiny velvet bow tucked onto one side of my head pinned up a small section of hair.

I had blinked at my own reflection.

Is this me?

My expression, wide-eyed in wonder, reminded me of a portrait I'd once seen of Emma Hamilton, Admiral Nelson's infamous mistress. The one used on the classic cover of *Wuthering Heights.* A foreboding shiver ran up my spine at the thought. I hoped things turned out better for me than they had for Emma or Young Catherine, in the end.

For the final piece of my transformation, Adriana appeared with new clothes, and the girls shimmied me into the flirty, skimpy dress. Once again, I had turned to the mirror to check my appearance.

I *did* look like a doll.

A sex doll.

Well, I thought, carefully walking into the gym, *I guess that's the point.*

With a crooked, nervous smile, I strode forward and immediately felt a little better when the applause and mock catcalls broke out. Someone had dimmed the gym lights considerably, so that it felt more like an intimate theatre, but I could see Adriana, Margot, Claire–who'd recently returned from Vegas–Hope, and Aspen.

And Graham.

Standing in the shadows so that I couldn't read the expression on his face. But something told me I wouldn't like it. Self-consciously, I tugged at the hemline of my dress, but nothing was going to make it any longer. I'd have to remember not to bend over.

"Isn't she spankable?" Margot cooed, making me want to die.

"Whoa, Poppy!" Hope teased, wiggling her slim shoulders in a sexy, *come hither* manner. "I'd fuck her."

I blushed to the tips of my ears, biting my lip as I smiled. I wondered if she meant it, or just wanted to make me feel better.

"How 'bout you, Graham?" Hope asked.

I felt each thump of my heart as I froze, flicking only my eyes in Graham's direction. It was too dark to make out his face. He was going to say something to humiliate me, I knew it. That could be the only reason for his unbearable pause.

"Poppy Greer!"

My head snapped toward the direction of the shout.

"Look at you!" Riley hooted, walking into the room and letting out a low whistle. "I always knew you were hiding underneath those pantsuits. Just *look* at you! Our own new-found asset. Gorgeous!"

I exhaled, relaxing my shoulders as the tension broke. For once, I was grateful for Riley's lack of filter and I turned toward him, ignoring Graham.

"Take it down a notch, Riley," Claire chided.

"Well, she does look stunning," Hope said.

"True. But you should always take your look for a test drive in public first," Adriana remarked, thoughtfully.

"Initiation!" Margot shouted, clapping.

Initiation?

"Let's go to… um… how about Off the Record?" Margot suggested, and everyone quickly began gathering their things.

"You're coming, right?" Adriana asked Riley.

"I wish. Carter's got me combing records on the Dubford case. I'll catch up with you later, if you're still there," he said, never taking his twinkling brown eyes off me.

"Aw…" Margot teased, running her finger down Riley's shirt. "Whatever will we do without a male chaperone? What kind of trouble will such a group of helpless girls get into all by themselves?" She licked her lips to show she relished the thought.

"You're killing me, Margot," Riley replied, but still his eyes remained locked on my scantily-clad form.

"Are you coming?" Margot asked Graham, who had since stepped out of the shadows. He nodded, once, curtly.

Of course, I thought. *As if I were an actual teenager and you an actual father, bent on reining in any fun I might have.*

The other girls only preened at the rare treat of Graham's attendance. Turning from stern to suave, he winked, offering Margot his arm. She happily slid to one side and Aspen quickly claimed his other.

CHAPTER 9

"**S**HE'S ONE OF us now. Get her a gray!" Margot exclaimed the strange order to our group, far too loudly for the sexy, subdued bar.

Several heads turned in our direction. Again.

We'd made a spectacle upon entering—five women noisily crowding into a bar usually did. Hope, Claire, Adriana, and Margot were all dressed to the nines—although, they possessed that kind of beauty, that perfect bone-structure, that commanded attention even when wearing a t-shirt and leggings.

"What's a gray?" I asked, picturing some kind of liver mousse, a pâté the other girls ate that was equal parts upscale and revolting.

"Marxon came up with it," Margot said, grinning. "It's a cocktail. GRAY. It stands for Girls Risking their Ass for You."

I cocked an eyebrow.

"Acronyms aren't his strong suit," Adriana shrugged.

"What kind of drink is this?" I asked when it arrived, eyeing the murky concoction with a grimace.

Adriana didn't answer, instead confirming, "Your flight

leaves at night, right?"

"Yes. Why?"

"You're probably going to want to sleep in tomorrow. Just make sure you hydrate throughout the day."

From the corner of my eye, I saw Graham watching darkly from a booth along the wall. Not scowling exactly, but not smiling either. It didn't deter several women in the bar from casting flirty looks in his direction.

I knew he'd try to be an actual *chaperone.*

"You have to drink it all at once," Hope said, wagging a finger. "That's the rule."

My eyes popped as I took my first sip.

Pure liquor. With only a little curaçao to change the color of the cocktail.

"Go, go, go…" The girls chanted and laughed as I knocked back the drink. As if we celebrated in a rowdy sports bar and not an upscale speakeasy. But I suppose when you bear resemblance to a group of goddesses descending upon the earth, management tended to look the other direction.

Correction: management–and every other patron in the bar–tended to look *in* our direction.

How could you not? High-heeled glamazons sounding as if they had a monopoly on fun, looking like they were all in on a secret you wanted to know.

And the truth was, they were.

Just not the kind anyone ever expected.

Was I one of them now?

Without cleavage, without a commanding height, without chiseled cheekbones?

I was.

Almost. Maybe.

For one mission, at least.

"GOOD THING RILEY ISN'T HERE to see you," Margot said, as I declined the suave, blond-haired politico who offered to buy me a drink.

I shrugged. "Riley flirts with everyone but he doesn't mean anything by it."

Margot shook her head. "He likes that you're not like the rest of us. Thinks you're unspoilt goods."

I barked a laugh. "I thought we'd established that I'm not a virgin. I wouldn't be doing this if I were."

"Not literally," she rolled her eyes. "You're not jaded, like the rest of us. He's into that innocence. Haven't you noticed the way he looks at you, ever since your date?"

"What date?"

Margot let her head fall back. "See! I knew you didn't even know it was a date, you're so naïve."

"What. Date?"

"When the two of you had coffee that night to review the specs on the Azorean shipment."

I wrinkled my nose. "That was work."

"Not to him. Not to anyone. Except maybe you."

"Ew. No. That wasn't a date. Are you saying Riley likes me?"

"I'm saying Riley is obsessed with you."

I laughed, loudly, spurred on by drinks. "He's not my type. But I'm thankful Aspen got stuck helping him tonight. Maybe the two of them should get together, although, I can't imagine a worse match."

"No one's your type!" Margot cried.

I laughed again, feeling increasingly tipsy. "One more cocktail and everyone here is my type."

Margot smiled. "Don't let Hope hear you say that."

I giggled, flattered. Hope was notoriously picky, worse than me.

"Besides, Aspen's got a thing for Graham," Margot said.

I snorted, letting my eyes roll. My head may have rolled a bit with it; I was feeling the drink.

"That makes sense. *They'd* make a good couple. The two of them both have sticks so far up their asses they think it hoists them high above the rest of us. And their heads are so full of nonsense maybe they'll just float away—"

Margot and I were facing the bar. I only half-felt the air shift behind me, indicating someone stepped up to order a drink.

"No, *Aspen's* head is full of hot air. Graham's is full of utter bullshit. Bullshit he feeds himself to believe he's better than everyone. And he feeds it to other people too, and they all believe it! EI6, *Elite* Intelligence, ha! He's just a stuck-up snob who covers himself in bespoke suits to conceal the commonness of his character. Or rather, lack thereof."

"Oh, I don't know. I rather enjoy the feel of fine tailoring."

I froze. I could almost feel the color drain from my face. *He's standing right behind me.*

"Perhaps you should try it sometime, Ms. Greer. The right tailor might be able to do something with the fabric of that dress. Or rather, lack thereof."

I turned to see his sharp eyes make a pointed sweep of my attire and I suddenly felt half-naked, tawdry. I crossed my arms over my body and looked at the floor.

"Graham," Margot chided, "an insult to Poppy's outfit is an insult to me. I'm the one who dressed her."

"My apologies," he said, tersely. "That was just the utter bullshit I'm known to speak."

My cheeks pinked as Graham threw my words back in my face. He raised his eyebrows, quite *unapologetically,* then turned on his heel and headed back to the table without getting a drink.

I felt Margot's hand on my shoulder. "You look lovely, Poppy. Don't let Graham get you down. He's just not used to seeing you like this and, you know. He's so *proper*."

I cleared my throat. "Right. Well. I guess… whatever. Let's have another drink."

I DIDN'T KNOW WHAT TIME it was when we all found a table. Not so much *found* as Adriana smiled, and the men occupying it leapt to vacate it on our behalf.

I barely remembered sitting down or what we discussed, not until Claire knocked over our drinks for the second time, and instead of feeling embarrassed, everyone laughed.

Everyone except Graham, standing above us along with Hope, because there weren't enough seats.

"Keep on celebrating like this operation isn't a disaster waiting to happen."

We all fell quiet at Graham's sudden words, low and sharp.

"Graham," Adriana warned.

"Everyone here operates in a moral gray zone, and you know it. None of us have any problem making the tough choices because the choices aren't tough, not for us. But her? Her compassion is a liability. If it comes to a choice, do you think she'll sacrifice the one for the many?" Without waiting for a reply, Graham continued, "This mission is more dangerous than Carter's letting on. He's gambling with her. She's had two weeks of training. What do you think is going to happen? It wouldn't matter if she had two years. She'll never stay in character, it's not in her nature. She's a sheep in wolf's clothing."

He leveled his cold stare at me. "The real wolves will smell you, Ms. Greer, and they'll eat you alive."

At the lack of protest, at everyone's uncomfortable silence, I panicked and paled. *Was he right?* Graham shook his head and walked away from our table, heading for the door.

Before I knew what I was doing, my feet carried me out and through the building. Following him onto the street, I blamed the alcohol for everything that happened next.

"Graham," I cried. "Stop."

He halted and turned, his broad shoulders tense.

"What is your *problem?*" I seethed.

"I should think I made that obvious," Graham declared, all arrogance and condescension. "In theory, I know you want to be logical, but in practice…" Graham shook his head with smug dismissiveness. "You're too ruled by your emotions in the moment. It could expose you or worse, get you killed."

"I'm not good enough to be an asset, Graham? I'm never good enough for a mission, a job… to dare occupy the same breathing space as the other girls. I'm *nothing,* right?"

A couple, alarmed at my shouting, quickly scurried across the street to Lafayette Park, as if we threatened to interrupt their amorous mood. Cars whizzed down H Street, but I didn't care who saw us. This would be the last time I saw Graham before the mission, and I'd be damned if I let him have the last word. To send me off feeling like… like… *this.* Doomed to failure.

When Graham spoke it was slow, measured. And what he said was completely unexpected.

Also, it was difficult to process in my drunken state.

"It would be preferable if you were a submissive, Poppy. You'd listen and obey." Graham sighed, spreading the fingers of his hand as if he sought to grab the right words from the air. "And it would be better if you were nothing, entirely disengaged. But you're worse than being just nothing."

Roughly, Graham raked his hand through his dark hair. "I don't mean nothing, I mean… plain. Normal. Vanilla."

He stepped closer. So close he invaded my personal space, forcing me to look up at him. I fought to hold my ground.

"You're a brat, Poppy. A tempestuous brat. The second someone wields authority over you, you seek to defy it. The moment you're issued a command, your instinct is to disobey. You think this is the easiest mission? It's the worst. For you, I can't imagine more of a disaster waiting to happen. You're the *most* ill-suited."

His declaration hurt, and alcohol, being a highly flammable substance, fueled the fire inside me. All I heard was *a disaster, ill-suited*. If I'd *only* been sober enough to fully process his words, I might not have so blatantly confirmed them with my own.

The sharpness of my tongue contrasted with the sluggish bobbing of my head as I shouted, "Well, you don't get to decide the missions I go on. You're *not* the boss of me, Graham. You're not ODX! You're not even American! Y–you think you still own us? What *is it* with you and that chip on your shoulder?"

God, I wish my rambling stopped there.

But it didn't.

The world spun and my words spun with it.

"Why do you always butt into ODX business?" I pointed, accusingly. "Is this you covertly trying to reassert British control in the colonies? You think you're King… King… George? You're not a king and I'm not your subject. You can't tell me what to do! We don't have kings here. And if you were my king, I'd… I'd…rebel. Start a revolution. That's what this is, do you hear me? This is me, starting a revolution!"

King George? Revolution?

The goddamn alcohol. Part of my brain knew my words didn't make any sense. But I seemed powerless to stop them.

"You can just… sod off, or whatever it is you say over there. Because I'm an independent nation–*woman*–and I'm not subject to your commands."

I didn't know half of what I was saying, but I remembered those last foolish parts of it, and then…

…*Blackness.*

My ridiculous tirade was a mortifying moment to have as my final memory of the night, but I had little recollection of what occurred after that.

I dreamed I nearly swooned or… slumped to the ground, drunk.

I dreamed Graham caught me before I hit pavement.

I dreamed he said something terrifying under his breath.

And then the scene cut, as dreams often do. The next thing I knew, the girls were helping me home and into bed, apologizing for plying me with so much alcohol. I forgot about what transpired with Graham, about the dream of his declaration.

I didn't remember it the next morning.

Not as I drank a thousand glasses of water to help counteract my hangover, nor as I threw the last of my toiletries into my luggage. Not even as I raced to the airport and caught my flight to Heathrow.

I didn't remember Graham's final whisper until so much later.

Not until Wistlock.

Until the threat became real.

When my legs gave out and his arms encircled me, I'd dreamed he'd rasped in my ear, *"I've never met a girl more in need of good strapping than you, Poppy."*

PART II
Lie Back and
Think of England

CHAPTER 10

ALL ODX EMPLOYEES were required to keep a valid passport up-to-date. But until now, mine didn't bear a single stamp.

It still didn't, technically.

I arrived in London under the name Klara Volkov, with her falsified papers for identification.

But the experience is all mine.

A three-hour delay had everyone pushing out the gate. I scurried along with the swell of bodies, worried my lateness would cause the Wistlock escorts to leave.

If I wasn't nervous enough about my first time out of the country, as well as conducting my first mission, the imminent promise of being torn from my cell phone made me feel utterly adrift and isolated. For several reasons, *no modern technology* was a strictly-enforced party rule. I wouldn't be reunited with my cell until the end of the last day.

At the arrival gate, I spied two burly men holding up a sign with Klara's name on it—*my* name on it—and sighed in relief.

"I'm sorry I'm late–" I began, but one of the men waved off my concerns, literally waving one large hand.

"Welcome to London, Ms. Volkov."

"Ah–thank you."

I ran my fingers through my hair, self-conscious about how terrible I must have looked from the long flight. I half-expected the men to size me up, but they didn't seem interested at all.

Just another year, another girl for the auction block.

"We'll be escorting you to Wistlock. I'm Tom, this is Billy." Tom quickly held out his hand. "Your cell phone, miss."

"Right," I said, plastering a smile on my face to hide my racing heart.

This is it, I thought, feeling the cold, comforting metal slip through my hands. *I'm on my own.* I stared longingly at the device as he slipped it into the pocket of his suit jacket.

My only line to the outside world and to ODX, taken from me–along with my travel bag, which I handed over to Billy. Everything I'd needed had been packed into my carry-on. Per the rulebook, clothing would be provided at the event.

Not that I'd get to choose what I'd wear. That would be up to whoever bought me.

I followed the men through the short-term parking garage and up to an old-fashioned Rolls-Royce, though I couldn't specify the model.

"Please make yourself comfortable, miss," Billy said, opening the door to the backseat for me. "We've got a long ride. You'll find bottled water and reading material in the caddy."

"Thank you," I said, ducking into the cabin to see a variety of fashion, gossip and home decor magazines. I had my own novel tucked into my purse but I couldn't possibly concentrate on words. As we left the garage, I could barely even hear the men over the pounding of my own heart.

Slow down, I soothed the overactive organ. *The auction hasn't even started yet.*

The wheels of the Rolls Royce spun, carrying us out of the sprawl and into picturesque countryside. My mind seemed determined to match the pace, spinning wildly as I imagined what was about to happen. On some level, I recognized the green pastures as gorgeous, but I took in little of their beauty. Two hours flew by in a blur. In what might as well have been twenty minutes, we turned onto a dirt road and I could see Wistlock towering in the distance.

I wiped my clammy palms against my pants.

It's time.

"WELCOME, WELCOME, AND HURRY, PLEASE!" a tall brunette with brick-red lipstick sang, ushering the girls into a wing of the castle before I had a chance to explore.

"I'm Natalie," she introduced herself, "and I'll be taking care of all of you this week. We're running behind schedule so we must hurry. Those of you just arriving will need showers and then it's straight to hair and make-up."

I felt guilty that my flight delay must have contributed to the schedule snafu, but then I realized I couldn't be the only tardy participant, or else they would have simply gotten everyone else started.

Natalie looked to be in her early thirties. She had a long, elegant neck, displaying a chunky gold necklace and shoul-der-length hair brushing her stiff shirt collar on either side. Paired with her black pencil skirt, she looked as if she could be conducting a business meeting. I wondered how she came about such an odd job, and what she thought of all this.

"Aren't you adorable?" she said, making me blush.

"T–Thank you," I stammered.

"The American?" she asked. "From New York? Klara, yes?" I smiled, nodding.

"Did you sleep on the plane?"

"Yes… ma'am?" I replied, and she laughed.

"Call me Natalie, please. That makes me feel old!" She threw an arm over my shoulder. "I'm only thirty-two. The men are insatiable their first night, I just want to make sure you're well-rested."

My laugh sounded more like a nervous squeal.

Insatiable?

NATALIE USHERED THE TEN GIRLS, including me, through a series of opulent rooms and into a more modern space, serving as a prep room. It looked like the backstage of a fashion show–not that I'd ever seen one, outside of movies. Men and women scurried about issuing orders, carrying colorful clothing and make-up tools, like the frantic behind-the-scenes of the opening day of an upscale event.

Which, in a way, I guess it was.

The girls ranged from looking as comfortable as if they were hanging out at a friend's party to fidgeting as nervously as I did.

Repeats and newbies, I figured.

"Right, into the shower," a man with a moustache told me, pointing in the direction of what I assumed were bathrooms.

Tentatively, I followed where he'd indicated and found a

communal area, not unlike a spa bathroom, with showers, toilets, lockers.

"They throw parties in here," said a voice behind me and I whipped my head around to meet the eyes of short-haired blonde woman. She had a cute, upturned nose and eyebrows so faint they barely existed. "Everything from self-pampering to weddings. When they're not serving the kink community."

I flashed a nervous smile.

"Castles are expensive to maintain," she added. "I'm Ingrid. And you are?"

"Klara," I said, pleased with how natural it sounded on my lips.

"You're new. This is my third time. I can show you what to do."

Her admission of repeat attendance pricked my ears. Could she be connected to the traffickers? I knew the culprit was likely male, but I didn't want to rule anyone out. We had no leads; everyone was a suspect.

"Are you washing your hair?" she asked.

I shook my head.

"It's gorgeous. You're the only redhead here this week. Plus, you're new. I'm sure you're going to fetch a good price." With a wink, she added, "Here's hoping your buyer has a cock as fat as his wallet."

THE AUCTION WOULD BEGIN AT seven, sharp, which supposedly didn't leave much time for everyone to get ready.

Correction.

The auction began at seven-thirty. The pre-sale, when men would browse the girls tied up on display, began at seven.

This year, I learned, all the girls would be draped in crystals of a different color—right down to the glittering pasties and jeweled panties.

A rainbow of submission, I thought, wryly. I felt as if I'd fallen down the rabbit hole and these brilliant oddities were just as curious as anything in Wonderland. But I was relieved to learn we wouldn't be *totally* naked for everyone to see. I wasn't ready for that. Not now, maybe not ever.

Not that I'd get a say in the matter.

"We have something special for you," a man said, coming up to me as I stood by the wall, clutching my robe tightly. "I'm Etienne, your stylist for the auction."

"Hi… and, thank you. I'm Klara."

"You're the only ginger this year. We have just the right color."

"Purple?" I guessed.

He shook his head. "Amethyst looks so beautiful on Eliza, with her dark hair and olive skin, no?"

I looked around at nine other women in various states of undress. It seemed all the colors were taken. Pink, purple, blue, green, black, orange, yellow, red. What remained?

"For our last two girls of the evening, you'll be silver and gold," Etienne beamed. "Or in your case, more of a rose-gold."

He pulled out a miniscule thong and two pasties, burlesque-style, for my breasts. Metallic thread held the champagne crystals in place and swirled along the rest of the tiny fabric in glittering, undulating patterns.

A crooked, nervous smile grew on my lips, because I tried, I *really* did, to make him see I appreciated the sparkling beauty of the items. But my stomach dropped, confronted with how little I'd be wearing.

At least it's something, I reminded myself.

"You get to keep the knickers," he said, winking.

Lucky me.

Etienne handed me the items and I realized he meant for me to change, now.

Right. No modesty here.

With a deep breath, I stepped out of my robe and quickly shimmied into the sparkling set. Another anxious smile pasted itself onto my face. It came out more like a grimace.

"Relax, ma chère, you look perfect." He shared a conspiring grin. "Almost perfect."

Etienne lifted a crystal necklace from a box. The dazzling jewels flashed in the light, splintering radiance in a thousand directions around me as he gave it a slight shake.

"Thank you, it's beautiful."

"This, you don't get to keep," he said, moving one finger in a twirling motion to indicate I turn around to clasp the necklace. With a flourish, Etienne finished adjusting what little covering I wore. Once his hands left my body, my arms immediately flew up, folding across my chest.

Etienne pursed his lips, impatient, and I lowered my arms. Then he pressed my shoulders back, a nudge not to hunch.

"Bearing is breeding," he said. "Remember that."

Bred for what? Is this a beauty pageant or a submissive auction?

A clapping sound resounded around the hollow, modern room, as Natalie called us all to attention.

"Queue, please, girls!" she shouted happily.

My stomach riled as if a storm raged within, threatening to make me regurgitate the meager food I'd eaten.

Don't puke. It won't endear you to buyers if you look ill. Certainly not if you hurl onto their shining shoes.

I fought the urge to cross my arms again as we fell into line. At least the pasties covered a modest area of my small breasts. I looked at my nine companions. How were they all so serene? Or excited? None of them looked ready to hurl, like me.

It's not real, I told myself, unsure why that made me feel better, but it did. *You're not* really *here as a submissive. You're here for work. It's pretend.*

It's all just pretend.

CHAPTER 11

THE AUCTION

*W*HAT AM I DOING?
Ten low platforms lined one side of the dark room. Each stood only a few inches high, I assumed, so that the men could get a good look. Every platform was built with square, wooden beams, rising up and crossing at the top. A soft glow emanated from a light installed into the base, illuminating each of the ten girls.

Dangling from the top and bottom corners of the beams were leather restraints.

I gulped.

My heart lodged itself in my throat, as if ready to spill forth from my lips in a scream to cut through the room.

Oh god. What am I doing?

I felt like livestock as we marched to our posts and Etienne guided me to the end of the row.

First. I would be auctioned first. Or last.

"You must calm down, ma chère," he admonished. "You've given yourself a flush all over your neck. This is fun, relax. You

Americans take everything so seriously. You'll give yourself a heart attack before you're thirty."

I wanted to argue that it was easy for *him* to say. He was wearing clothes. But me… someone was going to own my body for the next week. *My orifices,* I thought, forcing myself to face the truth. Whoever bought me could do whatever they wanted to my body–inside and out.

Despite my fear, the notion caused a frustrating tingle in my pussy.

Spreading my quivering arms, Etienne locked my wrists into the cuffs above my head. He spread my legs and repeated the action with my ankles. Then he produced a gag from somewhere.

"Helps complete the picture," he explained, shrugging one shoulder. "We used to use blindfolds, but some of the guests complained because they couldn't see your beautiful eyes."

I didn't know how I felt about that. On the one hand, a blindfold would have introduced a new kind of terror… but it also would have hidden some of my shame. Without one, I would be forced to witness everyone examining me, to watch the auction for my body as it unfolded, to look the men in the eyes. I wasn't sure which was worse.

Etienne fastened the gag around my head and under my hair, so as not to mess up the styling. I would have laughed if I wasn't about to cry.

Why truss me up like a beauty queen, only to tie and gag me like a slave? Why not just start all in leather or some other kinky costume? Was that the theme another year? Or did the men like to introduce the transformation themselves? Was the point to present some kind of untouchable goddess waiting to be ravished? Or was it simply some tradition I wasn't privy to?

Etienne laid a steadying hand on my shoulder. "You look magnificent," he said.

Then he chucked my chin adding, "Please calm down. Trust me. I'd bid on you if I were allowed."

My eyes popped and I failed to conceal it. I assumed he was either gay or long since immune to finding any sex appeal in the unending parade of naked flesh he must see at these events.

Etienne left and I had nothing to do but stare at the assortment of armchairs in front of me. Most were deep, leather Chesterfields. I counted fourteen. One for every man?

That meant four men would go home without a submissive.

I wondered what those unlucky few would do with their found time. I assumed they'd already planned a week's vacation for the party, but for all I knew, men of this economic strata didn't even need to work.

Oh god, oh god, oh god. What am I doing?

Someone turned on music from what appeared to be an outdated stereo. It had been wired to speakers throughout the room, but it wasn't an advanced sound system.

Keeping in line with the no modern technology rule.

It sounded like one of those sexy European-beat playlists to put couples in the mood, but softer, a little slower. I strained my neck to see how the girls to my right were faring, but I couldn't make out any faces from my angle. Only the subdued lights shining up on each girl were electric, the rest of the room glowed from various pillars and tapers someone had lit.

Two middle-aged men in dark suits materialized from a side door and I recognized them from the party information I'd been emailed with the legal documents. Victor Hall, a dark-haired man of average height, and Angus Ainsworth—a big, burly specimen with a mop of red hair more shocking than my own. They were the event organizers and possible suspects.

I wanted to study them both, but too soon, I heard the main doors open.

Oh god. It's time.

My hands twisted nervously, grasping at their leather binds. As the first men filed into the candlelit hall, I squeezed my eyes shut and fought to control my breathing.

Looking like a panicked wreck won't entice bidders.

Or maybe it would. *How the hell did I know what these men desired?*

Who cared? *Focus on the mission.*

I'd never felt more naked in my life. It wasn't just the lack of clothing. It wasn't just the fact that I'd been tied with leather straps. It was more than flesh. It was that my desire had been laid bare.

You're a submissive, my position screamed to all who entered. *You like it.*

I shook my head.

No. You're an agent. You're here for work.

I UNDERSTOOD A LITTLE OF what was about to happen, but things got murky around the sale price of a girl.

Actual money wasn't exchanged directly. Club "credits" were utilized, channeled through a series of unnecessary layers to complicate the transaction, so that it didn't seem directly related to... what might be construed as prostitution. I doubted the methodology would stand up in court, but I also didn't think many people knew about, or cared to get involved in, litigating what went on between a bunch of freaky, consenting adults, in the middle of some remote castle.

Or the organizers bribed officials to look the other way.

I let out a low laugh as I tried to wrap my head around what was about to happen.

I was selling myself at a submissive auction.

When in reality, I'd be operating as a spy on my first mission.

At an event where someone secretly used the party for the hideous crime of recruiting *actual* sex slaves.

The irony. The game. The muddled layers.

My heart beat frantically as the men continued to file into the room.

Lie back and think of England? More like, lie back and think of... *all that.*

Forcing myself to size up the buyers, I was pleasantly surprised. The group was fairly diverse in terms of age, ethnicity, and body type. But from a cursory glance, none of the men stood out as unattractive. At least, not hideously overweight or hairy or unkempt. I breathed a sigh of relief, before a feeling knotted in my gut.

But one of these decent-looking men might be our suspect.

I cast my eyes downward as the buyers milled about, many turning in my direction, making my hands sweat. The rapid rise-and-fall of my chest as my breathing sped sent sparkles from the crystal necklace to dance about the room. Servers appeared, bearing trays laden with cocktails and wine, and the guests started to drink as they circulated.

Why did I think I was capable of this?

I swallowed as I began to feel men pass by on their way to other women or coming closer to examine me. But I couldn't look up. Not yet. Not until my heart rate slowed.

I can't do this.

I felt a flush all over my neck and face. I tugged nervously at my restraints. I hated the way they pulled at my arms, pushing my breasts out, forward. The jeweled thong covered my sex, but I couldn't close my legs, so that my pussy felt equally on display, an offering.

I guess that was the point.

Here's a girl, a toy for your pleasure, gentlemen. Use her at your leisure.

I couldn't muster the courage to lift my gaze for some time.

Later, I wondered if I felt something at that moment. Something intangible, but no less real.

The heat of a gaze I despised.

I raised my eyes at the same time two men parted, revealing a third, dark-haired gentleman between them.

It's not possible.

My stomach dropped.

Graham Kellum.

CHAPTER 12

THE AUCTION

I WAS THANKFUL FOR the gag because it muffled some ungodly squeak of horror coming from my throat. A caricature of surprise, I blinked several times, attempting to clear the mistaken vision before me.

Graham fucking Kellum? Here?

It was like a dream—*no, a nightmare.* The kind where you find yourself naked in front of the class, or your colleagues. I would have preferred to be naked in front of my entire office, if only it didn't include *him.*

This isn't real. It can't be.

Reflexively, I tried to close my legs and cover my chest, only to find myself immobile, spread and tied. Still my hands twisted, trying in vain to cover my nudity, to free myself, to run, *anything.* Anything but stand in pasties and a thong before Graham.

What was he doing here?

He was looking *right* at me. I stared, dizzy, unsure if looking away would steady my vision or if he somehow anchored it.

A stupid notion; Graham wasn't my anchor, certainly not in this.

In that millisecond, a hundred thoughts raced through my head. Chief amongst them, I wondered what he would *do*.

Grin? Wink? Raise his eyebrows like he often did? Oh god… walk closer to me?

Surely, he'd do something insufferable–

Graham blinked, once, and looked away slowly. As if he stared at a blank point on the wall and simply shifted his gaze elsewhere, finding nothing of interest before him.

It hit me like a slap across the face, worse than if he'd flashed some sardonic grin to taunt me. The helplessness of my position, my nudity in front of a colleague, in front of *him*, wasn't something I'd forget for the rest of my life. Yet the moment seemed to bore him; he'd dismissed it.

Resentment coiled in my chest as Graham flashed a warm grin to someone nearby, stretching his hand to give a firm shake in greeting. He clapped another man on the back, clearly enjoying himself.

Calm down, I told myself, feeling like a total idiot. *He's only doing his job. He can't acknowledge you… and you don't want him to anyway. I mean, you don't care.*

But what was Graham's job here in the first place? Had EI6 put a man in play for this mission?

Oh, you bastard.

Suddenly, I knew exactly what happened. Graham trusted me so little he had wormed his way into the party, seeking to undermine my work. I'd bet money on it.

I couldn't help myself from staring as he strode leisurely up to the girl on the dais next to me, obviously admiring her voluptuousness. Ella, I'd heard her called.

So that's your move, I reasoned. *Bid on a girl and uncover the suspect before I do.*

A competitive rage boiled inside my chest and I deliberately held onto it, glad for the distraction from fourteen sets of eyes ogling my nearly-naked body.

I could do this. I could be a good sub. A good agent. The perfect asset.

The men started to approach the girls more seriously now, discarding their drinks by chairs of their choice and inspecting us, one at a time. I lowered my lashes provocatively, but the heat never left my cheeks whenever a man came close.

"I'm told you speak Russian?" one asked, and I nodded shyly. As the drinks continued, the questions grew bolder.

"Do you like to suck cock?" a fellow American inquired, brushing my shoulders with his fingertips. He smiled, taking my accompanying shiver for a *yes,* I suppose.

"Look at those lips," he said, titling my head to better see. "Perfectly made for cock, aren't they?"

Not yours, I hoped, trying to hide the disgust from reaching my eyes. The man had close-cropped chestnut hair and a stocky build. He wasn't completely unappealing, at least not until he'd opened his mouth. It wasn't just his words, but his slimy *tone.*

"I'm going to bid on you," he said, making my stomach sink. "And we'll put that mouth to use first thing."

Not him, I mentally pled, as he walked away and the next bidder approached.

The men were forbidden from touching our breasts, rear, or anywhere near the area between our legs. Not until we'd been purchased. But several men took the liberty to run fingers through my hair or down my neck, leaving me feeling manhandled without traversing regions more intimate.

By the time the inspection phase nearly finished, my arms had grown sore and the leather chafed my wrists. The buckle on my heel strap dug into my skin, and I longed to take off my shoes. I'd tried several times to find Graham again, but I'd lost track of him until he suddenly appeared to my right, examining Ella, sending my pulse racing.

He'd travelled downward… meaning I'd be next.

He did not turn his head, but slowly, his eyes swung in my direction. Everything about him was restrained, measured, predatory. He stared but did not speak.

I shifted my gaze downward. I couldn't stand the suspense. Of what he would say or do when he reached me.

Breathe, Poppy, I scolded myself. *Don't faint. He'll never let you hear the end of it if you faint.*

I refused to look, but my ears picked up the rustle of his suit as he moved toward my platform.

Not yet. I'm not ready. Please let him just skip me.

But there was nothing I could do, nowhere to run or hide, no way to cover any of my body.

My eyes remained glued to his overpriced shoes.

"Look at me," Graham commanded, voice low. He tucked his thumb and forefinger under my chin, lifting my head.

CHAPTER 13

THE AUCTION

I DIDN'T WANT TO look. Oh god, I wanted nothing less in the world. But I was a submissive, here to do as I was told.

On the dais, we were matched in height. Unwillingly, I lifted my eyes and gasped when I met his blue-gray stare—so cold it burned. That must have been the reason heat coursed through my body. I blinked, confused at the feverish sensation.

Graham gave no outward appearance of our familiarity. He turned my head left and right, inspecting. The act was subtle yet so condescending, I forgot my fear for the moment and started to get annoyed.

I was the one who was on assignment here, *he* had no right to be in this room. Did he?

Whatever. He was being an absolute prick and though he gave no sign of anything other than sizing up the goods, I knew he was secretly gloating or... or... thinking something awful about me. Tallying up my flaws.

I narrowed my eyes as I lifted my chin, defiant. In return, Graham tilted his lips into the ghost of a smile. Just a hair, but I caught it.

It was strange, as if we had a conversation only through our eyes.

Fuck you, my gaze said.

Is that so? his stare returned.

At least… I think that's what it said.

It may have been a darker challenge passing between us, because the next thing I knew, one of Graham's long fingers touched my clavicle and traced its way down the center of my chest, right between my breasts and down my stomach.

I may have gasped. I may have trembled. I may have leaned into it. I may have leaned away.

I didn't even know, only whatever reaction he'd caused pleased Graham. I could tell by his smug expression.

Ignoring my blush, I narrowed my eyes further as he reached the top of the jeweled panties, pausing, almost taunting. I noticed he wasn't wearing his usual family ring.

You can't go any lower, I thought. *Or go right ahead and get yourself thrown out. Have fun with my stomach. That's all you'll ever touch.*

As usual, Graham studied me with a hard expression I couldn't read. I hated his goddamn mask of stoicism. Not only could he read everything in *my* burning face, but now just about every inch of my body was bare to his examination as well.

Suddenly, Graham's warm hand reached for my waist and he squeezed, pulling me subtly toward him. Or did I… lean into his hold?

His lips twitched, and then his other hand grabbed my waist as well. For a moment, we both froze in a strange, silent combat. I suppressed the wiggle my hips wanted to give, the indication that his touch had any effect on me at all. I tried not to think about my nearly-bare breasts rising and falling as I panted, right beneath his eyes.

Unexpectedly, Graham dropped his hands and left, without saying another word.

ONLY ELLA AND I REMAINED for sale and I couldn't help but notice our differences. Ella's straight hair fell past her shoulders, dark and glossy. Her jade eyes and sculpted features conveyed a relaxed confidence. Unlike my modest handful, her large breasts had been created to perfection–I admit I stole a few envious glances. They were balanced by her hips, making a nice hourglass figure… whereas below my breasts I felt too straight, too stick-like, too childish. I knew it wasn't true; I had *some* curves. But next to Ella's ample eroticism, I was overly conscious of our contrast.

It *wasn't* because I noticed Graham noticing her. He clearly couldn't take his eyes off the woman.

But… I mean… how could he not?

From his relaxed position on his armchair, Graham crooked a finger to one of the attendants. The man bent down as Graham whispered in his ear.

He wanted to bid on Ella.

That's a relief.

Another man–Sanjay, I'd heard him called–followed suit; beckoning an attendant to make a bid.

Of the men remaining, Graham and Sanjay seemed the most interested in Ella.

I swallowed thickly, eyeing the other four men.

They are waiting for me, I realized.

Were they interested in me, or had they simply been outbid for someone else?

Of the four, one was a little too hipster for my taste, but that's not what I disliked. The man seemed young, about my own age, and for reasons I didn't want to examine too closely, I preferred someone older.

Out of the corner of my eye, I noticed the bidding between Graham and Sanjay become more contentious, but I didn't worry.

Graham always got what he wanted.

Focusing my gaze back on the four men who waited for me, I studied the others and decided on the one I preferred. Beneath his glasses, something in his eyes read as kindness; his smile came easy and warm. He was handsome enough, somewhere in his thirties or even early forties. The third man, with the auburn waves and Eastern European features, was my second choice.

Really *anyone* but the fourth man—the American who asked me about sucking cock. I caught his hand traveling to his pants, adjusting himself as he watched me.

A laugh, almost gloating, came from Sanjay. I looked over, perplexed.

My eyes flashed between Graham, looking surly, and Sanjay; proud.

He... won?

The attendant untied Ella's leather straps and escorted her off the dais... to be claimed by Sanjay.

My mouth would have fallen if it wasn't gagged.

No.

Without turning his head, Graham shifted his eyes to me.

Wait. No. This wasn't right.

Graham was here to buy Ella. That way we'd cover more ground. Or something.

Maybe he just wanted to make an appearance, I thought, calming myself. *Only scope out the situation from this point. Yes, yes, that must be it. He wasn't here to—*

Graham crooked his finger again, and the attendant jumped to do his bidding.

My eyes rounded....

He couldn't...

Graham whispered in the attendant's ear.

Did he just... make a bid on me?

No, no, please, no.

I felt faint. This was all a mistake. It wasn't supposed to happen like this.

What was he even doing here? Sitting languid, like he had a right? Insufferably proud, like a king on his throne?

It wasn't just that Graham was a trained assassin who could take out an opponent in a heartbeat. All the agents were. Graham wasn't even the strongest fighter, at least not physically. His muscles were well-developed—long and lean—but we'd contracted plenty of hulking, thick-necked bodybuilders over the years, who'd win a match in the boxing ring. What intimidated me most was what lurked behind Graham's calculated expression; the cunning he was bringing to more of an executive role, going forward. While I couldn't claim him as the prize-winning killer if it came to physical blows on the mats, I might concede to him having the sharpest, deadliest mind I'd ever encountered.

I resented how that unnerved me. How fearful I felt being pitted against it, and in such a disadvantaged position.

I must have been in a slight state of shock, because the five remaining men made bids on me, but I could barely even hear or see. The room refused to come into focus, my ears felt as if they'd been plugged. The auction seemed heated, intense, but I didn't know if it was because anyone desired me or if they simply wanted to stay at the party and I was the only option remaining.

I caught the hard set to Graham's face and knew he'd just increased his bid.

This can't be happening.

I needed to get a hold of a phone somehow, to call ODX headquarters.

I couldn't remember my training. What was I supposed to do if I suspected another agent was in play? Thoughts swam in my head, dizzying me.

Then one rage-inducing idea popped to the surface.

Maybe Graham had planned this all along.

Maybe he thought I was so incompetent, he arranged to buy me just to make sure I didn't fuck up the mission.

It felt like a physical blow to my core when the auctioneer gave a slight, formal bow of the head in Graham's direction, pronouncing him the winner.

Of me.

My heart lodged in my throat while my stomach raced in the opposite direction, sinking to my feet.

I was going to be sick.

I blinked, hard.

This can't be happening.

It meant…

I *belonged* to Graham for the week.

No, no, no.

My palms and neck began to sweat as the room suddenly grew hotter. I barely noticed Natalie untying me, helping me step from the platform. I didn't have to act. My knees turned to jelly and I stumbled, completing the picture of the frightened, docile submissive.

Natalie didn't remove my gag, but it mattered little. I was speechless. She gently turned me around and guided my hands behind my back, tying them with yet another leather restraint. Then she left me to my buyer.

Casually invading my personal space, Graham stepped close, all six feet towering over me.

His *property*.

With a metal collar in his hands.

The expression "like a deer in headlights" came to mind, as I couldn't stop myself from staring with dumb acceptance of my oncoming doom.

But where else would I go? What could I do? This was the mission.

Grinding my teeth against the gag, I felt hot, angry tears threaten to spill. I didn't want to admit there was any fear behind them, just total fucking fury. Trying not to grimace, I bent my head for Graham to lock the collar into place. I would have no way to remove it without a key.

His fingers gently caressed the back of my neck as Graham brushed my hair aside, unclasped my crystal necklace, and replaced it with his branded collar. It wasn't too thick or tight, and for that I was grateful, figuring I'd have to sleep in it if he so chose. One small metal ring hung from the center. Emblazoned above were the initials A.R., and I didn't understand what they represented.

I turned to look up at Graham, narrowing my eyes as if to demand, *what the hell are you doing here?*

He reached out and stroked two fingers down my cheek. Possessively. Condescendingly. A show of ownership.

I flinched and then, meekly, I bowed my head again, playing the role. *It's all part of the act,* I told myself.

Whether Graham was here for his own reasons or if he'd been assigned by EI6, the result was the same. His role for the week would be one of comfort, ease. To make demands of me. Mine was to provide his comfort, ease. To submit to his demands throughout the week.

It wasn't fucking fair.

My heart picked up speed as Graham leaned down to my ear. His stubble tickled my cheek and I smelled the piney, fresh scent of his body wash or aftershave… or maybe it was just *him.*

Graham answered the question that had been knocking around my brain since our confrontation outside of the bar: *Did he remember my drunken rant about rebellion, or had he been equally inebriated?*

Graham's voice was entirely too smug as he rasped, "Consider yourself under British rule."

CHAPTER 14

THE AUCTION–AFTERMATH

FOUR OF THE guests had been given suites within the castle, two found their weeklong-home in a converted carriage house, and the remaining four were directed to a set of guest units spreading out in a semi-circle at the rear of the castle.

I didn't quite know what to make of them. They could be called bungalows or cottages for their size, but they'd clearly been erected with modern design in mind. From the back, stone walls blended into the floor-to-ceiling glass like something out of a rehabber's dream, so that the structures meshed with the history of the property, while incorporating the best of contemporary architecture.

Our cottage rested at the end of the semi-circle and I didn't know if that came to luck, Graham's planning, or the fact that he'd obviously made some kind of last-minute entrance to the party. Either way, I liked the additional privacy. The nearest cottage stood twenty or thirty feet to our left. To our right rose one of several dense rings of trees the estate had likely planted many years ago.

Graham led me to our bungalow on a leash. Walking behind him.

I swear to god, I could feel his arrogance radiating off him as I stared at the back of his head. He'd fisted the leash around his hand a few times, shortening it; and once when I failed to keep up, he tugged to remind me, nearly causing me to stumble.

When my heels clicked out of time and I struggled to maintain balance, Graham turned around and caught me, making me wonder if he'd done it on purpose, just to make a fool of me or to force me to rely on him.

I'm going to report your ass, I thought. But, to whom? He wasn't under American jurisdiction and for all I knew, he'd been sent here; his mission, sanctioned.

What could I say, anyway? That the son-of-a-bitch enjoyed debasing me? He was just playing his role.

Better than I was, I thought with dismay.

We had delayed back at the castle for a drink—*correction—*Graham had an old-fashioned while I waited on tenterhooks to get back to our room and ask him what the fuck he was doing. But we'd been invited to hold off a few minutes as the staff prepared our quarters. I didn't know what that meant and Graham offered no explanation. He didn't say anything at all, and I certainly couldn't because he hadn't removed my gag.

Finally, after he finished his cocktail, he turned to me and asked, "Thirsty?"

With daggers in my eyes, I nodded. I needed a damn drink, badly.

But instead of ordering me something alcoholic, Graham untied my gag and lifted his untouched glass of water to my lips, pouring the liquid into my mouth as if I were a helpless child.

If he had noticed the fury behind my eyes, he gave no outward acknowledgement.

"Here we are," Graham said, approaching the door to our bungalow. He produced a key from his pocket, unlocked the door, and stepped back.

Even though he indicated I should enter first—a gentleman's move—I eyed him suspiciously as I passed. When I heard him step in behind me and the door close tightly, I spun around to face him. Alone, I could finally speak.

"Who do you think you are buying me like that?"

With lightning-fast reflexes honed from years in the field, Graham slammed me against the wall. He pinned my shoulder with one strong hand. The other *seized my throat and squeezed.*

He's going to kill me.

Wild-eyed, I pulled against my restraints to free my airway.

I didn't stand a chance. Graham was too strong, too skilled, even if I had the use of my arms. My instinct was to scream, and I might have if I could breathe. Terror coiled in my breast, my stomach, radiating out through my veins in a fight-or-flight call I couldn't answer.

My god, he hates me so much, he's going to remove me from this mission and make it easier for himself.

Suddenly, Graham released his iron grip on my neck—but that hand only grabbed my waist and pinned my bucking hips against the wall. I gasped and choked for air, too relieved for the moment to fight.

Before I could say anything or even sort out what was happening, Graham *slammed* his body against mine and covered my mouth with a bruising kiss, swallowing my squeal.

What was he doing?

His tongue—confident, insistent—forced its way past my lips. Astounded, I pulled my head back, trying to escape, only to meet with unyielding wall.

Oh my god, what was he doing?

Graham clamped his free hand beneath my chin, holding me steady. At the same time, he wedged his thigh between my legs, pressing up hard into my pussy and making me gasp again.

The message was clear: kiss me. Now.

With his strong body caging mine, I… complied.

I stopped struggling and relaxed my mouth, allowing the exploration he demanded. *Did it… feel good?* Every inch of my nearly-naked body pressed to the fine cloth of his suit: my breasts imprisoned against his chest and my sex spread helpless upon his thigh. Graham held my waist so tightly I worried it would bruise, something the party discouraged without consent.

My mind couldn't make sense of what was happening, only broken thoughts floated to my consciousness and they were too shameful to truly acknowledge. I might have forgotten to fight for a moment, forgotten myself. I might have forgotten everything and gone a little limp because, *fuck*.

He was a really good kisser.

A moan of pleasure sounded in my ears—was that me?

Graham thrust his groin against me, as if… he *wanted* to. As if an actual, real desire simmered beneath the surface.

But that was impossible.

At the same time, his hand tightened further around my waist and his kiss bruised my lips like he wanted to punish me.

Maybe he was. Manipulating me? Hurting me or shaming me?

At the thought, I tore my head to the side. This time, Graham allowed it, loosening his grip on my chin.

Panting, trying to understand what just happened, I felt him lean forward. Not to capture my mouth again, only to bring his lips to the ear turned in his direction.

The timbre of his voice dripped with malice as he whispered, "Please keep your pretty little mouth shut until I sweep the room."

The… what?

It took several long seconds to understand what he said.

I was an idiot.

Of course. We didn't know if it was safe to talk and the first thing I did was break cover.

Oh god, I was a fool.

Graham didn't want to kiss me any more than I wanted to kiss him. He just needed to shut me up. We were acting. Pretending for the week. I had gotten carried away and–

"I want you on your knees in the center of the room."

My pulse, having just slowed, quickened once more at his disciplinary tone.

Graham hadn't removed his body from mine and I didn't like the way it made my skin tingle. But he spoke clearly. Louder. For the benefit of any potential devices, recording our conversation? Or maybe… video-recording?

Graham released his iron grip on my waist. His warm breath caressed my ear as he spoke.

"If I have to repeat a command, Klara, you'll be punished."

CHAPTER 15

AUCTION AFTERMATH

FUCK, FUCK, FUCK.
Why did his voice make goosebumps rise all over my skin?

"Go. Kneel. Until I tell you otherwise."

Just do as he says, I consoled myself. *Once you sweep for bugs, you can return to normal. You're not really going to be his submissive for the week.*

Burning with shame, shaky legs carried me to the room's center and I lowered myself to my knees. I looked down, noticing how having my arms tied behind my back pushed my pasty-covered breasts up and out. Or was that arousal that caused them to swell and lift?

For several agonizing minutes, Graham worked around the room doing god-knows-what. Then he busied himself with unzipping one of his bags and withdrawing items I couldn't see.

My head snapped when I heard a beep. A *modern* beep.

Huffing, I rolled my eyes. Technology wasn't allowed, but the rules didn't apply to him?

Once again Graham worked his way around the room, including disappearing into the adjacent rooms I hadn't yet seen. Finally, Graham returned to his bag, re-packing whatever device he'd previously removed. Without urgency, he crossed back to the center of the room, directly in front of me.

By this time, my knees ached and I thought my teeth would crack from all the grinding. I wasn't sure what was worse—staring at the seat of his pants, gazing down at his shoes, or looking up. Each felt subservient its own way.

I didn't have to make a decision when Graham's hand found my chin and tilted it up in an act of manhandling I resented. To make matters worse, he studied me as if I were his property, as if we weren't pretending. He took his time while I was forced to pose, nearly naked, blushing furiously.

I hated to admit that I felt intimidated, and I didn't think Graham was even trying. He just *stood,* naturally, casually, and it did funny things to me. His body was so solid, so threatening… and yet, he wasn't an overly large man, he just… had an aura. Something about the way he positioned himself with a wide stance, shoulders back… the way he carried himself with such confidence. A part of his being hummed with an undercurrent of power. I couldn't say it was entirely cocky because it was so damn casual, effortless. As if it said, *I will have my way,* without him actually saying it. And everyone fell in line, awed by his gravitas, and Graham bent people to his will.

And now I was going to be one of them.

The questions screamed in my mind as I bit my tongue.

Why are you here?

Can I get up?

Speak?

Put on some damn clothes?

I wouldn't ask, wouldn't show myself to be foolish again. *But he had better start explaining.*

After studying my face for a long minute, Graham released my chin. By this time, I was clearly scowling.

"The room is clean, but I want you to listen. Do not speak. Do not move."

Reflexively, I opened my mouth anyway. Graham raised his eyebrows at me, a chiding sort of expression. I snapped my mouth shut.

I'm going to smack him when this is over, file a report…

But once again I thought, *on what grounds?* If he was here on assignment, this was all just part of the mission. He didn't even *want* to be assigned to me. He was only here because he lost the bid on Ella.

God, not him, I prayed, as if divine intervention could change my circumstances.

Being nearly-naked with Graham felt worse than being fully-naked in front of a hundred strangers. His eyes seared every inch of my skin in a way no other man in that room had. It was as if he *took* something more from it. Worse, something in me engaged in the dynamic, without my consent. Like his eyes drank in my flesh, fed on it. Like he stripped it away, yet what lay beneath bared itself to his scrutiny in equal measure. Like there existed something traitorous in my body, *giving,* even in its stillness.

"We can speak plainly in this room, but we are not going to."

What? Why?

"Even seasoned actors often do not break character between shots—they exist in and inhabit their roles at all times. Agents with years of experience over you maintain the same level of commitment. Do you honestly believe you can waltz into your first mission and flip the act on and off like a switch?"

I opened my mouth, unsure what I even planned on saying, when Graham cut me off.

"We'll have none of that American arrogance."

My eyes rounded, popping out of my head. *If that's not the egotistical pot calling the kettle black. If you're not the very embodiment of arrogance–*

"EI6 has partnered with ODX for this mission. That is all you need to know. We will not speak of this again. Even if I hadn't bought you, *which I have,* I possess far greater experience in the field than you. I am in charge from here on out. There will be no second-guessing my decisions and no backtalk. You are a sub. I am your Dom. I've indulged your behavior in the office, but that ends now."

His tone was clipped, business-like, and more powerful than ever before.

Fuming–partly because he wasn't entirely wrong–I bit my tongue. I expected Graham to meet my anger with his own in return, but there was nothing at all like rage in his expression–just a frustrating calmness to his face. That part of him I knew, but there was something else there now, too. Something unfamiliar and frightening gleamed behind his eyes. The same fear I'd felt when he'd grabbed my neck came creeping back.

Tersely, he instructed, "We'll remain Dom and sub at all times during the week, even in private. I will be your lord and master both outside and inside these walls. You will be obedient, just as you would have for any other man who might have purchased you. From this moment on, you will address me as 'sir.' When I issue a command, you will obey without question. Do you understand me, Klara?"

I hated the way he spoke to me. I hated that I couldn't do anything about it. I hated that it made something warm burn in my core.

"Yeah," I mumbled, knowing it was a bit petulant.

Calmly, with control, Graham fisted my hair, giving my head a firm yank backwards. I gasped.

"Klara, understand that I can easily break you." It was a dangerous voice I didn't recognize. "You will bend to me or I will break you, and I can assure you the latter will hurt more. But, either way, you'll submit to me."

My heart started pounding again. *Were we pretending?*

"S—stop it, Graham," I whispered, feeling like I didn't know him, like he'd put up even more walls between us than usually existed. "I—I don't like this. You're scaring me."

"You should be afraid." His voice dripped with ice. "Being afraid of me is the smartest thing you've done since you took this mission."

Graham pulled my head back further. "But if you do exactly as I say, I'll be the only thing you have to fear this week."

Calm down, I told myself, fighting the shaking I could feel starting in my hands. *He's not* really *going to hurt you.*

Is he?

I forced myself to swallow both my fear and my pride as I grit out, "Yes, sir."

Graham let go of my hair and said, "Try again."

Oh, fuck you.

I took a deep breath, determined not to fall in this simple task, determined to show him I was a competent asset.

"Yes, sir."

When Graham nodded, satisfied, I felt bold enough to continue.

"May I ask one question, sir?"

He strode forward, tilting my head up again, this time with only a finger.

"You may."

I licked my lips and croaked, "What about clothing... am I to be... nearly naked all the time? Sir?"

It was harder than I thought to maintain eye contact on that question. Failing, I looked down at the lapels of his dark suit.

"Yes, Klara. It helps remind you of your place."

He said it so plainly, almost indulgently, as if he did me a favor. He let go of my chin, stepping back as he next spoke.

"Both when we leave this room and while we remain in it, you will wear the clothing I choose for you. Which will be very little."

I gulped. All I wanted to do was crawl into the corner and hide. Find the bedroom and dart under the covers and never come out again.

How could I do this? Bear a week of being Graham's submissive? Wearing whatever he selected, doing as he bid? Pretending...

Oh god, would I have to... to touch him? Feign obedience and pleasure in.... sexual acts? Would *he* touch *me?*

Certainly, sex was out of the question. Improper. Unprofessional. *Wasn't it?*

I gulped again.

"May I ask one more question?"

"One."

"This wasn't planned, was it? It was a mistake. What I mean is… you were bidding on Ella and you lost. I–I'm not the one you came for, am I?"

My voice broke as I spoke, too humiliated to continue smoothly, and yet, I couldn't tear my gaze from Graham's face. I needed to know the truth.

He stiffened and then replied, roughly, "No. This wasn't the plan."

For some strange reason, his reply almost stung.

I swallowed any misplaced sense of rejection and straightened my spine.

This was good. It meant he hadn't come from a false belief that I couldn't handle myself. It meant he detested this arrangement as much as I did.

A need to seize control, to assert one final power, rose within.

"Good. Fine. I will obey you and defer to you as the lead on this mission and as my… Dom… I understand that some touching, some intimate acts cannot be avoided. But there will be no *full* intimacy between us. I mean… intercourse." For some reason, I spoke as clinically as possible. Perhaps to keep it clear and business-like. "I accept that your hands may touch my body in order to maintain cover, but your… ah…"

Sighing at my own ridiculous skirting of the matter, I simply cut to the chase and said, "Whatever happens, I expect you to keep it professional when it comes to your penis. I expect you to keep it in your pants. I don't want you to try and fuck me."

That muscle feathered in Graham's cheek.

"For once we're in agreement about something."

CHAPTER 16

BEDTIME

"**Y**OU'LL BE SLEEPING in this room," Graham said, leading me to the smaller of the two bedrooms and allaying some of my fears. He'd finally untied my arms but grabbed me halfway between my hand and my wrist, pulling me along.

I nodded, refusing to give him the satisfaction of silencing me. I simply wouldn't speak, silence *my* weapon.

Perhaps I set my mouth, petulant. Easy for someone like Graham to read. He gently-but-firmly took my chin between his thumb and his forefinger again—a move I quickly realized I was going to have to get used to.

"Don't sulk, Klara."

I bat my lashes and flashed a half-smile, as if I didn't know what he was talking about.

"Do you need me to spank you before bed in order to behave?"

What?

In a heartbeat, I flushed crimson. My mouth dropped and I seemed incapable of breathing.

He wouldn't.

Would he?

I tried to slow my pounding heart. I licked my lips, then bit them. I looked around, *anywhere* but at Graham. He couldn't do that to me. He had no right. I wouldn't allow it. I would fight him.

"Answer me, Klara."

I studied Graham's solid body under his dark, tailored suit. He towered several inches over me; he could easily flip me onto my stomach. Or my back.

I shook my head. "No," I whispered, mortified.

"No, what?"

"No, sir."

"Klara, don't test my patience or I'll be forced to test your limits. And I can assure you, your bottom will smart for it. The whole sentence, please."

Jesus, could he just not *say these things?* Impossibly, my face burned hotter.

"No, I do not need a spanking tonight in order to behave, sir," I said, closing my eyes.

Graham released my chin and walked over to the closet.

"Your clothes are in here. The rooms have been fully stocked with a variety of outfits to suit all tastes, we had only to wait until they brought those assigned to you. Each morning I'll come to wake you and dress you as I see fit."

He paused and I realized he waited for my confirmation. "Yes, sir," I murmured.

"Let's get you into something for bed," Graham said.

"I'm going to bed?" I scoffed, bristling. I thought we might discuss the mission or… *something.*

Graham raised his eyebrows at my tone. "Yes. You've had a long day and I have work to do."

I felt like a prisoner in my own cottage. I knew it wouldn't have been any different, had someone else bought me. I just thought… thought maybe I'd be staying up my first evening. That my new owner and I would get to know one another… maybe drink some wine together…

Be grateful, I told myself. *It's better this way. You don't have to do anything sexual.*

Then why did even the simplest act *feel* sexual when Graham did it?

He rummaged through the closet, pulling out loose, cotton shorts, and a matching tank top. I exhaled, pleasantly surprised. I worried he'd find a latex ensemble and I'd pass a fitful night's sleep in something better suited to a dungeon.

The pleasantness quickly abated when he next spoke, moving toward me.

"Let's get you out of these garish pasties, shall we?"

Graham reached up and I instinctively crossed my arms over my breasts.

"Hands down, Klara," he ordered.

But why? I wanted to demand. *Did we really have to pretend* this *hard?*

For a few seconds, I debated whether or not to uncross my arms. But I feared two outcomes if I disobeyed. One, my inability to adhere to remaining in character would mark me more inept than I'd already shown myself to be; and two, that Graham would make good on his threat to punish me if I didn't obey.

Slowly, I lowered my hands to my sides, refusing to acknowledge the tingle in my pussy as Graham reached for my nipples and peeled each of the pasties off my body. I scrunched my eyes shut, clenching my teeth.

He can see all of my breasts now.

"Arms up," he commanded.

Was his voice huskier than usual?

I raised my arms and Graham slid the white tank top onto my torso. I knew without looking that my nipples poked through, hard.

Because I'm anxious. Not because I'm aroused.

"No!" I suddenly cried, hands rushing to protect my modesty when Graham's fingers tucked into the waistband of my jeweled thong. "I—I can do it myself."

Was I afraid of him seeing my most private areas or seeing… that I was wet?

That couldn't be it.

Because I wasn't.

I wasn't.

"Klara, I won't have you questioning my orders at every turn. I find it tiresome. Move your hands this instant and keep them away. If I have to tell you again, I'll remove your panties and you can sleep with nothing."

I groaned and let go.

This can't be happening, I thought, for the umpteenth time.

Slowly, the bastard pulled down my underwear, kneeling as he reached my feet. All of my senses heightened, tense, readying for… I didn't know what. My pulse raced in anticipation of an event I didn't know.

"Step out," he ordered.

I whimpered as I obeyed. Something felt so final about

losing the minimal covering my thong provided, even if it was already around my ankles.

Graham removed my shoes and guided my feet into another, softer pair of panties. He reversed his previous motion, pulling them up onto my legs. When he reached my rear and smoothed the underwear into place, I shivered beneath his touch. He repeated the process with the shorts, condescendingly patting my bottom, like a parent to a child.

Was he doing all this to get me used to my new role or because he enjoyed it?

"Thank me, Klara."

"Thank you for dressing me, sir."

It came out through clenched teeth, not as submissive as I intended. But I was annoyed he hadn't unlocked my collar.

"Sir…" I began, resenting the word. "May I please remove this collar to sleep?"

"No." Graham tapped my nose, another patronizing gesture making me see red. "You will wear it at all times throughout our stay."

"Why does it say A.R.?"

Graham paused, cocking his head. "Archie is a friend of mine. It's his collar, his place I took here. This was a last-minute decision from above; there wasn't enough time to get the letters changed."

Oh. *But still, why did I have to wear it all the time?*

"Now, to bed. You're jetlagged. Stay in your room until I come get you in the morning."

Graham nodded his head toward the twin bed. Obediently, I climbed inside, settling under the covers. I was used to my own Queen-sized mattress at home, but I had to admit the bedding here was more luxurious. Cool, hotel-quality sheets enveloped me, making up for the lack of space. The down comforter, much like most of the room, was soft-white. I supposed the cream and white décor had been chosen to be a blank slate. I wondered if Graham's room looked similar. He hadn't offered me the opportunity to explore.

Again, like a child, Graham tucked the covers beneath my chin. My eyelids drifted shut and I realized with some resentment he was right. Up until then, I'd been running on adrenaline, but I was hideously jetlagged.

I felt Graham stand over me, hovering for a moment… watching me? Then he left, switching off the lights and plunging me into blissful darkness.

CHAPTER 17

SOMEHOW, I KNEW it was very early when I woke. I felt completely refreshed, and, at the same time, completely on edge. Inviting as the bed was, too much weighed on my mind to attempt sleep any longer.

I crossed to the closet and shuffled through unappealing options until I found a white, terry robe, typical of upscale hotels. I put it on, figuring Graham wouldn't complain if I still wore the sleepwear he'd chosen, underneath. Hearing no sounds from his room, I quietly crept into the living area, finally taking the time to assess the bungalow.

From the shared space, floor-to-ceiling windows and French doors led to a patio out back, but Graham had closed the curtains the night before, providing total privacy. The room itself was large, easily fitting two small sofas, a coffee table, a desk, and a dining table to the left. The modern space was done in dark, tasteful tones—deep browns and grays, giving it a chic vibe. A wide, arched doorway led to a small kitchenette on the right. Another two doors led to a closet and a shared bathroom, complete with a small tub. The bedrooms stood to the left side of the room. Mine, apparently, didn't warrant an ensuite. I'd be bathing in the shared powder room or in Graham's room, I thought, with dismay.

Rummaging through the kitchen, I found a small packet of instant coffee that would have to do. I hoped something richer might be offered at breakfast. Or perhaps no one had thought beyond tea? But surely, with an international clientele, I'd be able to get my hands on something more potent, because this wasn't going to cut it. Strong coffee and strong alcohol were the only way to handle the forthcoming week.

I'd been so lost in thought, staring at that sad little packet of insta-brew, that I didn't hear Graham come up behind me.

"Were you given permission to leave your room?"

I started, whipping my head around. Graham had crept up to about two feet away, still in sleep pajamas consisting of a soft t-shirt and drawstring pants. The thin, black material clung distractingly to his muscles. Something about it reminded me of clothing he might wear to spar on the mats. Or maybe it was his stance.

"I—no. Sir."

I hadn't realized he was serious about me needing to wait for him to even leave my bed—that seemed a bit extreme. I wanted to make a sarcastic remark but thought better of it.

"You will do nothing without my explicit permission this week. It's for your safety and mine."

"O—kay," I replied. But I wasn't really sure what he meant. If I couldn't leave my room, did that mean I also needed to ask permission to brush my teeth? To shower? Pee?

"I just left my room to come into the kitchen, Graham. It's not a big deal. I mean, sir." My declaration might have come out with impatience behind it, if not sarcasm.

Graham's expression didn't change; if anything, it hardened.

"Klara, I'm going to spank you."

The words fell like a hammer on the anvil of my heart, heavy and loud, reverberating around my brain and ringing in my ears.

"What? No." I shook my head vigorously and took a step back.

"Yes. I can see that we have to set the tone for the day over my knees. Come here, now."

"You… can't."

"That's exactly the attitude I'm going to eliminate. I can do anything I want to you for the duration of the week. The sooner you learn your place, the better. A hard spanking is just what you need."

I heard his words, but my brain refused to fully process them. My body understood better—it shivered.

This wasn't what I expected the week to be like. A little fun play for some imagined infraction. No matter what happened, I still had the power. No matter who bought me, *I* would secretly be playing *them*. My buyer could think he was thrilling me or breaking me, but it didn't matter, it was all an act. I was going to let him believe it while I worked to manipulate him behind each submissive bat of my lashes.

I was the spy. I had control. I was never really going to give it up, not truly.

And now I felt it slipping through my fingers. Now everything had been upended.

Including, soon, my rear.

This wasn't play.

This was real.

And it frightened me.

I studied Graham's toned arms, his muscular chest. In an instant, all of it became a threat, a force to be feared.

"Klara," Graham's voice came as a low warning that went straight to my spine, sending tingles down its length. "Remove your robe, pull down your shorts, and come here now. If I have to do it for you, I will get the hairbrush."

CHAPTER 18

DAY ONE—MORNING

"NO. I–I CAN'T. You can't."

We were spies, colleagues. Pretending to be regular people. Pretending to be Dominants and submissives. Pretending to get along.

A game within a game within a game…

Somehow each cancelled the other out, like a double negative. A *quadruple* negative? What remained didn't feel like a game at all, pretense stripped in a circuitous route. Until my pulse raced, my heart sped, my skin prickled with a sense of friction raw and real and *risky*.

The very air between us crackled with it. My hair stood on end, as if from this electricity, and I tensed in anticipation of the storm.

Was he threatening to punish me to maintain the cover as his sub, or to keep me in line as his subordinate in this mission? Both? Or something else entirely?

Fruitlessly, I searched the room for somewhere to flee; I scoured my mind for some excuse, some refusal.

Without a word, Graham turned and crossed to his black bag on the dining room table. Ominously, the sound of a zipper's pull filled the room. When he turned back to face me, he held a flat, wooden hairbrush in his right hand.

Just seeing it, I gulped. A swarm of frenzied butterflies released in my stomach, fluttering wildly, as if trying to escape. My eyes darted back-and-forth between Graham's face and the wicked-looking object.

"This could have been easier on you. I want you to remember that, Klara. You brought this on yourself."

Entirely too business-like, Graham pulled back one armless chair. Seating himself, he said, "Come here now and place yourself over my lap. Disobey me and I'll get my belt. You've already earned a hand-spanking and the hairbrush. I suggest you do as you're told, or we'll increase your punishment to include a firm strapping."

My mouth dropped as the room suddenly swayed.

He couldn't be serious.

He was.

When Graham made a move to rise, as if to retrieve his belt, I scurried to his side without hesitation.

Tears of humiliation pricked my eyes and I broke out in a sweat just staring at his powerful lap. It felt impossible to push myself to lay across it. Even breathing was a challenge.

"Don't… don't do this…" I begged, aching to break my role but fearing the consequences. *Graham, we're colleagues,* I wanted to shout. *You're taking it too far.* Licking my lips, I looked helplessly at his stern face, pleading for a way out.

Perhaps understanding that my body had turned to stone, he reached for the tie on my robe and loosened it, before pushing the garment off my body.

Suddenly, my muscles began working again and I stepped back. And back again.

"*No.* Don't you dare do this Graham. You *can't* do this."

When he rose, I bolted toward the door.

I didn't even make it halfway before he caught me around my waist, lifting me off the floor like I weighed nothing. I was only 5'3" and slender; Graham was nearly six feet tall and muscled. It wasn't a fair match.

"Don't you dare, Graham. I swear, I'll report you!" I screamed, kicking my arms and legs. I thrashed like a wildcat as he sat with quiet, patient force, flipping me face-down over his knees.

"Let me go! I swear if you spank me, I'll report you!"

To whom, to where, for what exactly–I didn't know. And I'm sure Graham knew it was an empty threat. But it was all I had. I certainly wasn't going to seize control physically.

I felt totally ridiculous. Shame coursed through my veins like a drug, stealing my breath and making me clammy, coloring me to the tips of my ears, my forehead. It only worsened when Graham set about adjusting me, pushing me further up so that my ass sat squarely in his lap, my feet dangled helplessly, kicking at the air. At least I was able to brace myself with my hands against the floor.

To my horror, I felt the air on my backside as Graham tugged down my shorts, though not without difficulty as I was pressed flush to his thighs and wiggling to free myself.

"No," I groaned, squirming, "let me go!"

But Graham pressed his arm against the small of my back, adding pressure until I realized my struggles were useless.

"Perhaps we'll have an exercise writing lines this evening, but it won't be a report," he said.

What does that mean?

"Next time, if you obey, maybe I'll allow you to keep your shorts on."

Bullshit.

"Why are you being punished, Klara?"

Oh god, why couldn't the earth open up and swallow me whole right now?

"Please," I whined. "You can't do this."

A sharp smack hit my rear and I yelped, though more from surprise than pain.

"Why are you being punished, Klara?"

"Because… because I disobeyed you." My face burned hot at the forced confession. "Because I didn't listen to the rules and I left my room."

"And what kind of punishment do you receive when you're a disobedient little girl?"

Please don't make me participate in this, I thought. *It's too humiliating.* But I knew what he wanted to hear. Graham wanted me to say something like, *I get spanked.*

Resentment boiled up in me, seizing my tongue. Foolishly, I spat, "You use the opportunity to show me what a prick you really are. As if I didn't already know."

I didn't immediately regret the words. For one glorious moment, they felt *fantastic.* To show him I wouldn't be broken by a mere display of his dominance. I had spirit, *dammit,* I'd earned this mission and I–

The next smack that hit my bottom stung much more than the other. Worse, it was accompanied by several more in rapid fire. And several more after that. Hard, sharp, insistent.

"Ow, stop! I swear to god, Graham, you better stop!"

Graham continued smacking my backside with his large, open palm. It particularly stung when he hit the region between my bottom and my legs–legs I hadn't stopped kicking. My panties rode up into the crease between my cheeks and I wondered how much he could see.

"Stop, wait! Let me up! You can't do this!"

When this is over, I told myself. *When I'm safely off his knees and out of spanking range, I will tell him what a fucking asshole he is, how much I hate—*

As if he could read my mind, the next smack hit my thighs and I jumped, crying out. He gave me an identical smack on the other thigh and I yelped again.

Returning to my rear, Graham continued spanking once every other second—and I couldn't believe how much it hurt. Wiggling only seemed to make him hit harder, so I tried my best to stop. Instead, my little cries and whimpers grew.

When Graham finally ended the punishment, relief washed over me. I tried to catch my breath and didn't immediately understand when I felt his hands on my panties, tugging them.

All at once, it hit me.

My spanking wasn't over.

"Wait, no!"

"No?" Graham asked, pausing. His tone sent chills down my spine. For some reason, what I said was very wrong.

"Did you just tell me *'no?'*"

"I—no. Yes. I'm sorry?"

"Klara, you will never tell me no again, is that clear? This spanking is long overdue. My only regret is that it can't be more severe. Though you've earned it, I'm saving the belt, for now. We need to pace ourselves for the week."

What did that mean?

I thought I'd die of embarrassment when Graham pulled down my panties. Squeezing my legs together, I prayed he couldn't see anything in between.

Something cool rubbed up and down my cheeks and it took a delayed moment to recognize the object.

Oh no.

No.

The evil-looking hairbrush.

Torturing me with slow circles, as if to juxtapose the pain it would soon inflict, Graham lectured as he caressed.

"You've earned yourself this dose of the hairbrush, Klara. You've earned far worse. However, because this is your first time, I will be merciful."

The blood rushing in my ears made it hard for me to hear him.

"Graham… don't do this," I begged.

"You're only confirming that you still need to learn."

The hairbrush left my bottom and suddenly smacked back down against my flesh with a sinister *snap*. I squealed and squirmed but Graham was ready. His strong hands pressed into my back, holding me down.

"You are free to kick and cry, but if you try to escape the discipline I provide, I will be forced to tie you down and double the punishment."

I groaned. He would do it.

When Graham started spanking again, I forced myself to accept it, to not fight him. Oh, I kicked. When that wicked hairbrush fell on my unprotected rear *again and again and again.* I moaned and wailed, trying to lessen the pain somehow. I knew I put on a show, but I didn't care. I didn't even care that my legs scissored, exposing myself to Graham's eyes. I cared only that he'd stop.

I didn't want to cry, but tears welled in my eyes.

"Please, sir, please!"

Graham ignored me.

Was a spanking supposed to hurt this much? Jesus, would it have been better if the girls prepared me by giving me a taste back in training?

I grew desperate, babbling, hoping something would stop the insistent rain of stinging blows to my fiery cheeks.

"Please, I'll be good. I will listen. I will do as I'm told. I understand you're in charge, Graham, sir!" The frantic words tumbled from my lips in a jumble, as if I searched for the magic phrase that would make him stop.

But he didn't.

I would surely bear marks. I guessed the rules about consenting to bruising didn't apply to him, to our dynamic. Over and over he spanked, often concentrating right on the area where I would later sit down, laying one awful smack directly on top of another. The pain became unbearable, I howled at the fire in my bottom. I begged, no longer caring if it made him smug, if he won.

"You're in charge, Graham. I'm your submissive, I will do anything you say. I will obey you, please, sir!"

I'd say *anything* for him to stop the relentless punishment.

At some point, I stopped fighting the assault of the hairbrush. My legs no longer thrashed. But even then, he pushed me further. Only after another minute of laying limp over his lap, when I could feel the tears pooling on my eyelashes and threatening to spill, did he finally still his punishing hand.

Please, let it be over, I prayed.

I blinked, causing a stray tear to fall down my cheek.

Slowly, the world returned, expanding beyond only Graham and his discipline.

It was morning. We had a full day ahead of us. I would be a model of submission. My bottom was on fire. My pussy was…

Oh, god.

I felt slick between my legs.

Could he see it?

How was that possible when I'd just endured terrible pain?

No, please. After what I'd just suffered, I couldn't bear this new humiliation.

"Are you going to submit in totality today or do I need to teach you a lesson with my belt?"

"No, sir," I whispered, failing to hold back my sob. "I'm sorry I disobeyed you, sir. I won't do it again. Please don't belt me."

I hated Graham for his threat.

I hated that I had to beg him not to do it.

I hated that it aroused me.

I couldn't handle any one of these feelings, let alone all three.

A second tear ran down my cheek and I sniffled audibly.

Graham's hand touched the lower curve of my ass, closer to my pussy than he'd previously dared. Stiffening immediately, I wondered if he could see or feel any wetness between my legs.

He withdrew his hand and I panicked.

Had he touched something? Was he examining it? Or was it my over-active imagination?

"I'm pleased you respond so well to discipline."

Oh god, oh god, oh god. Did he mean my contrition or my wetness? Or both?

I suddenly realized I wasn't alone. Through Graham's soft fabric I could feel a rock-hard—*rather large*—bulge beneath me. But… that didn't mean anything. Graham was probably just turned on by seeing a naked girl's bottom. It happened to men, involuntarily.

What was my excuse? I'd been spanked.

"We'll start each day in this manner. You will bring me the hairbrush and ask me to spank you. You will drape yourself across my knees."

Please no. Please just let me die of this unbearable embarrassment.

Graham rested his hand on my burning right cheek and left it there, making it difficult to concentrate.

"If your behavior has been exemplary, you will only receive a few swats with the brush. If you decide to disobey me in any way, you'll receive a harsh reminder of why that is a bad idea. Just like today."

I couldn't breathe. *Every morning?*

"It will set the tone for the day and serve as a reminder of who's in charge, who makes the rules."

I couldn't do this every day. But I had been too humbled to argue. Especially not when Graham wielded a hairbrush right above my sore bottom. And why wasn't he moving his hand? Was it a threat? Or just a form of gloating—*see, you're mine to touch any way I like.*

"We need to get you in the right frame of mind, Klara, and you need to stay there."

I frowned, once again perplexed. Did he mean that as his sexual submissive or his professional subordinate—or both?

"Who does this bottom belong to?" Graham asked, stroking my rear in a way that soothed, that felt nice, that confused the hell out of me.

"Y–you?"

"Is that a question?"

I swallowed. "No, sir. It belongs to you."

Just when I thought things couldn't get worse, Graham slid his hand between my legs and *cupped my pussy.*

Graham. Graham fucking Kellum. My colleague.

I wanted to protest that this couldn't be right; he took pretending too far. But all I could do was groan.

There was no way his hand wouldn't be wet.

Please don't mention it, please don't mention it.

"And who does this belong to?"

Was he serious? Was this getting me in the right frame of mind or… real? It felt…

I must have taken too long to reply because Graham *squeezed.*

Oh my fucking god, Graham Kellum squeezed my bare pussy and I–goddammit–moaned.

Covering my slip, I quickly replied, "You, sir. M–my p–pussy belongs to you."

And now I just wanted to die.

I'd never go on another mission. I'd never return to work after this. I was leaving ODX. I could never face Graham again. My face burned so hot with embarrassment, I wanted to plunge it into a tub of cold water.

For a moment, Graham didn't move, his firm hand just held me between my legs. I would have given anything to see his face or know what he was thinking. My thoughts seemed to spiral downward, tailspinning somewhere dark and dizzying me.

Terror that he'd punish me further. Fear that he'd say something about my obvious wetness.

Longing for him to stroke me.

I despised that one the most. That my body couldn't hide the yearning for his hand to move, to rub, to relieve the agony in my core. His fingers were *right there.* I struggled not to clench, not to show him by any further action that I was turned on.

I wasn't. Not by him. Not by *this.*

"Breathe, Klara," Graham ordered, in a strangely soothing voice. "Breathe."

I hadn't realized that I wasn't breathing much, if at all.

Slowly, Graham removed his hand and I exhaled a sigh of relief. Or frustration.

"Let's try this day with perfect obedience. Would you like me to pick out something for you to wear?"

"Y–yes, sir. Please pick out something that would please you."

"Well done," Graham praised, giving my sore rear a gentle squeeze, sending conflicting signals throughout my body.

"You will stand in the corner until I tell you time is up."

"Yes, sir," I replied, inwardly groaning.

Inelegantly, I struggled to right myself, surprised when Graham's hands grasped my waist. For half of a second his arms tensed and it seemed as if he acted to draw me closer to his chest before changing his mind.

Instead, he rigidly guided me into a sitting position that kept six inches between us. I moaned at the pain in my bottom but did not dare protest.

"Look at me." Graham's voice was low, firm.

Meeting his eyes after the punishment I'd just experienced was the last thing I wanted to do, but the fire in my bottom told me I better fucking listen.

When I lifted my gaze, my heart skipped a beat. If I didn't know better, I'd think something like lust darkened Graham's blue-gray eyes. Neither of us moved for a moment, transfixed.

"Into the corner," Graham rasped.

I blinked, clearing my eyes from some spell, some fairy dust temporarily clouding my vision. *Right. The corner.* More shame. With a resigned sigh, I peeled myself off his lap and shuffled to the corner.

"Hands on your head," Graham instructed.

Why did this keep getting worse?

Closing my eyes, I did as I was told, using the time to lecture myself. *Don't give him more reason to punish you or to think you're a lousy asset.* Do what he doesn't expect and surprise *him.*

Pressed to the wall, bottom on fire, I made a vow to try to obey before he could even command it. I would beat Graham to the punch and prevent any further justification for disciplining me.

Which made me wonder… *had he ever done this before?* He acted quite comfortable with it.

Dammit. Was that better or worse?

I couldn't believe how much a spanking hurt and I couldn't believe I'd just received my first one over Graham's knees.

"You may turn around."

With a deep breath, I turned to face him, bared to his gaze and desperately wanting to hide.

On the bed, he'd laid out my outfit for the day: a postage-stamp mini skirt, kitten heels, and a barely-there thong. The only portion of the outfit that fully covered me would be the shrunken t-shirt and even that looked midriff-bearing if I stretched.

Okay. Be submissive.

"Thank you, sir. I hope it pleases you to see me in this."

"I'm sure it will," Graham replied, narrowing his eyes with suspicion. But I guessed I impressed him enough that he allowed, "You may shower and change alone. Your toiletries are in the hall bath. You've got fifteen minutes for whatever you need to do. I'll be in my bedroom, waiting. Don't dally."

Dally? Why did everything he say sound like something an old man would say?

As soon as he left, I raced to ready myself, as if I'd impress him with how speedily I could complete the task. Digging a wristwatch from my bag, I saw I used ten minutes to take a hot shower, brush my teeth, and put on some minimal make-up. Then I darted back into my room to dress.

Graham was waiting in the living room when I finished and he stiffened when he saw me. Was he angry? I smoothed down my skirt.

"Stop fidgeting," he admonished, and I immediately stilled. To my surprise, Graham put his arm around my waist and pulled me to his side. I had thought perhaps he'd require me to walk behind him on a leash again. But this felt… intimate.

Frowning, I re-asserted an inch of space between us. It did not go unnoticed.

"Walking next to me is a privilege, Klara. With one word, I can make you crawl."

Forgetting myself, I grit out, "You think you're the good guy and you say things like that?"

Graham cocked an eyebrow and his voice grew deeper, more ominous than usual.

"I'm not the good guy."

Fuck, the way he said it. My knees weakened. Graham was right. I was afraid of him and perhaps that was wise. Swallowing, I relaxed my body back against his.

"Let me do the talking today. Don't speak unless you're spoken to."

I nodded. I could handle that.

Perhaps it gave me false confidence. I started to think I could manage whatever was thrown my way.

The fates must have been laughing at me.

PART III
Down the Kinky
Rabbit Hole

CHAPTER 19

BREAKFAST WAS SERVED in the main dining area, buffet style. Because I'd awoken early, we arrived early, despite having taken time for a discipline session.

I wasn't even close to hungry. Ironic, after struggling to adhere to Adriana and Margot's strict diet the past two weeks to slim down my tummy, all I needed to tie my stomach in knots was to sit across from Graham Kellum with my bottom burning.

Meeting his stare was nothing short of torture.

As if he knew, as if not even my own meals could be within my domain of control, *"Eat,"* he said, pushing a basket of bread in my direction.

Dutifully, I took a hard cranberry scone from the container and nibbled at one corner. Or maybe the little red berries were currants; I couldn't taste anything anyway.

This whole scene was strange, surreal, making me want to pinch myself. It was one thing to have a few drinks and engage in kink under the cover of night… but this? I didn't particularly enjoy the public nature of the event, and I wondered what Graham made of it. He was notoriously private; group fetish fests couldn't be his favorite way to spend the day. Eying couples strolling into the sunny breakfast room, I wondered what they'd gotten up to the night before, what they'd make of the red marks trailing down my thighs, who might secretly be yearning for a different Dom…

Graham sighed. "You're having a cocktail."

My eyebrows shot up, hopeful.

"If you don't relax, we'll both be sorry. Now, what do you usually drink at brunch when you're on holiday?"

"Uh… any kind of champagne cocktail is fine. I don't suppose you'd consider bringing over the whole bottle?"

Graham shot me a look and crooked his finger at one of the waiters. God, I hated the pompous way he did that. Was he playing a role or did he naturally beckon people in such a manner?

"She'll have a bellini," he said to the server. "I'll have a coffee, black."

The waiter bowed and hurried to fetch our order.

I quickly polished off my drink and felt *much* better when the champagne went to my head. It also took my mind off the pain in my bottom.

Once we'd finished eating, Graham led me into an adjacent library. *This is too fucking weird,* I thought, stumbling behind him in heels and a miniskirt at nine o'clock in the morning. It was like a never-ending walk of shame, and everything about my attire felt stranger for being surrounded by such luxury. Rich, damask prints, heavy curtains, and hand-woven oriental rugs. Antiques and objects d' art that likely graced the castle for generations. *If these walls could talk.* I imagined the castle being haunted by seventeenth-century ancestors looking on, shocked and appalled at what had become of their proper, country manor.

Throughout the day Graham and I socialized, which, thankfully, didn't require much conversation on my part. Graham slid into conversations, commanded them, and always left the other guests laughing and extending invites for "drinks" back in their rooms. Each time, I stiffened, afraid at what sounded like a thinly-veiled offer to engage in partner-exchange. But Graham always found a way to be politely vague about any potential acceptance, and both relief and gratitude washed over me. We kept an eye out for Victor and Angus, our prime suspects, but they were busy coordinating some kind of formal affair for the evening.

It wasn't until the late afternoon that my world turned upside-down once more.

Still mingling, we entered one of the rooms set up like a dungeon, and found a few couples already playing. Nearest the door, a sandy-haired man in his mid-to-late forties stood above his sub, whom he'd cuffed on her back to one of two tables.

Graham shifted his eyes briefly to mine and I read the warning in them, though I didn't understand it. The message was clear: *be on your best behavior.* Graham's posture tensed, then forcibly relaxed.

"Graham, old boy, where have you been hiding?" the man asked, and I knit my brow before remembering to smooth it. *Was this one of his friends?* But no, Graham had been ill-at-ease upon entering.

"Though I might hide away too if I'd bought that filly," the man said, snide. "She looks delicate enough to break from one turn about the castle."

I bit the inside of my cheek to keep from frowning at the insult.

"She does require the hands of an expert, to bend without breaking," Graham remarked. "But such a reward it is when she's *bent*, far exceeds any imagined return on investment."

I bit harder into the inside of my cheek, this time to keep from smiling. For *once,* I appreciated Graham's wit, as it was finally on my side. I tightened my grip on his bicep as a *thank-you* for coming to my defense.

"Randson, this is Klara, my sub," Graham said, introducing us.

"How are things at the club?" Randson asked, suddenly changing the subject.

"Business as usual," Graham replied.

"Yes, it must be tiring," Randson remarked, with what sounded like false, exaggerated sympathy. "How about we distract ourselves with a little amusement? Please, join us."

Graham nodded, but I didn't understand what was happening until I felt him guiding me to the open table.

Oh god. *Why?*

At Graham's nudging, I scooted up onto the surface and laid down. Fighting the rising panic, I gave Graham my arms and he cuffed each down in succession, above my head. Taking my ankles in his hands he did the same for my legs, until I was spread, helpless, and breathing erratically at the predicament. I looked at the girl tied up to my left, but she kept her eyes downcast.

Randson offered Graham a glass of something alcoholic I couldn't see. After the men toasted, the blond stranger asked,

"Would you like to hear Allison sing? She has the sweetest voice. Would you like to sing for us today, Allison?"

She did not look up as she replied. "Yes, master. If it pleases you, master."

Allison wore a black bra and panties, resembling a bikini with accessible ties. I understood why he'd chosen the outfit when Randson tugged the top and Allison's pert breasts spilled out for our view. I quickly looked away, but I could see out of the corner of my eye as Randson repeated the process on her bottoms, so that she lay bare before the men.

In a move that looked so harsh I clenched my pussy in sympathy, the blond Dom seized Allison between her legs, grabbing roughly with his hand. She began moaning, so I assumed he'd inserted his fingers into her, but again I averted my eyes.

I wish I'd had another glass of champagne, I thought, not wanting to face this sober.

I looked over to Graham and I wasn't sure why, but he seemed… pensive? Concerned? I *knew* that look. His face was a cipher but something calculating was going on behind his eyes. When he caught me staring, his expression quickly relaxed, and I wondered if I imagined it.

"That's my wanton little slut," Randson cooed, but there was no affection in his speech and his near-repulsed tone of voice repulsed *me.* I didn't judge Allison for her obvious pleasure at it, but I was thankful he hadn't purchased me as his submissive.

"Such a dirty, fucking whore, aren't you?"

"Yes…" she moaned. "Please touch your dirty whore."

Throughout her rocking, Allison kept her eyes downcast. I heard the wet, squishy noises and, embarrassed, wished I could close my ears.

How did I wind up here?

"You've got one minute to come and I want to see and hear the best orgasm you've ever had. Entertain us with your squeals like the whore you are. If you fail to please me, can you imagine what I'll do to this pussy later?"

Squish, squish, squish.

Allison didn't need to hear more. "Yes master, yes, yes!" she cried and *damn* if she didn't deliver. I couldn't help but look. Her body convulsed so hard I thought she'd break her bonds. The table creaked with the motion. Couples from the far side of the room turned in her direction to watch, mesmerized.

When something hit my nose, I realized I could *smell* her pleasure.

Well. This is a day I will never forget.

One final, throaty wail signaled the end of her peak. Her bucking suddenly ceased. Allison slammed back onto the table, a dazed and satisfied grin on her lips.

Randson wiped his fingers on his trousers and gave Graham a snide smile.

"She's a glorious instrument, isn't she? But then, I'm the master player, no?"

"Exquisite," Graham agreed, curtly.

"Shall we hear how finely you've tuned her strings?"

It took my brain a second too long to understand what he asked.

Oh god.

Graham was much faster; he already knew where this headed before it began.

No.

Randson wanted me to go next. Was this some kind of dick measuring contest? Only, instead of dropping trou and seeing who had the bigger cock, the prize went to whose submissive put on a greater show?

Shit, shit, shit.

Fucking *men.*

Maybe Graham would find a way–

"It would be my pleasure," Graham replied, smoothly. "And hers."

Oh god.

He couldn't be serious. He'd find a way out.

My heart was a hummingbird, tiny wings beating rapidly in my breast.

This can't be happening.

Graham stepped close to me.

But it was.

I couldn't stop it.

"Look at me."

His voice pulled me back from the edge of panic.

I gazed up into his dark expression, expecting I'd find something there–a secret, a plan. But the merciless look in his eyes told me to abandon that hope.

Oh, fuck, oh god. Was Graham going to… *pleasure me?*

I gulped.

No, no, no. Colleagues didn't stick their fingers inside each other during missions. They just did not.

"Keep looking, Klara. Eyes on me, little one."

Jesus, what was he saying?

"I'm going to allow you to preserve some of your modesty. I'm feeling generous after your efforts this morning...." He said it saucily, then trailed off, implying… something that didn't happen?

"But, Klara, if you dare look away, I'll tear your skirt off and call every man in this room to stand here and watch you writhe. Do you understand me?"

I gulped again, nodding vigorously. But I didn't understand. Was he trying to make this easier for me by dangling the threat of something worse? Or was he being an ass, as usual?

I kept my eyes locked on his, not bothering to conceal my panic. Was it better or worse to have to look?

Oh god, oh god.

I didn't want to come. I didn't want *him* to make me come. Not Graham, my colleague, a man I loathed. I would have preferred to have been forced to bring *him* to an orgasm, rather than surrender my own. And worst of all, I didn't want to *look* at him as I did it. Holding his gaze would expose not just my body, but all the twitches of pleasure, all the ecstasy as it floated across my face.

As I *gave* it to him? As he *took* it?

No, no, no.

I couldn't bear it, I couldn't.

My chest rose and fell in great, heaving breaths as Graham slid his hands beneath the handkerchief passing as my miniskirt. His touch felt warm, confident. I didn't know what he planned, I assumed he'd push aside my panties—but I gasped when he fisted the material and ripped them off.

His eyes seemed to... twinkle? Was there mischief beneath them?

Was some part of him enjoying this?

Of course he is, I thought. *He hates you and he's debasing you. What's not to like?*

I bit my lip to hold back the natural protest as Graham stroked my thighs, closer and closer to my pussy... readying me?

No, no, please.

I begged both for him to stop and for it to… stop feeling good.

Unconsciously, my hips bucked. I whimpered in shame.

Just go with it, I tried, mentally switching tactics. *That's what they want. A show. Give it to them.*

I didn't fake the moan when Graham's fingers first caressed my slit, though I know I flushed crimson.

Oh my fucking god. Graham Kellum's hands are stroking my pussy. For the second time today. Only now, with the intent to invade.

He ran the tips of his fingers up and down my wet folds several times and it shouldn't have felt as good as it did. My eyes must have fluttered without me realizing it, because Graham chided, "No, Klara, *look at me.*"

I refocused and the next moment, he drove one finger deep inside me. I can't be blamed for the sound it tore from my throat. I hadn't had sex in months yet I'd been bombarded with erotic material the past two weeks, hijacking my mind, revving it up. Then I'd been plopped into this castle, this entire party, designed to heighten my arousal. On top of all that I'd been spanked until I was frustratingly soaked this morning, with no release.

Fuck.

It was obvious.

I'm as tight as a bowstring and I need to be plucked.

No doubt Graham knew. Nothing escaped him.

The high-pitched gasp coming from my mouth signaled my rapture and I noticed that son-of-a-bitch smirked. He quickly added another digit—which only made me gasp in ecstasy a second time.

When Graham curled his fingers, I swore I'd never felt anything so blissful in my life.

My hips rocked, meeting his thrusts, and the walls of my pussy clenched on their own accord. He passed his thumb over my clit and I saw stars. My legs shuddered as he teased it again, rubbing in calculated, expert circles.

I stopped paying attention to the moans falling from my lips. I thought only about meeting the pleasure Graham coaxed from my body and the increasingly difficult challenge of keeping my eyes open. He thrust his fingers in and out, driving me wild. It always took me a long time to relax enough to come, but Graham summoned my pleasure with a god-like power for which I despised him even more.

I could feel the orgasm begin to build when he inexplicably slowed his fingers.

What... why? Weren't we putting on a—

"Beg," he said.

—show.

Oh.

Oh, no.

"Beg, my little one."

He wasn't going to allow me equal participation in chasing my orgasm the way Randson did Allison. He was going to require I humble myself even further.

"P-please," I stammered. My legs strained, seeking a way to meet his fingers, to find more pressure, bucking up at nothing, shamelessly.

"Please what?"

"Please, sir. Let me come."

Graham pushed his fingers into me *hard* and that unfamiliar wail tore once more from my mouth.

God, please, don't stop.

I might have murmured the words aloud. By the time Graham brought me close to orgasm the second time, I no longer cared if anyone saw. I didn't even care if it gratified Graham to debase me like that. I ached only for release.

And still, he denied me.

"*Please, sir,*" I repeated at his prodding, and my humiliation didn't end there. Graham made me utter horrible things. I said them all, desperate to come.

"*My p—pussy belongs to you.*"

"*My pleasure is at your will.*"

I had just enough of my wits about me to feel hot shame on my face, but not enough to outweigh my desire for release.

Oh. My. God.

I don't know how many times he pushed and pulled me, dancing at the edge of my orgasm before he finally allowed me to come. By the end, my head lolled like a drunkard, partially due to the near-impossible task of keeping my eyes on him while pleasure washed over me. I couldn't hold back my moans if my life depended on it. Though Graham preserved some of my modesty by allowing my skirt to remain, I could preserve none of it myself as the orgasm shuddering through my body might have been the best I'd ever had.

Graham's hand worked my pussy like a command. Like he knew exactly how to draw the most mind-blowing pleasure from me and he took it with each skilled motion of his fingers.

Holy. Fuck.

I felt myself shudder as I peaked, somehow the experience enhanced for being completely restrained.

Spent, breathless, my mind blanked for several moments during and after my climax. I lay boneless on the table. I was aware the men spoke, but I couldn't even make out the words.

Consciousness returned slowly, and with it the unpleasant awareness that Graham had not withdrawn his fingers from inside me because my core squeezed a few final times around them, greedy for more. My own sticky wetness dripped out onto the table.

My first cohesive thought was pure and thorough mortification of what Graham had just witnessed.

As I came, I'd closed my eyes, and he must have known I couldn't help it. At least it was some small measure of privacy, but part of me wished *I* could have seen *his* face at that moment.

Are we done? I longed to run back to our room and hide for the rest of the party. *Please, oh please, just let me hide in my room and never see your face again.*

My eyelids fluttered open as Graham very slowly slid his fingers out of me. He brought them to his lips and I watched, wide-eyed, as he licked them.

Correction. Licked *one* of them.

"Would you like to taste my triumph, Klara?" he asked, having saved a digit for me.

No. I absolutely would not.

"Yes, sir."

Graham traced my lips with his finger, then dipped it inside, forcing me to suck the tang of my own juices.

"Good girl," he praised.

I fucking hate you, I thought. *More than ever.*

But my body clearly needed to get the message.

CHAPTER 20

"**Y**OU'LL BE ACCOMPANYING me to a formal dinner this evening," Graham informed me, settling back in our room.

I barely had the courage to meet his eyes after the day's humiliation. *Was he going to say* nothing *about what he'd just done to me?* I knew we were playing at being Dom and sub, I knew we were on a mission, but we *both* knew what we were outside of this.

Fucking *colleagues*. Who'd one day have to see each other again across a conference table.

And he'd just… stuck his fingers inside me and… *oh god.* This wasn't *fucking* normal. I needed him to apologize or acknowledge it or *something*. I felt trapped in my own head; the walls Graham built around himself as my Dom were starting to make me feel so alone, so desperate.

"White tie," Graham said. "A few dresses were offered. I've already selected yours."

I huffed, annoyed that I wasn't allowed to even see the options.

"You mean black tie. I'm wearing a gown?"

Graham flashed a quick grin and I didn't immediately know why, but I could tell I didn't like it.

"White tie is the more formal of the two. Tails and waistcoats. White shirt, white bowtie. Don't worry, we'll be skipping the top hats and canes. Although I'm sure a few of the gentlemen will be bringing a cane of some other sort," he remarked, wryly. "You'll be wearing a gown, with gloves. Just remember to remove them before eating."

I stared, having no idea what Graham was talking about.

"It's more typical here, I suppose," Graham mused, waving his hand. "But I'm surprised you haven't been to any traditional weddings or state dinners in D.C."

State dinners? Was he serious? *Why yes, I'm on the president's short-list of attendees when visiting dignitaries are in town.* And for fuck's sake, the last wedding I'd been to had a backyard barbeque theme.

I bat my lashes and switched to Russian, speaking in a language he couldn't understand a comment that loosely translated to: *I don't need to put on airs like some arrogant people do.*

Graham stilled, becoming eerily quiet.

He couldn't have known what I'd said, could he? I quickly scanned my memory for some mention of his studying Russian, but I didn't find any. *I suppose my tone was hard to miss,* I thought, pursing my lips.

"I seek to educate you, Ms. Volkov. By sharing knowledge," Graham said, taking his time as he stalked forward. I instinctively backed away, feeling the threat. "And how do you return the favor? By taunting what knowledge you can withhold? Teasing. Like a brat."

I opened my mouth, scoffing. He was twisting it. When he put it that way, he made me look like the bad guy. But I knew without a doubt that he'd been smug about *his* knowledge, lording it over me.

"We won't have any outbursts like that at dinner. Do you need a reminder of who's in charge?"

I shook my head, quickly looking down. Maybe I *had* been a little bitchy about it.

Graham reached his hand beneath my hair. He grabbed a fistful and tugged my head back, forcing me to look up at him. It didn't hurt, but the threat was unmistakable.

"Let's try finding a better use for your mouth, shall we?"

My breath caught. *Did he mean…*

"An apology, Klara."

Oh. Right.

"I'm sorry, sir," I whispered, without feeling behind it.

Graham studied my face.

"On your knees."

My lip jut, petulant, while I stared daggers. Nothing I'd done had been *that* bad. He just wanted to reassert dominance, to wield authority over me.

Graham removed his grip on my hair to rest his hands on my shoulders, guiding me to my knees. His fingers found my chin, forcing it up. I fisted my hands, fingernails digging into the flesh on my palms.

"I'm sorry, sir," I apologized through clenched teeth.

"Show me."

I sucked in a sharp breath. Again, my thoughts headed in one direction with his cock at eye level. Unbidden, my mind pictured the act of fellatio, of Graham's sizable erection

I had felt beneath me that morning. Some unwanted, innate reaction had me licking my lips at the image. *Did he mean…*

"I—what?"

"Kiss my shoes," Graham instructed. "Each."

Seething, heat exploded across my face. In a strange way, debasing myself by kissing his shoes was worse than if he expected to be orally serviced. I once again wanted to die. Or kill Graham. Either. Both.

But the two of us couldn't exist like this, couldn't go on for a week.

Steeling myself, I bent low and brought my lips to Graham's goddamn overpriced shoes. Subserviently, I kissed one, then the other. I renewed all my vows to find *some* way to report him *somewhere*. I would detail everything he'd done—the spanking, the… well, I'd skip the part about how he made me come. But surely making us pretend in private was taking the mission too far.

I shot back to my feet without waiting for permission.

"Don't sulk," Graham chided, taking my arm like he owned me and tugging me to my bedroom closet.

I couldn't endure a week of his cocksure manhandling. I was so angry the blood racing through my veins felt hot, reminding me of the expression *blood boiling*.

Even if my pussy tingled in spite of it.

"STOP FIDGETING."

Graham's voice carried that warning tone again. He looked dashing in his tailcoat and I'm sure he knew it. He'd dressed me in the gown he'd chosen. My palms sweated beneath the long gloves at the prospect of facing a room with people who'd seen me nearly-naked, possibly heard me orgasm, and now would judge my formal table manners.

It was too much.

The black dress clung to my skin and dipped down my front, revealing cleavage artificially pushed up by a padded bra. A slit ran up one leg high enough that I worried with each step I'd flash something intimate. The gown ran just the wrong side of appropriate, and I had a feeling the other subs would be dressed similarly—in a nod to formal attire while still being obviously dressed for the party's kinky theme.

At Graham's order, I stopped fidgeting with my metal collar, but I still wanted to scream. He didn't understand. I needed a break, I needed to breathe. It was one thing to submit to a stranger, it was another entirely to submit to *Graham*.

I felt even more trapped in my mission, knowing he was *right there,* that he knew the truth about everything... but I couldn't share the burden. He wouldn't talk to me like an equal, a co-worker. It made me feel more isolated than if a complete stranger had purchased me. It made it all harder, instead of easier. The auction, the spanking, the forced climax. It was all too much and I felt emotionally drained.

I can't do this, I thought, wanting to scream or cry. *I can't take one more step.*

Suddenly, Graham's fingers found my chin, tilting my head up. I didn't want him to know I was on the verge of tears. But my lip trembled. I hated that I needed something from him, that at this time, only he could give it to me.

Graham's thumb reached out, lightly brushing my cheek.

Say my name, I willed, unsure why I wanted to hear it. I just needed to be seen, known. To feel less alone. To feel like I wasn't losing myself down this rabbit hole.

"You've never looked more beautiful," Graham said, voice husky.

My eyes snapped up. Was that a genuine compliment? It wasn't my name, it wasn't even acknowledgement of our past, not really. But it was… hint enough. Even if I grasped at straws, I didn't care. I held onto it like he'd thrown me a life preserver in the midst of the ocean. Had he known? Had he seen on my face that I was at my wit's end?

Graham leaned down to my ear. I could feel the rough caress of his stubble. His hands grasped my waist, drawing me to him as I let out a small gasp.

"I've got you," he whispered.

My heart seemed to skip a beat at those three little words. No one had ever said anything like that to me before. There was something more compelling about hearing it than even *I love you.* Possessive and protective at the same time.

I've got you.

My shoulders relaxed and I allowed myself to lean into his hands, overflowing with gratitude for the comfort and security the vow provided, even if only for a moment. I clung to that vow. Tossed about in a savage sea of raw exposure, of vulnerability that brought me to my knees, Graham was my anchor. Whether I liked it or not.

"Thank you," I whispered, staring into his blue-gray eyes. Graham was so close, I could see the fine lines crinkling their edges. His lips were inches from my own. I could feel his breath. See how the light reflected on his thick, perfectly-styled hair. He'd slicked it back for the affair.

Graham drew closer, leaning down… and before I knew what I was doing, my eyelids fluttered, my mouth parted…

Graham pressed a soft kiss to my forehead. He quickly straightened.

Returning to his stern lecture voice, he said, "I expect you to obey every one of my commands without hesitation. Like a good girl. Is that clear?"

I took a steadying breath. "Yes, sir."

He held out his arm, formally. I tucked mine within, and we left our bungalow together.

"There are going to be social dinners each evening," Graham remarked, as we crossed the grounds leading back to the castle. The night was warm, with just the slightest breeze. "Not everyone will join, but it's in our best interest to do so."

Of course, I understood. We needed to continuously mingle, to find out as much as we could about everyone here.

"Most of the dinners are themed. White tie, primary school role play, fantasy cosplay, masquerades…"

"Like a cruise or an all-inclusive vacation," I quipped, smiling.

Graham shot me a look. "Well, yes. But more refined."

I arched one challenging eyebrow in his snobbish direction. Cruises might not be the height of elegance, but neither was a dinner party with girls in Japanese sailor uniforms crawling around their master's feet.

"Perhaps refined is not the right word," Graham admitted, a smile threatening to curl his lips. "Regardless, you will conduct yourself with both refinement and total submissiveness."

"Yes, sir."

THE DUCK WAS DELICIOUS. THE dinner was draining.

Maybe Graham was right; I couldn't handle the pressure of maintaining cover. Posing as a submissive while probing for information. Trying to remember the dual roles and trying not to *feel* anything. Or maybe it was only difficult because Graham had bought me and he made me feel so… so… out-of-sorts.

When Victor and Angus first appeared to give a welcome speech, I second-guessed every glance I cast in their direction. *Was it too much? Was Graham judging my skill?* And, over dinner, whenever Graham looked in my direction, I shifted nervously, brushing back my loose waves of hair. *Did I look enticing? Pretty?*

Did it matter?

Dinner had been set up on circular tables back in the same room where we'd had breakfast, only now the hall glowed with candles. All the guests arrived in similar attire, as I suspected. Two or three of the submissives eschewed the rules and donned short, tight dresses, better suited for clubbing, but most girls wore risqué gowns and elbow-gloves.

Like a puppy dog, I trailed Graham around the room as he mingled and followed his lead. At least, not speaking much gave me a chance to ruminate on the two primary suspects—the event organizers. I'd already taken a disliking to Victor, who openly leered at my breasts. But Angus's compliments seemed polite-to-a-fault, and it raised a tingle in the back of my neck. *Was he faking it to hide his true nature? To lure unsuspecting women to offshore soirées?*

"Thank you *so* much for coming, we're honored to have you here in our humble manor," Angus gushed, clasping Randson's hand in a shake. The large man dwarfed the scrawnier Randson—he pretty much overshadowed everyone. Angus's head, with its shock of red hair, bobbed several inches above most other Doms. From the look of it, I'd guess he even had to duck to enter some of the older rooms of the castle.

"And you!" Angus said, turning to another man. "I'm delighted you've joined us. I hope you find everything to your liking. You'll notice we've planted new rose bushes this year..."

Victor barely listened to his co-host. "Ah, the after party," he announced, seeing guests begin to funnel to one side of the room as staff pushed tables to the other.

Jesus, what was happening now?

The candles were blown out and soft lights from the wall sconces flicked on in their place. Upbeat music began, piped into the room in the same fashion as it had during the auction.

I looked nervously at Graham, but my eyes widened when I saw what was occurring behind him. Couples started to dance and the girls either voluntarily stripped off their dresses or the men helped them out of their gowns.

My heart picked up speed as I looked back to Graham.

Couldn't anyone keep their clothes on at this fucking party?

Well, the men did. Full white-tie. While the girls twirled in... what was looking to soon be nothing at all. They giggled as they spun, joyous, inebriated.

Graham met my eyes, holding them steady.

Are you ready? His gaze seemed to ask.

No, I thought, desperately. *Not again.*

I scrunched my face and closed my eyes as Graham slid the straps of my dress down my shoulders. My skin met cool air as the gown pooled at my feet. I stepped out, obediently, and Graham kicked the garment to the wall.

At least it's dark.

I whimpered when he unhitched my bra, baring my breasts to the world.

Here it comes...

But Graham didn't reach for my thong. Instead, he wrapped one arm around my waist and pulled me close, pressing me to his chest. He swept me into a turn, holding me too near to be formal. When the turn ended, he didn't let go. After a moment, I realized he wasn't going to. I wore my heels and my black thong, giving the room a good view of my ass, but he kept me close enough to shield my breasts and panty-covered sex from prying eyes.

Because he knew I didn't want to be so exposed again?

Or was he playing a role? The possessive Dom, the one who didn't want to share, who didn't want others to see his property?

I buried my head against Graham's chest, knowing I was inches from semi-public nudity again; knowing that at any minute, if Graham decided it, I could be dancing bare. *Hell,* I could be putting on a show, if ordered. If Randson challenged him again like that afternoon. If Graham couldn't–or didn't want to–find an excuse to prevent it.

I clutched his back tighter.

What if another man *had* bought me and commanded me to dance naked? Was Graham right? Was I ill-equipped to handle this mission?

After three songs of awkwardly-tight dancing, Graham whispered, "We're walking back to the room now. Klara, you must keep your arms at your sides. Don't disobey me."

Fuck.

I understood. My dress was long gone, the bra had been kicked aside during the dancing. To dress me back up would draw curious attention at my prudishness. I was going to have to make the trek bare-breasted.

I gulped and nodded.

Thankfully, when Graham broke us apart, he quickly turned me toward the exit. Wrapping an arm around my waist, he escorted me to the rear doors of the castle. We didn't meet anyone until a male member of staff scurried across our path and I cringed, shyly turning my face toward Graham's side.

When we reached the moonlit lawn at the back of the castle, I breathed a sigh of relief. Even though it felt strange being half-naked on the open grounds, we weren't likely to be seen again on the short walk to the cottage.

"TIME FOR BED," GRAHAM SAID, not five seconds after we'd entered our bungalow.

I blinked, stunned.

"Go. Undress," he pointed toward my room. "I'll be in shortly. I have some things to take care of."

Graham started walking to his room, leaving me. Suddenly, everything I'd been bottling up since he bought me came spilling to the surface. I couldn't do this any longer. Pretend that we were strangers. Be all alone. Be so... locked out of his thoughts. Just as I had before we left for the evening, I felt like crying once more.

"Please, wait," I pled. "I can't do this."

I didn't need or want to accompany Graham into his bedroom. I just didn't want to go to my own feeling so alone.

Graham paused, but he didn't turn around.

"*Please.* I can't keep acting like this. Like we're not both here for the same reason. Please. Talk to me. Let me in."

Graham turned around, giving me hope. For a moment he glowered, saying nothing. But the longer he paused, the more I despaired. I was ashamed to hear myself whimper, fighting back the tears.

"Klara…" Graham sighed through his nose, clenching his jaw. He spoke slowly, authoritatively. "If you feel comfortable, you'll lose the sense of danger and you'll slip up. I know you. Every Dom has to maintain a bit of mystery, a threat. In this case, it's more important than ever. And especially with someone like you."

"You're wrong," I argued. But I really wanted to shout something else. *You scare me, Graham, it doesn't matter how close I get.*

"I'm not."

"Then punish me!" I cried, surprising even myself. God, was it the alcohol? We'd had our fair share of cocktails that evening.

Graham narrowed his eyes and tilted his head.

Did his overly-cautious mind think I was toying with him or playing some angle?

Desperate, I threw myself onto my knees, half-crawling to his feet.

"Punish me. Degrade me, debase me, I don't care." I looked up at him, trying not to cry. "Just let me in. If you have to frighten me more for it, if you think you have to hurt me to counterbalance this… this… perceived closeness, then do it. I don't care. Don't shut me out. I can't do this alone, Graham. Sir."

Graham studied my face but said nothing.

"Please," I begged, clinging to his trousers, not caring what it took. "You think I'll forget myself. Slip up. Get lippy. So balance it out. If you tear down walls in some places, build them up in others. I don't care. I'm giving you permission. I'm asking for it."

My heart pounded against my ribcage. I knew what I was suggesting wasn't even close to right, wasn't the proper way to play. At this party or in any BDSM scene in the real world.

"You want me to punish you, harder than I already plan to," Graham rasped, "in exchange for relaxing the rules a bit, in private?"

"Yes! Do whatever you feel is necessary. Only… talk to me. If you have to do it when I'm draped over your knees, fine. Just please, Graham, sir. I… I… need you. In this."

When the tears came, I couldn't figure out if they were from shame or exhaustion or… relief. Everything was so damn confusing. I was suggesting adding yet *another* layer, another game within a game. A lie wrapped in a truth wrapped in a lie, dizzying me until I couldn't sort out what was real any longer.

A perversion of the perverse.

Graham knew it too. I could read it in the tension in his shoulders, the continued clenching of his jaw. But something darkened behind his eyes.

For whatever reason, he wanted it.

My submission.

To punish me.

For *me* to want it, in whatever dark way I had of suggesting it.

I honestly didn't know how far he planned on taking our roles, in private. But I had given him a twisted way of taking more.

Or had I given myself a twisted way of asking for it?

Graham's fingers found my cheeks, brushing away the tears.

"Go to your room and take off the rest of your clothing. You may get under the covers. We'll discuss Victor and Angus before bed. I have my opinions on each of them. I'm curious to hear yours."

I let out a breathless laugh, blinking back tears. "Thank you, sir," I whispered.

"I'll have to punish you harder tomorrow morning."

"Yes, sir."

CHAPTER 21

"**Y**OU HAVE FIFTEEN minutes to get ready. When you're done, you will exit the bathroom without any clothing. You will crawl to me. You will hand me the hairbrush and ask me to spank you. You will place yourself over my knees. When I've sufficiently disciplined you, you will thank me."

My face burned hot, beet red. All the more for how utterly at ease Graham issued commands. As comfortable as if he simply ordered how he wanted his breakfast eggs prepared, while I struggled to breathe.

You bargained for this, I reminded myself, swallowing hard.

I did as instructed, quickly. Clutching the bathroom door frame and peeking around, I saw Graham had already dressed for the day in gray pants and a collared shirt. Ominously, he'd rolled up his sleeves, revealing toned forearms. No longer gelled, his dark hair sat loosely on top of his head with just the slightest wave. His ever-present stubble completed the picture of cool, effortless masculinity.

He was sitting in the same armless dining room chair he'd spanked me in the day before. Cringing, I stepped out from behind the door, dropped to all fours, and crawled buck-naked across the floor.

To Graham fucking Kellum.

Who looked… kind of… handsome. Or he would, if I didn't know him as a total prick underneath that chiseled jaw and all the rest of the fortunate bone structure.

The only thing I wore, the only thing I *ever* wore, was the damn silver collar. Which was worse than being naked.

Swallowing again, I spied the hairbrush on the coffee table. I crawled over to pick it up, giving Graham an unobstructed view of my ass, then crawled to his feet. When I handed him the brush, he tilted my head up to look at him as he so often did.

His cold, blue-gray stare was deeper and more intense than before.

Fuck, fuck, fuck. I was wet. Already.

Why? Certainly not for him.

I'd gotten what I'd wanted last night; we'd spoken as colleagues for at least half an hour. Graham believed Victor was most likely the sex-trafficker we were looking for. I insisted it was Angus—no one was naturally *that* polite, fawned over guests to *that* extent. It was definitely forced for some reason. Graham and I finished debating, ending in a stalemate. Then he tucked me into bed and shut off the light.

He held up his end of the bargain. It was time for me to honor mine.

Dazed, I stared at his formidable lap.

Why was this all so confusing?

I chewed my lip, debating. I couldn't do it. Couldn't ask for punishment, to willingly place myself over his knees.

"Graham, I... I mean, sir, I... I'm sorry. I know we had a deal but. I can't."

My heart thumped with renewed speed. Inching back, I protested, "Can't we find another way? I mean... it's not fair. I shouldn't have to be punished just to speak with you on equal terms."

"Klara. You're the one who struck this deal."

"I know, but... I don't want a spanking."

Even if my pussy thinks I do. My brain knows how much it will hurt.

"I don't want a spanking," I repeated. "It's not fair."

Not that it mattered to Graham, self-proclaimed "bad guy," after all.

His eyes held that dangerous warning I knew too well, his face set in that stony, villainous expression. He'd barely moved a muscle but I felt the danger.

Instead of capitulating, like I should, fear made me irrational. Wringing my hands, I looked for a way out.

It's too embarrassing. Too painful. And it wasn't *fair.* If someone else bought me, I wouldn't know them and would never have to see them again. But Graham...

"I *can't.* Sir, please. I don't want a spanking." I folded my arms across my body and shrunk backwards.

"No, no, *no!*"

Graham rose and scooped me up off the floor. Knowing where he planned on depositing me made me fight even harder to free myself, but of course it didn't do any good. Flipped like a child across his knees, I let out a groan and pressed my legs together.

"I shouldn't be surprised at your behavior. You really are a brat."

"Graham, sir, please understand–"

This is all new to me.

It hurts.

I don't want this.

You make me nervous.

Even if I'm somehow wet.

Not you. Anyone but you!

Goddamn, I'm just… hella confused.

I didn't know what I wanted to say.

"I–I… I'm sorry," I whined, thinking it best to show contrition when my bare bottom was within striking distance and his strong hands were wrapped around my midsection, allowing no escape.

Why didn't I just obey when I had the chance?

I hung my head, defeated. Graham said nothing, perhaps biding his time, letting me wage the private war I was having with myself.

He would have his way. I could either submit and make it easier on myself or make it harder.

"Will you p–please spank me, sir?" I finally whispered.

Graham didn't miss a beat.

"Why are you being spanked, Klara?"

"To keep me in line. Because I need to learn my place." My voice came out breathless, sultry. *Was I saying the right things?* "Because you decreed it would happen every morning and it's your right."

Fuck. I was definitely aroused in spite of myself and my fear of that awful, impending smack I knew I'd receive any moment.

Graham tapped the cool hairbrush against my rear–a warning.

I guess I'd get no warm-up this time.

The first smack hit me and I jumped. It was harder than yesterday and right on my sit-spot.

"S—sir," I breathed, battling terror, adrenaline racing through my veins.

"As we discussed, you were already going to receive a harder spanking than originally planned, more than a maintenance spanking. But now you've gone and made it even worse by refusing to obey. You need a good, thorough dose of the hairbrush. Do you agree?"

Fuck. No.

"Y—yes, sir."

Graham wasted no time in bringing down the brush again with unmerciful force.

By the time he finished, I was howling. The spanking was brief, but relentless, and this time he brought me to tears. It wasn't full-blown sobbing and wailing, but unlike yesterday, several tears escaped down my cheeks. I'd flailed my legs and Graham smacked deeper in the crevice between my bottom, as well as paid more attention to the tender skin on my thighs.

Yet, I also felt a funny lightness I couldn't explain. A strange... release. My limbs took on a weightlessness, a willingness to be guided.

When Graham helped me into a sitting position on his lap, I didn't fight it. In the back of my mind, I worried my shameful wetness would show on his pants. But I couldn't seem to care too much, almost as if I were slightly drunk. I quietly sobbed into Graham's chest and I must have thrown my arms around his neck when I turned, but I didn't remember doing it. At the same time, my hips rocked, pantomiming sex. I immediately stilled when I realized it.

"Shh…" he said, stroking my back. "Are you going to be a good girl today?"

"Yes, sir," I moaned, playing my role. I knew it was all just a game to get me in character yet it felt almost… natural.

But it wasn't. Of course. Graham was only manipulating me to put me in the right mindset and to wrest control of the mission–likely just to prove my incompetence and to claim success under EI6.

Any affection was a ploy I shouldn't fall for.

SCATTERED ABOUT THE ELEGANT DRAWING room were numerous chairs, some already occupied by other guests. One large, stone hearth climbed halfway up the far wall, though no fire was needed on a summer's afternoon. Graham chose an overstuffed armchair toward the richly-curtained windows facing a green, rolling pasture outside.

"Come. Sit on my lap."

Feeling like my limbs were made of mud, I shuffled over to his side. Gingerly, I tried to position myself so that I'd maintain modesty, but it was no use. The short dress Graham had chosen for me rode up in the back, pressing my bare, sore rear to his muscular thighs.

The act of sitting in his lap made butterflies take wing in my stomach. The sensation only increased when Graham reached up, stroking the nape of my neck, playing his role in front of the guests milling about after breakfast. I begrudgingly followed his lead, nuzzling closer, and caught his clean, masculine scent. *Funny how other couples could engage in depraved acts before me, totally naked, but the simplest touch of Graham's felt laced with more erotic tension.*

At the same time, a small but growing part of me resented having to submit to the morning's discipline. I had that uncomfortable feeling again that Graham could almost read my mind as he idly stroked my silver collar, reminding me who was in charge.

Was Graham right? Was I a brat?

After the spanking I'd been eager to jump at his commands. Now that we'd eaten breakfast and time had passed, the recollection of our professional roles came creeping back. The memory of all the times Graham sauntered around our office as if he owned the place, the stinging pain of moments he talked down to me, and worst of all—when he worked against me, like trying to prevent me from going on this mission in the first place.

"Tell me what you see," Graham whispered into my ear, surprising me. I pulled back and searched his face for a trick. The look in his eyes told me he meant, *professionally.*

Was that how this would work? Was I allowed to speak as his colleague when he permitted it? We were secluded enough in our corner that I *could...*

The truth was, I liked cataloguing things and I had noticed a pattern as other couples strolled between the rooms. Had he been watching me watching them? Graham stroked his lips, looking at me expectantly.

"There seems to be... subcultures within the subculture."

Graham said nothing, so I continued.

"Preferences. Cliques," I whispered in his ear. He stroked my back, keeping up the guise of an affectionate couple. "Some of these people know one another outside of the event, others gravitate based on a particular fetish under the kink umbrella. Over there, on the far side of the parlor, the group that went straight for the leather attire… they're more into the master/slave dynamic, I think. And that group still poking around the buffet," I continued, subtly shifting my head in that direction, "some of the girls are wearing knee-highs or frilly skirts. I'm guessing they like little girl play. At least, the men do. If the sub didn't previously know her buyer, she doesn't have much say in the matter, I suppose. If he wants her to call him daddy, she best reply in kind."

"Oh?" Graham mused, idly tracing his fingertips down my leg, searing a path of fire in their wake. Pulling back, he stared at me like my conversation truly interested him. Like he was interested in *me*.

It's just pretend. But he's a damn good player.

"Since we don't have much time, I think we should focus on one person from each group, to start," I whispered. "Pump him or her for information about the others."

Graham nodded, curling one side of his lips into a pleased smile.

"And what's my subculture? Where do you see us fitting into these tidy little groups you've made?" His eyes bore into me as if they could see through me. For some reason, my heart began thumping at his question.

What was Graham, really? He lied so well, I wasn't sure how much of what he did was him embracing the role, how much of it was real, or how much of it was him simply relishing putting me in my place to show me how ineffectual I was.

Struck by the power in that gaze, I replied, "Straight-up Alpha Male. A real old school dominant who wants a straight-forward submissive to bend to his will. Traditional. Not to be trifled with."

"Is that so?" he asked, face frustratingly impassive.

"It is," I insisted, lifting my chin.

"And yet you keep *trifling.*"

"Well, I'm a brat. You said so yourself. We're a mismatch."

"Is that so?" he repeated.

I frowned. "What is this, some kind of Socratic method of questioning? Yes. *It's so.*"

It came out a lot brattier than I intended, which made Graham's eyes flash.

It wasn't my fault; he goaded me into trouble. Got under my skin and made me say things. As if I could throw him out from inside me, along with my words. It never succeeded, it only seemed to work him deeper into my veins; it only ever proved him right on some point of contention. I should have learned to just shut my mouth.

"P… please don't spank me again, sir," I whispered, fidgeting on his lap.

"Shh…" he spoke low into my ear, tucking back a strand of my copper hair. "I will never punish you for answering a question honestly."

I hadn't realized my hands clutched imploringly at the shoulders of his blazer, not until his words had me relaxing them. Conflicting emotions—resentment and gratitude—warred within me and I struggled to make sense of the bizarre sensation. Half of me wanted to smack Graham for lording over me his power to threaten, and half of me wanted to kiss his feet for his mercy. I fisted and flexed my hands, unable to decide if I wanted to wring his neck or cling to it. Was he manipulating me into such a perplexing position? Was this the stirring of some kind of Stockholm Syndrome?

God, it was only day two and I already couldn't handle my feelings.

Worse, it felt like the less I mastered them, the more *he* did.

CHAPTER 22

DAY TWO–AFTERNOON

I JUST WANTED TO go back to the office and never see Graham again. I would never be able to face him in those brightly-lit halls of ODX, never. Each passing hour only made it worse, I only suffered more embarrassment from which I'd never recover. By the time this week was over, we wouldn't be able to stand in the same building without me wanting to die of shame. Scratch that–the same country. He needed to stay in England and never set foot on American soil for the rest of his life. I certainly wasn't ever coming within landing distance of these shores in the future.

"I need to use the ladies' room," I said, finishing up lunch. "May I please be excused?"

At least some of my appetite returned, though I attributed it to the famish I felt after two days of struggling to exhaustion over Graham's knees. Physically and emotionally, he left me spent. Perhaps that was his intent.

I can't stand up to him if I can't even stand.

Graham nodded permission and I tottered off in my high heels to find the nearest lavatory. He said he enjoyed seeing me in heels. Again, I credited that to his need for control. *I can't run away from him if I can't run.* Or maybe he simply had a shoe fetish. Who knew what went on in his head? He shared so little and lied so well.

Halfway down the dark and windowless hall, I realized I hadn't chosen the correct direction. Not as richly appointed for guests, it looked like this area of the castle led to staff quarters.

"Is the little ginger lost?"

I jumped and spun to find Victor Hall standing close behind me—too close.

"Tell me what you're looking for and I'll help you find it. For a price."

His watery-blue eyes weren't looking into mine. Like before, they were firmly affixed to my breasts—and lower. He wasn't a tall man, maybe only 5'6", and in my heels we were almost evenly matched.

"I—uh, yes, sir. I need to find the bathroom, please."

Instead of answering, Victor stepped closer.

"I know where to direct you." He smiled, I think, but it was half a sneer. The leer in his gaze reminded me of Randson. Maybe Graham was right, maybe Victor was our suspect. Perhaps he and Randson even worked together. Yet I still couldn't push Angus's aggressive kindness from my mind. It was just the sort of cover-up behavior I'd suspect from someone hiding something.

"But what price are you willing to pay?" Victor asked, rubbing his square jaw, as if in thought.

"P—price?" I said, dumbly.

Victor inched forward and I realized he was backing me toward a wall. Nothing he did was overtly inappropriate or against the rules, but the threat remained.

"As I said. I will tell you where to go, for a price." He stretched his arm to the wall beside my head, blocking me without directly touching me.

I didn't like this, *at all*. Part of me felt like I should flirt with him—it's what a good agent would do. But part of me was revolted by this man. It was deeper than his actions, it was as if I picked up something distasteful by an unknown, sixth sense. My subconscious registered what my conscious did not, as if a rancid scent caught my nose, too subtle for my olfactory system to identify. Or like someone blew an unnaturally high-pitched sound, similar to that of a dog whistle. One primal part of me somehow *felt* the noise, while the other functioned, largely unaware.

I gulped, stalling for time, while Victor leaned closer.

"I... I..."

"Victor!"

The sharp call came from down the hallway and Victor instantly straightened.

Natalie.

I sighed in relief. She charged down the corridor, short, glossy hair swinging against her collar.

"Are you scaring the submissives?" She laid a gentle hand on his bicep, speaking like a stern teacher would *tsk* an errant pupil. "You know that's not allowed. Leave that to her Dom."

"Just helping the girl find the loo," he replied.

"Angus needs you in regards to that contractor for the roof leak," Natalie said. "Some kind of fee dispute."

"The work of the landed gentry is never done," Victor remarked haughtily.

"Sorry," Natalie shrugged. "I tried to handle it but It's above my pay grade. He insisted on speaking with the owners."

Victor gave a curt nod and walked off. Natalie watched him go down the long corridor, then turned to me.

"Are you alright?"

"Yes… thank you."

"He's harmless, really. Just gets caught up in all…this," she said, waving her hand. "What man wouldn't, right?"

"Right," I whispered.

She paused, then scrunched her red lips. "Ah… oh, I have to ask if you want to, but please don't… lodge a complaint? No one should touch you but your Dom, unless you both grant permission… but sometimes the men get carried away. But it's your right, of course."

"No, I'm fine, thank you. He didn't touch me."

Natalie flashed a big smile, exhaling. "I am really sorry." She gave me a squeeze, then made to leave.

"Wait!" I said. "Can you please help me find the bathroom?"

She rolled her eyes. "He wasn't helping you find it, was he?"

I forced a grin. "Not really."

"Ugh!" she looked up again, exasperated. "This way."

Natalie wrapped an arm around my shoulder and led me down the hall.

"SIR, I'D LIKE US TO talk. As… as… *civilized* people."

Graham and I were back in our bungalow, taking a break after lunch. I wanted a frank discussion of what transpired with Victor in the hallway and I didn't want Graham to shut me out of any theorizing.

Graham raised his eyebrows, smiling on one side of his mouth.

"I mean, as professionals. About the mission."

"Alright, Klara. But you remember our deal. You may speak freely only when I'm assured that it won't lead to any slip-ups later." He put his hands to his chin, as if considering. I folded my arms, feigning impatience though my pulse began to race.

"I'll allow you to speak as plainly as you like. As long as you're in a position throughout that reminds you of your place."

"And what position is that, *sir?*" I grit out, fighting the rising heat creeping up my neck.

His only reply was a cold smile. Graham left my bedroom and, from his own, I heard him unzip his black bag. When he returned, he ordered, "Take off your shirt and lay down on the bed."

"Are you serious?"

"Klara, you can't even follow the simplest commands. Do as you're told or you're telling me I need to make this worse for you."

I could have screamed. *Professionals don't behave like this.* "Fine. *Sir.*"

Huffing all the while, I took off my shirt and bra and laid down on the bed. One look from Graham and I lowered my arms, giving him an unobstructed view of my bare breasts.

Jesus, colleagues shouldn't see each other naked, ever, let alone this often.

"Give me your arms," he said.

I reluctantly obeyed and Graham set about strapping my wrists into the leather cuffs he attached to each bedpost. Panic began to rise within me as he hadn't yet deigned to explain what was to happen to me and I now had no way to fight him off.

Not that I ever did.

"I think we'll leave these here for the duration of our stay," Graham remarked, indicating the cuffs. Then he removed two small metal devices from his pocket.

"Nipple clamps," he said, watching my face to purposefully delight in viewing its immediate flush.

I gulped.

"We can speak as long as you wear them. But I'll be tightening them throughout."

"You're a sadistic prick, do you know that?"

Graham took my whispered insult like a compliment.

"Is this some kind of revenge for getting assigned the mission when you didn't think I had the capability? Cruel punishments for getting one over on you?"

"Now, Klara," he chided. "If you think this is what it looks like when I set my mind to cruelty, you really don't fear me as much as you should."

Goddammit. The *way* he said it. My mouth ran dry and my cunt, wet. I shivered with fear *and* a frustrating excitement. *Why?* Why did his words do that?

My small breasts felt heavy, aching for touch. But I didn't want *Graham* to touch me. I didn't. Just in case there was any confusion about my hard nipples, I looked away, frowning, almost snarling with disgust.

I snapped my head back when Graham snapped the nipple clamp onto my right breast.

"Ow!" I shouted, jumping.

He clipped the small, padded clamp onto the other breast and I hissed. Graham let me sit there for a minute, adjusting, groaning... *moaning.*

Damn, did I like it?

"Now, what was it you'd like to talk about, my dear?"

Fuck if I could remember. God, this mission made a mess of my head. I certainly couldn't report Graham any longer, not when my bargaining contributed to upping the stakes.

Well, yes, I had to discuss the specs while he tightened clamps on my nipples… it all makes sense if you understand the context…

I wouldn't be telling anyone about this, *ever.*

"Victor…" I began, squirming as I spoke, "that incident in the hallway I told you about. I—I know what you're thinking. That it only points more to him as the trafficker. But I still think we should spend more time investigating Angus. Although Randson gives me bad vibes too. What's the deal with you two, anyway? How do you know each other?"

My words came out jumpy, breathless. It was hard to concentrate with all my attention focused on my throbbing nipples.

Graham paused, tapping his tongue to his lips as he decided what to reveal.

"We know each other from school, but we belong to different clubs now. I'm a member of the Reform Club, he belongs to another, even more exclusive. Old money and typical entitlements. He likes to think he's better than the rest of us because of his lustrous ancestors."

I blinked at both Graham's unexpected openness and the idea of him not being totally overprivileged compared to someone else.

"You *are* old money. Didn't your great-grandfather build the family fortune or something like that?"

Not that I'd ever been asking anyone about Graham. It was just… common knowledge around the office. *Adriana mentioned something once,* I thought.

"That doesn't make you old money," he said, shaking his head.

It does to me.

"Right… so how far back does it have to go to be 'old'?"

"Further back than my surname and its accompanying fortune. You have to understand the lot. I could earn billions more than Randson and still wouldn't be an equal in his eyes. He rather despises me *more*, the more I earn, seeing as how his family has no further streams of income and the shared pot does nothing but dwindle under his inexperienced hands."

Did I detect a hint of impatience or annoyance belying Graham's measured tone? I couldn't help but gape. It was a secret side of him I'd never seen before, and it helped me understand the tension that came out around people like Randson, our own greasy little *Tom Buchanan.*

"Well aren't you quite the Gatsby?" I teased. "Tell me, what sorts of businesses do you have, aside from operating as a secret agent? Are they legit or scandalous?"

"That's a story for another day," Graham said, reaching over and sliding the ring down further, tightening my nipple clamps. As payment for information received, I supposed.

I hissed again, panting, feeling beads of sweat form on my brow. Graham knew what he was doing. My nipples had adjusted to the initial pressure and it wasn't as painful, but tightening caused renewed distress. We locked eyes in a silent challenge as I realized Graham gave me an out, a way to cry mercy. But I wouldn't take it.

Games. We were always playing games. And either way, he always won.

I pursed my lips, using my nose to breathe through the heightened agony. I stilled my pain-pleasure writhing to mere squirming. Regardless, heat pooled low in my belly and I squeezed my legs together, frustrated.

"So has Randson always disliked you?" I bit out, looking at Graham with what I hoped was flint in my eyes.

"More or less. He resents that outside of his tiny world, none of that status matters. That I can outspend him. I can buy the better room here, the better girl."

I blinked at the sudden compliment then narrowed my eyes, remembering what he'd taught me.

"I know exactly what you're doing Graham Kellum." I would have wagged a finger, had I a finger free. "Don't forget–you trained me. You're distracting me, diverting my attention. I think maybe you carry a bit of a chip on your shoulder when it comes to boys like Randson always trying to make you feel less-than. So you're throwing out a crumb, wanting me to chase it, to ask what you mean."

Graham shrugged, non-committal.

Oh, I've got you, Graham Kellum.

"Okay, fine, I'll bite," I said, shaking my head, helpless to do much else. "What do you mean about buying the better girl? Did Randson want to bid on me?"

"He did. And to deter him, I hinted that I wanted Ella *or you.* I knew he wouldn't risk pitting himself against me and losing."

"But… why? Why not just let Randson have me? Then we could have guaranteed to work in separate teams and cover more ground. That was the plan, wasn't it?"

Graham stiffened. "He would have hurt you. You saw him with Allison. He's not the right master for you."

And you are?

I looked away, suddenly shy, despite having my aching breasts on display right beneath his face… his mouth…

"I–I can handle myself," I mumbled. It sounded like a bald lie, so I did what Graham just did. Deflected.

"Besides, you hurt me anyway."

I knew it wasn't *entirely* true. I knew it wasn't playing fair.

"Only what you need, Poppy. Never more than you can handle."

My heart momentarily stopped.

He said my name. My real *name.*

If that wasn't enough, Graham reached over and thumbed my lips, gently rubbing along the bottom curve. I sucked in a breath, unsure why the act felt so erotic, so dominant. Blood swelled my aroused mouth, making me feel I wanted to be kissed or… to suck on something. I wondered if he'd dip his fingers inside. I wondered how I'd react.

Were we playing? Why did it feel so real?

I snapped out of my thoughts when Graham suddenly pulled the clamps off my nipples—an act that hurt a lot more than when they'd gone on.

I cried out, arching, yanking at my leather cuffs. My hips bucked up, seeking the friction down below I so desperately needed.

I realized once again, to my horror and displeasure, Graham made me soak my panties.

CHAPTER 23

DAY TWO–EVENING

"YOU'RE STAYING IN tonight," Graham said, curtly, almost annoyed. "You are not to leave the cottage under any circumstances. I have to join up with some of the men who've organized a game night after dinner. Doms only."

My mouth fell and I threw up my arms. "Sir. You can't just… I mean… why do you never tell me anything until the last minute? Where are you going? Why? I don't understand. You don't seem happy about it."

He cocked his head. "It's required. Part of my role here. Need I explain more?"

I got the message. *Mingling. Observing.*

"No, I just… what am I supposed to do while you're out? There's no television in this room, everything is so outdated. Am I to just sit here and patiently wait for your return, like a dog?"

Graham bit back a smirk at that. "If you were a good sub, yes. In any position I instructed."

I blushed, hating the way he continually reminded me of his power.

"But we both know you're not very good at doing as you're told."

I bat my lashes coyly and shrugged.

"Your dinner will be arriving shortly. After, I've arranged for you to have a massage."

"A massage?" I looked at Graham as awe-struck and suspicious as if he'd just suggested I spend the night partaking in a limitless shopping spree at Cartier.

"Yes. The hotel has a range of spa services on offer. A member of staff will be coming to the room tonight to give you an hour-long massage. Take a bath first, if you like. Read a book or listen to some records." Graham nodded in the direction of the old record-player and handful of uninteresting novels–the only entertainment the room provided–in a side table I hadn't explored until that afternoon.

I chewed my lip, *very* suspicious. "That's almost… thoughtful. Why are you being nice? And why don't you seem to want to go?"

I wasn't asking because I wondered if he didn't want to leave me. I wasn't.

"Why do you ask so many questions and not simply *obey?*" Graham sighed. "I don't enjoy copious amounts of alcohol, especially on a mission, and heavy consumption to keep up with the revelry will be expected. I am sure many guests will be sleeping in tomorrow."

Oh.

"So why are you being generous?" I asked.

"I'm keeping you out of trouble. Just remember to keep your lips tightly closed when the masseuse arrives. I won't be here to manage you. Can you be a big girl and manage yourself for a few hours? Or should I spank you to remind you?"

Was Graham being intentionally more of a prick to prompt misbehavior or to test me?

"I can manage," I replied, folding my arms and ignoring the rush of blood between my legs.

THE KNOCK ON OUR BUNGALOW door came at eight p.m., sharp. Earlier, I'd eaten the room-service Graham had delivered as he was leaving—a simple dinner of baked chicken and rice, with a side of green beans, and a chocolate layer cake for dessert. Alone, I'd taken a luxurious bubble bath and wrapped myself in a terry robe to prepare for the massage. Yet a surge of nerves ran though me, annoying me. I'd gotten so used to Graham's presence, I felt a little worried being on my own. I'd almost peeked into his bedroom before biting back my curiosity, sure he'd somehow read the exploration on my face and punish me for it.

At eight o'clock, to my surprise, Natalie stood at our bungalow door, smiling sheepishly.

"Hi," I said.

"Hi," she replied, biting her lip in a manner I worried would smear lipstick on her teeth. "I'm sorry, but we're short-staffed tonight. I'm your masseuse. I hope that's not too weird? I actually do have my certification, or I did, though I let my license lapse…"

She held up a bottle of red wine, smiling wider. "I'm not bad though, and I brought wine for after, if you'd like a little drink."

A night off from Graham's demands, a massage, *and* the prospect of unchaperoned drinking? The evening just got even better.

"Not at all," I replied, "You are *most* welcome. Please, come in."

THE MASSAGE WAS HEAVEN, *exactly* what I needed. Natalie reminded me to hydrate before hitting the wine and she searched the tiny kitchen for a bottle opener. She eventually found one, but the cabinets failed to contain any wine glasses, so she apologetically poured the alcohol into two juice cups. I didn't care, it would taste the same.

Raising her glass, Natalie toasted, "My candle burns at both ends; it will not last the night–but ah, my foes and oh, my friends, it gives such lovely light!"

"Did you make that up?" I asked, laughing.

"Nah. It's a quote from Roald Dahl. It's my favorite toast." Natalie plopped onto the couch with a happy sigh. I took a seat on the opposite one, drinking a long gulp.

"This is good," I sighed. *And it's nice that Graham isn't here to monitor my intake like some conservative old biddy.*

"Swiped it from the reserve," Natalie said, winking. "Don't tell Victor or Angus, they can be inventory freaks."

"Angus seems nice…" I mused, hoping to casually lead her into divulging more.

"Totally," she replied. "He does a lot to keep this castle from collapsing over our heads, it's not his fault if he's tight-fisted. He's an absolute doll."

"And Victor is not?"

Natalie rolled her eyes, smiling. "Ugh, he's a good man underneath it all. He just gets worked up at these parties."

I took a sip of wine to cover my reaction. *Was Graham right?*

"Well, it's good he has you to keep him in line," I said, hoping I wasn't saying too much. Luckily, Natalie grinned again.

"I'd like to think so," she said, raising her glass.

IT WAS PAST MIDNIGHT WHEN Graham came through the door. He tossed his key and wallet onto the side table where they landed with a *clink* and a *thud.* I lifted my head just in time to see him run his hands through his hair, once.

Since Natalie left, I'd been lying on the couch in the darkened room, staring at the ceiling. I wasn't tired enough to pass out, but I was too inebriated to focus on words. The book I'd optimistically opened lay face-down on the rug beside me.

At Graham's entrance, I sat up. Perhaps too quickly; the room spun a little, so I focused on Graham. He looked handsomely disheveled. His hair lay tousled, loose, atop his head. He'd stripped his blazer and rolled up his shirtsleeves, giving me a clear view of his broad shoulders, his strong chest. In return, he stared at me, saying nothing. I shot to my feet, guilty for no reason. He had a strange look on his face.

"H–how was your night?" I asked, cautiously.

Graham didn't answer. He blinked. "You're drunk."

"So are you," I countered, moving from nervousness to annoyance pretty quickly. I wasn't sure if I was right, but he confirmed it when he next spoke.

"I don't fancy this state of diminished clarity, but it's my right to seek it if I choose."

Only Graham would talk like that when intoxicated, I thought. *His mental clarity couldn't be* too *diminished.*

"Well. I can be drunk too. If I want."

It wasn't the witty comeback I'd hoped. I wasn't even *that* drunk. Just fired up–or getting there.

Why was Graham being antagonistic suddenly?

I blinked. Did he seem taller or... more rugged than usual? Manlier, somehow.

"Actually, no, Klara, you can't." Graham bit out the words, harsh, stalking toward me. Was it the alcohol talking? "You can do nothing without my permission. You're not just my subordinate in work, you're my submissive here. Not to mention, of your own free will you made a deal to obey. Curious, that."

Shit, what was happening here? Something was happening, and the liquor made it difficult for me to grasp. Had Graham worked himself into a state? Was he intentionally provoking me? And *goddammit,* why did he look so... masculine... tonight?

Also, what was that strange scent on his clothing?

I stomped my foot, narrowing my eyes. "You keep reminding me of my position."

"You keep forgetting."

"You like this, don't you?" I seethed. Was the alcohol goading me on? "Having me unable to defy you. Forced to... obey."

Graham cocked his head, eyes narrowed. He stood very close now.

"Tell me, Poppy, what is it you like? What causes your soaked pussy whenever I assert my authority over you? Is it your desire for me as a man or your desire for bending to my will? Both?"

My mouth dropped. I fisted my hands to keep from slapping him—an act I was sure would send me over his knees and bawling in no time. *Jesus Christ. He couldn't say that... he didn't really think that. Did he?*

"N—neither!"

Oh god, please let this be the whiskey talking. I could smell copious amounts of it on him.

"You're a terrible liar," he mocked. "Don't you think it's a little thinly-veiled to ask that I punish you in order to have me level with you, as a colleague?"

"*What?* You didn't give me any other choice, you wouldn't let me in! It was the only thing I could think of to make you speak with me and it *worked*. Don't put this on *me*. This is *you*."

A dangerous, eerie stillness came over Graham, measured out in my thumping heartbeats.

"Strip. Now."

"What?"

"Remove your clothing. Don't make me repeat myself."

I scrunched my face, nearly snarling. But I forced my hands to move, first discarding the loose tank top I'd put on for sleep, then shimmying out of my shorts. Pausing only to grunt in protest—ineffectually—I slid my panties down and off my feet, baring myself for Graham. I kept my hands at my sides, though I fisted them again. I paid no attention to my breasts, high and full. Nipples inexplicably hard.

"Put your hands behind your head."

I stared daggers at Graham as I reluctantly lifted my hands and locked them behind my head, a move that forced my chest out further.

"Legs spread. Shoulder-width apart."

Another huff and I obeyed, feeling the heat of Graham's gaze searing every inch of my bare skin. Slowly, he stalked around me in one circle; a lion eager to devour prey. I knew it for what it was—purposeful torture; the beast playing with its helpless food before eating it. Tension between us rose to unbearable levels; the only sound in the silent room was my shaky breathing. It took every inch of willpower not to break form, to force myself to accept his inspection. My toes curled, rooting myself to the ground. I wanted to run to my room but I knew exactly where that would land me—over his knees. I wouldn't give him the satisfaction. His restraint was too tenuous, the veil between us thinned by liquor. Like All Hollow's Eve, when the curtain between the living and the dead shrinks to breachable thinness and dark creatures penetrate the gaps, seizing upon the innocent in frenzied hunger. Such a flimsy veil hung between us now. Diaphanous, blowing so insubstantially in the air the merest act—a puff of breath from his mouth, a delicate sigh from my own—could drive it to pieces.

Heart hammering, I pursed my lips and gazed up with total obedience. I instinctively knew any defiance would give Graham the excuse he needed to punish me.

He reached out and grasped my silver collar, giving it a slight tug—a show of ownership. My breath caught but I didn't flinch or pull away. Graham encircled the engraved "AR" with his thumb, a look of displeasure on his face. Could it possibly… bother him that I wore another man's initials? Did it bruise his ego?

He suddenly dropped his hand. "Bend over the table."

My stomach flipped.

"Remember what I said about repeating myself," he warned, when I didn't move fast enough.

I quickly walked over to the dining room table and folded myself over it, pressing my bare breasts to the cool wood.

"Spread your legs wider," Graham ordered forcefully. "Show me your pussy."

Holy fuck, could he just not say *those things?*

Clenching my eyes shut, I opened my legs, revealing all of myself to him. I didn't waste any foolish hope on thinking the dim room shielded me. I knew I gave Graham unobstructed views of everything private on my body.

"Good girl," he praised.

I heard him move closer, *felt* his nearness. I sucked in a deep, shaky breath as goosebumps rose on my skin.

"Should I check?" he rasped. "When I give you an order, you pout your lips, indignant. But what does your cunt show?"

Oh my god. I couldn't breathe when he said things like that.

Please let this be the alcohol. Please don't remember any of this in the morning.

"What would those boys in your office think, if they knew? Just because you blush at your depraved thoughts doesn't mean you don't have them. Your mind is fucking filthy. Tell me, Poppy. If I ran my fingers down your slit right now, would they come back wet?"

"I–I–"

Not my name. Please don't use my real name. I didn't want to admit anything *or* have him check. Both options were intolerable.

"Do you think I even need to test by touching you?"

What did that *mean? Was it... obvious?*

For tortuous seconds I lay there, bent and bare, dutifully awaiting his decision. But he didn't touch me. Graham stood right behind me, making me tense with anticipation, biting my lip as I waited to see what he would do next.

No part of me *wanted* him to do something. Did it? *Fucking alcohol.*

"Go. Go to bed. Now," Graham suddenly whispered.

I'd been so conditioned for submission, my first reaction was fear that I'd displeased him. That he was going to punish me. When I realized he meant to leave me alone–to not touch me–my fear was quickly replaced by confusion and disbelief.

"Now." Graham growled the command. I shot to a standing position, sparing him only the briefest of glances as I scurried to my room. His face had that strange look again.

What the fuck just happened? Graham couldn't be completely drunk–I don't think a man like him ever got that out of control. But he was definitely... looser than usual. What struck me most was the look in his eyes... slightly unhinged, almost mad. Both unfocused and obviously focused on *something,* as he stared in the distance.

Back in my room, it suddenly hit me what the strange smell on Graham's shirt had been. *Cigarette smoke.* I flashed back to when I'd caught him smoking in Carter's office. It struck me as odd now as it did then, because the Graham I knew didn't smoke.

CHAPTER 24

DAY THREE–MORNING

I COULDN'T SHAKE A feeling of inescapability about how the mission happened. Secretly, I had wanted the chance. I bore a resemblance to Klara. Graham didn't trust me, or ODX, to handle it. He was outbid, pairing us up.

All of it fit together, like pieces of a puzzle. A dark puzzle, displaying a hauntingly disturbing scene once complete. Or better yet, like dominos. Inevitably toppling, knocking one another down as they went, but falling in the *wrong* direction.

Towards Graham.

Shirtsleeves rolled up on his firmly-pressed shirt, long legs bent languidly in front of him as he sat in the dining room chair, hand tapping his lap, expectantly.

Fuck, shit, dammit.

I played one game for the agency, one for the party, one behind closed doors. A tornado, a hurricane, a tsunami.

And when I looked at Graham—an earthquake splitting the ground beneath me, sucking me to unknowable depths.

It was more difficult than I would have imagined. To stand fully naked, to willingly drape myself over his lap, to expose my rear to punishment.

But I was determined not to earn an additional spanking like I had our first two mornings here.

Third time's the charm, right?

I squared my shoulders, forcing my legs to move toward his side. Without giving myself a chance to back out, I nearly threw myself over his lap. The slight tremble in his stomach told me the bastard suppressed a chuckle.

That wasn't the only thing I felt against my midsection. *Did he know? Did he care?*

God, this was confusing.

We'd both awoken late, sleeping off our hangovers and missing breakfast. Some big event took place that afternoon, though Graham hadn't been forthcoming on the details, making me nervous. On the plus side, he said nothing about the night before either. I certainly wasn't going to bring it up. In fact, we'd returned to a rigid, slightly more formal manner of dealing with one another and I thanked my lucky stars for the reprieve.

"You're a good girl, Klara. I won't be administering additional punishment this morning."

"Thank you, sir."

To my surprise, Graham gave me a hand-spanking only—no brush included. It still hurt and his hand was more intimate than an implement, but it wasn't enough to bring me to tears.

At least, not until the end.

"Spread your legs, Klara."

I froze.

"W–what?"

"Spread your legs. We need to get everywhere the spanking will do the most good."

So much for formality. Jesus, did he just sit there and think up new ways to humiliate me?

Groaning, I parted my legs. I hated doing so in the bright light of day and *this* close to his gaze.

My head jerked back and I gasped as Graham smacked slightly *between* my legs. He did it again, bringing a sharp sting to the tender skin on the other side.

"Keep your legs open," Graham warned when I instinctively closed them.

Fuck, shit.

I could feel the instant wetness pooling. I wanted nothing more than for Graham to somehow develop selective blindness, to be unable to see my shame. With parted thighs, there was no way to hide it. When I stood, he'd have the evidence upon his trousers. Oh god, he'd probably have to change. Would that disgust a man so impeccably dressed all the time? That I'd have soiled his lap like a filthy slut? Or did he enjoy bringing me low, because, underneath it all, he felt nothing but contempt for me?

Please let this be over soon, I begged. *I need clothes. I need to hide. Why did Graham constantly insist on having me naked while he got to wear enough clothing to have a business meeting?*

By the time he'd finished smacking my vulnerable inner-thighs to his satisfaction, I was mewling strange noises, indistinguishable moans, toeing the line between pleasure and pain... sometimes arching up to meet his hand, sometimes digging my hips against his muscular legs in an attempt to burrow away from the blow.

Confusing as fucking hell.

I WAS STILL FACE-DOWN OVER Graham's lap, backside smarting. He hadn't let me rise but didn't continue to spank me either. I twitched nervously under his gaze, vulnerable to more punishment... or pleasure. I didn't think he'd appreciate me requesting to get up, but I felt the need to say *something*.

"So… what's the big event today?" I asked, grasping at any conversation to dial down the tension.

"We're having tea in the gardens. A themed tea, as it were."

I blinked, stilling. There was no way this could be a usual tea. Every event was a kinky mockery of its namesake.

"Tea?"

"Yes, and we're late today. We'll need to hurry. You'll be dressed in a… well, it's a bit complicated."

"Sir, *please,* I need a moment to catch my breath. This is all… you can't just… just spank me and then expect me to sit through high tea as if nothing occurred."

"Afternoon tea," Graham remarked, stroking my thigh lightly.

"What?"

"Afternoon tea. High tea is a supper for the working class, an occasion with hearty fare, to serve as dinner. Afternoon tea is a pleasant diversion in between meals. People often confuse the two." Graham spoke in a clipped tone, professor-like.

I craned my neck to look up at him, eyes narrowing. I badly wanted access to the internet, just to see if he was right.

He smiled. "You don't believe me, do you? You want to verify the claim?"

God, I hated how he got in my head.

"Why do you always have to be such a know-it-all?" I huffed, letting my head fall back down. With my bottom still exposed to his hands, I bit my tongue to keep from saying anything worse.

"Would you prefer it if I didn't share the knowledge I've accumulated over the years? Why does it bother you so?" Graham continued his gentle stroking of my sore thighs as he spoke.

Why *did* it bother me? I loved meeting a variety of intellectuals and experts in D.C., learning from people who knew more than I did about one subject or another. And Graham wasn't even haughty when he said it, at least, not all the time. If I thought about it, he was actually kind of nerdy when he got into lecture-mode; it was almost another side to him I'd never been privy to. *So why did it bother me?*

Because you make me nervous enough as is, a pesky voice in my head answered. *And when you exhibit even more ways to make me feel an imbalance of power, I become embarrassed because I want you to think me...*

Think me what?

Intelligent? Educated?

Why did I care what Graham did or did not think of me?

"Shall we make a wager?" he asked, voice mischievous. Was he taunting me?

"If I'm right, you accompany me to afternoon tea at The Savoy when this is over. If you're right, I'll join you for a 'high tea' down at the pub."

Face-down I scowled freely. Was he trying to placate me? Or worse, mock me? I'd just been bared and bent over his knees, and now he taunted a bet that sounded something like a date, like something people did *before* they stripped and probed one another. People who actually liked each other.

I racked my brain, trying to figure out the jest... surely, if I accepted the bet, there was a joke in there somewhere, something to make a fool of me. Like he'd done in our meetings. And on the training mat. And in the interrogation room. And countless times at Wistlock.

"I'd be willing to make a wager," I said, carefully. "But the stakes are too high."

I felt Graham's hand still against my leg.

"I'd rather not see you again after this is over, if you don't mind. Not at the office or anywhere else. May I be excused now? I have to use the bathroom."

Graham said nothing. His hand left my thigh.

I jumped off his lap without waiting to be dismissed. Then I paused and turned around, remembering. "Graham. Do you smoke?"

"No. Yes. *No.* Why?"

"Because you were smoking that day in Carter's office, when he assigned me this mission. And again, last night… I smelled cigarette smoke on you."

Graham sighed. "I almost never do, no. I don't like it, I don't like dependencies of any kind. But I engaged in many vices under cover in Taipei last year, and smoking was one of them. I've all but kicked the habit and only accept a cigarette when I'm offered one if I'm especially stressed."

"Oh." That made sense. Carter was a known chain-smoker, but I'd never seen Graham so much as carry a pack. Though I could understand it would be a difficult habit to break if he'd been forced to engage under cover.

"So… how often would you say you smoke? Like, how many cigarettes have you had in the past year?"

Graham looked at me. "Two."

"Oh."

Two. When I took the mission and last night? I stared at Graham, wondering if I was connected to those events or if it was just a coincidence.

PART IV
The Devil You
Don't Know

CHAPTER 25

FOR CRYING OUT LOUD.

I was Poppy-the-Bloody-Shepherdess. As if a designer got their hands on the antiquated style and worked an ensemble somewhere between Lolita fashion and slutty American Halloween costume.

Periwinkle bows dotted the backs of my white thigh-highs. My frilly skirt bounced with stiff white ruffles, revealing the bottoms of some strange pantaloon contraption Graham laced me into. The top—part corset, part bustier—laced tightly around my midsection and propped my breasts out to near-exposure. In fact, if I moved suddenly, my nipples *would* spill out. The bodice was trimmed with white and blue ribbons, matching the bows in my pigtails Graham insisted on fixing himself. Lastly, though out of place, I wore my silver collar to which only Graham possessed the key.

I looked ridiculous.

And I spent a good, long minute *looking* in the mirror at my own dazed expression. Wondering how the hell I'd wound up here. If I'd look back on this and laugh someday. And finally, blinking away an annoying part of me that found the outfit almost pretty and playful, in spite of my discomfort.

When he exited his bedroom, I'd expected Graham to wear something formal-but-old-fashioned as well.

He did not.

Were I a better agent, maybe that would have set off warning bells. But at the time, I was distracted by the way the thin linen shirt draped from his broad chest. The veins and muscles running through his arms beneath rolled-up sleeves. Below the white shirt, Graham wore casual, cream trousers. He looked *slightly* historical, just left of modern-day. But the key I'd missed was that his clothing was loose, easy for moving about.

For running.

Chasing.

SIMILAR, STRANGELY-DRESSED COUPLES DOT-TED THE pasture to the right of the castle. The sun beat down happily: a bright, beautiful day in the English country-side. A sweet day that should never see the likes of perverse petticoats and fetish frocks.

This is so weird, I thought, for the hundredth time. *It would be so much easier under the cover of night.*

"Let's sit here, in the shade?" I asked Graham. "It's too hot and I like this little tree, with the heart-shaped leaves."

Graham nodded and I busied myself with opening the picnic basket the staff provided. On the blanket Graham laid out, I spread out our food: little wedges of cheddar cheese and crackers, various finger sandwiches, apricot pastries, pastel macaroons and petit fours. The kitchens even provided hot tea in a thermos, though I couldn't imagine drinking it in this weather.

Why, on the hottest day we'd had so far, must we have scalding tea in the sweltering sun? I'd have killed for some ice, maybe a little sugar… like a refreshing sweet tea I drank whenever I visited my aunt in the south. I only nibbled at the food and sipped the beverage—it was too hot for having an appetite.

"Thank god for the shade," I remarked, tugging at my overly-tight corset.

"It's an Eastern Redbud," Graham said, lifting his chin up to the tree. "In the spring she'll bear vibrant purple flowers. It's quite lovely."

I put down my finger sandwich and cocked an eyebrow. God, it wasn't just *what* he said, but the *way* he said it. People didn't talk like that. At least, not the men I'd been around in D.C.

"Are you just making that up?"

He shrugged. "No. I spent a summer studying trees."

I tilted my head, searching his face. There it was again—that side to Graham that wasn't as smooth as the others I'd seen over the years. The side of him that was knowledgeable in a bookish, almost dorky manner. The side that didn't fit with the deadly agent I knew stalking the halls of ODX.

"Who *are* you?" I asked, shaking my head. "You talk like Mr. Darcy, you fight like James Bond…" I trailed off, because the next unacceptable thought that popped into my head was *you fingered me to orgasm like a sex god.*

I cleared my throat, blushing.

"I thought you pegged me a Gatsby," Graham remarked, dryly.

"Well. You're a chameleon. But I guess that's why you're good at your job. Right now, you're like a walking encyclopedia. My own personal google."

He chuckled, stroking his beard. "We contracted a surveyor for the grounds surrounding the house one summer. I wouldn't stop following the guy around. Made a nuisance of myself, the way my mother tells it."

I shook my head again, unable to picture the tall, rugged man across from me as a small child, dogging someone's heels through the lawn and pestering a stranger to expand his arboricultural knowledge. It sounded almost... cute.

"The grounds? Let me guess, you possess a stately manor, handed down through the generations? There are multiple wings and grand staircases and sprawling gardens."

"I possess a stately manor my great-grandfather purchased from a man who sold *his* ancestral home to move his family to Australia. There aren't true wings to the house, but there are a few dependencies—other, smaller houses on our land."

Of course there are. Why have one house when you can have multiple?

Looking around, I pointed to a cluster of blueish buds and challenged, "Okay. What's the name of this flower here?'

Graham shrugged one shoulder. "I'm afraid I don't know many flowers. Only trees."

"Reeally..." I drawled, raising my eyebrows. "Well now. That's interesting."

"Why is that, Ms. Volkov?"

"I don't know. But there's a hidden meaning in there somewhere."

"Such as?"

"Such as… you took the time to learn the trees, but not the flowers. It's like… maybe you admire sturdy, serviceable things, and you can't see or appreciate the beauty of what might be dismissed as ornamental on first glance."

"I assure you, I can see and appreciate beauty." Graham didn't move a muscle, except for his lips, and his gaze was intense enough to make me shift nervously, readjusting my bustier to ensure it covered my nipples.

"Speaking as one who's named for a flower," I said, clearing my throat and ignoring that funny feeling in my breast, "I'm offended you haven't taken the opportunity to learn about us."

Graham idly stroked his stubble. "Why did your mother name you for a flower? Is there a story there?"

"Not really. She was sure I'd have red hair and so she named me for the red poppy. My mother's a bit of an optimist. It worked out for her; it usually does. I don't know that it worked out for me."

"Why not?"

I shrugged. "I don't love the symbolism. The poppy flower is associated with death and dying. It's kind of depressing. She could've picked a rose or even a dahlia. But nope, it's Poppy, the red herald of death."

Graham stared.

"What?"

"I was just… listening. You've taught me something I didn't know."

I barked a laugh. "What, it happens so infrequently, you're surprised? God, it must be boring for you to know everything. No wonder you don't like conversing with people. What can anyone else possibly bring to the table?"

Graham looked as if he were about to speak, but out of the corner of my eye, I saw guests beginning to pack up their picnics and stand.

"What's happening?" I asked. "Is it over?"

"The chase."

Graham said it in a husky voice, banishing all trace of the bookish boy I'd just conversed with about trees and flowers.

"What's that?" I asked, freezing.

"You have to run in the forest. I have to catch you."

Graham was changing before my eyes, too predatory, too hungry. Or maybe it was simply my remembering that he was bigger than me… stronger… faster. That he was my Dom and, no matter how intellectual he seemed, he could flip me over his knees in a heartbeat.

"Oh, well… that's not so bad."

Graham's lips twitched with dangerous amusement.

"What? What am I missing?"

"If the man catches the woman, she's to be dressed in costume and paraded through dinner this evening."

I smacked my hands against my forehead, covering my eyes. "What does that mean exactly?"

"As an animal of the gentleman's choosing."

I let out a long, deep groan. "That's just great, just fucking fabulous."

"Klara. Watch your mouth."

My stomach flipped. He'd fully affected that dominant tone again.

"I'm sorry… sir."

"If the man cannot catch his prey, he must do penance," Graham added.

"Penance?" I looked up, cocking an eyebrow.

"Yes. It keeps things interesting. If, for any reason, the predator cannot catch his prey, he must wear the animal costume and humble himself throughout dinner this evening. Quite the reversal of fortunes."

"Is that... does that ever happen? I mean, I don't expect any man here would be keen on that outcome."

"Apparently, it has, to great hilarity. Though it's admittedly rare."

I licked my lips. Graham read my thoughts all over my face.

"Klara. You can't win," he said, shaking his head and grinning.

"Are you sure about that, sir?"

God, what I wouldn't give to put Graham in his place. To have *him* degrade himself for once.

Excitedly, I bit my lip, eyes shining.

"Technically I'm still a field agent, remember? Not yet quite a desk man."

"But almost..." I teased. "Look at you. Past your prime. Is that gray I see threatening to thread your temples, old man? Forty is just around the corner..."

It wasn't true. Plenty of men and women far older than Graham ran the field without any difficulty, and I knew Graham's promotion was an opportunity for bigger and better things. But I wasn't above mocking him for it to get a rise out of him.

I tied my skirt up to not impede my steps. "While I... I'm young and spritely. Plus, I am just *dying* to see you in some animal costume, humiliating yourself on the floor. I think I have more motivation than you do."

"I wouldn't be so sure about that," he said, licking his lips wickedly.

Springing to my feet, I grinned, "Okay. Do your worst. But I get a head start, right?"

"A full thirty seconds. But I'll be generous Klara," he held my eyes. "I can give you more than the other men."

I sucked in a breath, knitting my brows. It almost sounded like a pick-up line. I think Graham realized it too because he quickly amended, "You can have a full minute."

"Catch me if you can, old man," I teased, waving my shoulders back and forth. "I mean, *sir.*"

Graham shot out his arm, catching my wrist.

"I know just the costume you'll be wearing tonight." His voice took on a lower, husky timbre. Goosebumps rose on my arms.

"I hope it's adjustable," I countered. "Something that can stretch to fit the *male* torso."

Suddenly feeling bold, I leaned toward his ear and whispered, "Does it have a tail, Graham? How would you like to wear something like that? Remember, you always have such a stick up your ass anyway, it shouldn't be a problem."

His fingers tightened around my wrist, enough to hurt. Graham turned his face another inch toward mine. The scruff of his beard brushed my cheek and I had to suppress a shiver.

"Oh, Klara, my pet. I might have felt bad about it, but no longer. Yes, there is a tail. And yes, I shall enjoy introducing your lovely bottom to it." His other hand reached for my backside as he said it, squeezing one cheek.

The fuck?

How could he just… talk like that?

I *did* shiver then and slightly swayed. My knees turned to jelly and I think Graham tensed, ready to hold me up if I swooned.

Why couldn't he just keep his face pressed to the side of mine? Instead, he had pulled back, leaving me nowhere to hide from his gaze. The humiliating words reddened me to my scalp, but Graham only cast me his smug, raised-eyebrows expression.

How did he go from discussing the properties of trees to boldly threatening to put a toy in my ass? God, had the sun ever been so bright? It gave me nowhere to shelter as Graham searched my face. My heart beat so fast I feared he'd hear it.

Was this playing our roles… or real?

It didn't matter that the picture in my mind terrified me and I would do anything to avoid it. The heat, low in my belly, told me I found *something* sexy about it.

There was only one thing I could do.

Win.

Firmly, I resolved, "Is there a time limit? Because I might not be able to outrun you, but I can hide."

FASTER, FASTER! I SCREAMED AT myself, heart racing as I ran through the woods.

An unfamiliar exhilaration seized me, made me grin widely, even made me giggle with a thrilling fear.

I wouldn't think about the consequences if I failed—I couldn't. I just had to win. I didn't know how far the castle grounds extended through the woods, but hell, I'd run as far as the next property if I had to.

Couples scattered about toward the east, so I ran west. Quickly, as if I were flying away from the others, away from Graham, away from all the punishments and the pleasure and the pretending.

Don't look back. Don't waste time.

I hesitated only a moment when I reached a small stream. Then I jumped into it, based on the brilliant idea that I'd seen escapees do it in movies. As if Graham were a bloodhound who would sniff me out.

Jesus. The water was so much fucking colder than I imagined, piercing my skin like needles. I gasped loudly, then cursed myself for being so foolish as to give away my position.

Why is everything so cold in this country?

At least the sun was hot, if only for one day.

Instead of crossing directly, I let the stream carry me down a bit, then emerged, hoping I'd hide my trail. For all I knew Graham was an expert tracker who could hunt me down from my footprints in the dirt, who could somehow know it was *me* and not another girl.

A mix of mud and rocks made up the bank, soiling my once-pristine shoes *and* lodging the scree into my delicate flats, causing pebbles to scrape my skin as I ran.

Ignoring both, panting, I sprinted across the open grass to the cover of trees ahead.

Not thirty seconds after I ducked under the branches, I heard him behind me, coming out of *fucking nowhere.*

"No!" I shouted.

Graham's arms encircled my waist, lifting me off the ground. I clawed at his forearms, refusing to believe he had me.

The next thing I knew, we were both on the ground. Graham pressed his torso flat against mine, reminiscent of when he'd pinned me on the mat, back in training.

Only this time, we were both wet and nearly naked.

I'd been caught. Game over.

What little clothing I wore had soaked through, sheer and sticking to my body. Graham had removed his shirt and rolled up his pants to cross the stream, so that I could feel his skin rub against mine… his hard, wet, muscles…

"No…" I whined, even as I laughed, pulling to shimmy my wrists from his grasp. "I don't *want* to wear a costume!"

"Better you than me."

"You're such an ass! Dammit!"

Beneath the cool air of the trees, drenched, my teeth began to chatter. In response, it seemed as if Graham tried to press closer, to warm me. His solid frame held me against the springy grass, stilling my shivering. I let him. But only because I needed the warmth.

"I found another way to look at your name," Graham said suddenly.

I met his blue-gray eyes. We were pressed so *awkwardly* close.

"And what's that?" I whispered.

"Death, personified. As in, the Lord of the Underworld and the Maiden of Spring. Instead of thinking about funerals you could think about the myth. You're familiar with Hades and Persephone?"

Wordlessly, I nodded, mouth parted, color rising to my cheeks.

Don't think it, don't think it, I warned myself.

But was *he* thinking it? How did he even *know?* That wasn't common knowledge, was it?

Dammit, I couldn't stop my mind from picturing it. If anyone was some kind of devil, it was Graham Kellum. *For fuck's sake,* he'd just pinned me down in the forest like he ran up from the underworld, hellbent on capturing me. His dark hair, his height, his sharp features... *fuck.*

It was all too on-the-nose once he'd said it; impossible to unsee.

Was this another game? Teasing me? Manipulating me? Using his vast knowledge to subdue me?

I swallowed. "I–I'm cold. We better go. I need to get out of these wet clothes. I need... the sun to warm me."

Wordlessly, Graham lifted himself off me.

Again, I flashed back to when we sparred on the mats and he'd pinned me in a similar position. This time, extending his hand, Graham offered me help in rising. I hesitated for a moment, looking up. Graham stood over me, framed by trees, a god of the forest.

Tentatively, I placed my hand in his.

Because it was the sensible thing to do. Refusing would lead to punishment. Not because he really had subdued me, somehow.

CHAPTER 26

"**I** C-CAN'T... SIR," I stuttered. I shook my head, eyes downcast.

I didn't remember what happened to Persephone at the end of the story, but I was pretty sure receiving a butt plug from Hades wasn't in the original Greek text.

I didn't want to make this harder for Graham, either. *Was that Stockholm Syndrome?* My inability to just obey commands caused the rise of guilt, because maybe Graham loathed every second he had to touch me, to lead me, and he was just sucking it up better than I was. I wondered if Graham had his own an internal debate on how to best proceed, how to handle me. Did he hate having to do these things and act forcefully to make it easier on us both? Or did it come naturally?

Could punishing me be what he wanted anyway?

Fuck if I could sort any of this out.

I really didn't want to make Graham's job, or this mission, harder than it was by refusing to do as I was told. But this wasn't happening to *him*, it was happening to *me*.

"Klara," he said, sharply, and I knew my moment of hesitation was over. "Remove your clothing and get on all fours. Now."

I had to do it.

This was the assignment.

Graham was in work mode one-hundred percent of the time. Walls up. I needed to follow suit. To relax into my role and *be* submissive. Graham was right… I hated it, but he was right. That night we had our fight outside *Off the Record*—all of this was harder for me because my instinct was to buck orders. I wasn't a natural submissive. I was a brat.

Graham probably flattered himself to be the only man here to meet that challenge, to bend my will to his. But did he understand that he was the *only* man here I desperately wanted to *not* have to obey?

He wore that merciless look as I followed his orders, slowly removing my robe. I stripped the camisole and the matching, silken shorts I'd put on after showering. I had delayed the inevitable by taking a long time to blow out my hair into loose waves, as the stylist had instructed. A shining curtain of coppery red hung down my back. Then I stalled a bit longer as I carefully put on extra make-up for the evening.

When my fingers reached my panties, I couldn't stop myself from casting Graham a pleading look, but he only raised his eyebrows, impatient. Steeling myself, I pulled down my underwear and stood naked before him. I knew better than to cross my arms over my breasts.

The main part of the costume didn't look so bad. The black one-piece resembled a swimsuit, with a trim of short fur, and an ominous slit up the back. I didn't even mind when Graham showed me the headband with the two slightly-pointed ears for my head. It all looked rather silly, but not particularly revealing. I wondered if Graham had chosen it over a two-piece to make it easier on me.

But the first part I needed to wear... I cringed just looking at the ridiculous object in his hands.

"Onto the table," Graham instructed, pointing at the coffee table in front of the couch.

My eyes welled with tears of shame. *Stop being a baby,* I scolded myself. *This is the mission you signed up for.*

Except, I didn't sign up for it with *him.*

I crawled onto the table so slowly I received a smack to my rear.

"Your reluctance to obey just earned you a spanking."

I groaned. *Is he doing this on purpose?* I wondered. *No one needs this many spankings.*

"Legs spread, Klara."

I *hated* this part.

He could see everything when I obeyed. Behind me, I heard the *click* of a plastic cap and knew Graham had opened some kind of lubricant.

God, why? Why Graham? In what kind of world did a girl find herself spread naked on a table, waiting for her colleague to shove a butt plug up her ass?

I whined when Graham's finger circled my rear entry.

Only in the world of espionage could two coworkers wind up in a position like this, I thought, face burning so hot I felt light-headed.

"Please..." I croaked. "I can't do this. We made a deal. Help... help make it easier for me. Tell me something."

A pause, and then Graham said, "Graham isn't my first name."

Like a doctor using a simple game to distract a child while getting a shot, Graham used my surprise to insert his finger inside me. I groaned when he entered me, driving the digit in slowly, but firmly. As my hips bucked forward in an attempt to escape the intrusion, Graham used his free hand to grab my waist and pull me back.

Fuck.

My body didn't know what to make of the strange pain-pleasure sensation.

"W—what do you mean?" I stuttered, as Graham pulled his finger out and drove it back in, again and again. "What's your name?"

This can't be happening, my brain insisted, despite the all-too-real sensation of my colleague's finger probing me, intimately.

"Graham is actually my middle name," he said, adding more lube and bringing two fingers to me.

"Nooo…" I begged, but my plea fell on deaf ears. Graham worked a second finger into my rear. I told myself it was necessary; he was helping me expand. But as his fingers painfully stretched me and he took his time, I wondered if it gratified him to hear my whimpering, my confused moans.

"W—what's your first name?"

Stiffening, I felt the firm tip of the butt plug against me.

"Please, wait," I begged, knowing it would be useless.

It was.

"My given name is Cian," Graham said, pushing the first third of the plug into me. I fought to keep my hands on the table. Every inch of me wanted to smack Graham's hands away, to rip the painful apparatus from me and hurl it across the room.

"That's it… you can take it…" he coaxed, but his words didn't help me *at all.*

I wanted to die of embarrassment. I couldn't make sense of the shocking sensation going on behind me or the stunning news that Graham wasn't really Graham.

"No, please, sir."

"Good girl. Open up for me."

Graham pushed further and I felt myself stretch, forced to accept it.

"Wait, wait, please!" I begged, terrified.

"Shh…"

Graham pushed even further and I gave up fighting him. Desperate to focus on anything else, I asked, "So your real name is Cian Kellum?"

"You can see why I use my middle name."

"It does… sound like an outlaw or a bootlegger," I said, grinning in spite of myself.

At my amusement, Graham pushed the full length of the plug inside me. A pitiful whimper tore from my throat, more from humiliation than pain, though the size of the plug was definitely uncomfortable.

Cian? I tried to picture Graham as a Cian and couldn't see it.

I knew better than to move until I was told, and I didn't have the will to go anywhere anyway. I continued to kneel on my hands and knees, trying to regulate my breathing and not think about what I looked like.

"Is it true?" I panted. "Or did you just tell me a story to distract me?"

"It's true. Though how I got the name is another story. And now for your spanking."

How had I forgotten?

"Please, don't spank me," I whispered. "This is bad enough."

"And who determines what is enough, Klara?"

My head fell. "You do, sir."

"Bottom up," he commanded. "You've earned yourself the paddle for hesitating to follow my orders."

Bullshit, I thought. *Hesitation wasn't* that *bad.* But I hurried to comply, not wanting to earn further punishment. I heard Graham moving about the room and I arched like an obedient girl awaiting chastisement. Obedient *minx,* I corrected, feeling the plug inside me with every breath.

"I expect you to hold position through all ten strokes, counting and thanking me for each," Graham warned, lifting the tail up and out of his way. "If you fail to obey, I'll be forced to give you extras. If you fail to remain on this table and I have to tie you down, we'll start over, doubling your punishment to twenty strokes. And we'll go up to the next size in tails."

My eyes rounded. I could not take twenty strokes of a paddle and a larger plug. White-knuckled, I clung to the edge of the coffee table, determined not to move.

The first slap of the paddle shocked me.

"Ouch!" I cried. It wasn't a large paddle, but it stung. Graham wasn't going easy. He hit with a targeted force on my lower cheeks, to avoid the tail.

"One, thank you! Sir!"

The second, third, and forth strokes hit on the fullness of alternating cheeks and smarted terribly. But I didn't falter in my position.

The fifth stroke hit my thigh and I bent, collapsing with a cry.

"Raise your bottom, Klara," Graham said sharply.

"Five! Thank you, sir," I said, quickly arching back.

Cruelly, Graham laid a smack to the other thigh and I hissed.

By my ninth stroke, tears pooled, but I behaved.

Graham did not.

That son-of-a-bitch laid the tenth stroke directly on top of the ninth, and harder than any before.

I broke position, shooting up to rub out the sting and fighting back sobs.

Graham didn't need to say a word. Realizing what I'd done, I threw myself back onto the table and, I hoped, his mercy.

"We'll repeat that stroke and add another. The penalty for disobedience."

My stomach sank. Steeling myself, I offered Graham the target he wanted and braced for pain. When he hit me in the same spot, now for a third time, I shrieked and the first tear leaked, but I made myself hold position.

"I'm sorry, sir! I'm sorry I hesitated to obey you," I babbled.

It was the same place of contrition Graham always took me to. Near-hysterical apologies. Ready to say or do anything. I just wanted to please him. There remained a rational, analytical part of my brain, suspicious that Graham purposefully managed me this way, helped me direct my attention away from my embarrassment and focus it only on him. But I couldn't hold onto the thought with the burn in my bottom.

"Good girl," Graham praised, running his fingers softly down my back. I arched further, grateful for the gentle touch amidst all the pain.

After a few seconds, I felt the disappearance of his fingers. I nearly jumped out of my skin when he took the paddle and gently tapped it against my tail, sending reverberations through the butt plug. My brain overloaded, trying to sort through the pain, to pleasure, to… whatever this was.

"Are you ready for your penalty stroke, Klara?" Graham asked.

"Yes, sir," I said.

He brought the paddle down and I learned that penalty strokes, by Graham, were delivered with a sharp snap to the inside of a lady's thighs.

Without mercy.

I yelped and faltered, arms buckling, but Graham took pity on my reaction and didn't declare further discipline.

"Please, no more. I'm sorry, sir. I'll be a good girl, sir." The pleas fell from my lips like whispered prayers to a god, *a devil.* I was barely conscious of my words and unable to stop them.

Graham placed his hands on my back once more, stroking. He reached further down, caressing my reddened bottom. I feared he'd do something cruel, like squeeze or run his fingernails down my tender, burning skin, but he only palmed my cheeks gently, soothing.

"Shh…" Graham whispered. "You're absolved."

What were we *doing?*

A part of me knew that leaning into Graham Kellum's touch on my bare ass was the oddest thing in the world. But I sought his comfort with gratitude. I sighed into the compassion he doled out like it was a gift from the gods he bestowed upon me.

"You took your punishment so well," he praised. "I'm proud of you."

What the fuck kind of mind fuck was this? His words made my heart flutter. Made me beam, proud as well. And *that* made my head spin.

How did Graham do that? Shouldn't I be mad at him for punishing me when I didn't even really need another punishment? *Or... did I?* But that was entirely beside the point. The point was... why did it perversely please *me* to make Graham proud of how well I accepted *his* discipline?

As if he could read my mind, Graham thread his fingers through my hair and pulled my head back, pulling thought from it in tandem.

All thought other than, *yes, sir. How can I please you, sir?*

I moaned at the rough yank and arched my bottom high, an offering.

"Are you ready to eat, my pet?"

"Yes, sir," I breathed. "If it pleases you, sir."

I CRAWLED ON A GODDAMN leash at Graham Kellum's feet. The plug in my bottom rubbed with every move I made and my cheeks still glowed a light red. Never in a million years would I have thought it possible. Never in a million years could I have dreamt up a more humiliating scenario.

No matter what happened, I'd never be able to face him at work again. He'd seen all of me, every secret place on my body. Seen me hobbled and humbled and prostrate at his feet in humiliating ensembles.

Cian Graham Kellum, I corrected, wondering how many other people knew his real name, why he used his middle name in the first place, and why he'd deigned to tell me the truth.

At least Graham didn't require me to crawl across the open lawn, or through the castle halls, and I had exhaled at the reprieve, appreciatively. But when we reached the hallway leading to the dining room, he had tugged my leash downward and, groaning, I sank to my hands and knees.

No matter what I enjoyed behind closed doors, I didn't like this public display of subservience. Graham couldn't be keen on openly sharing kinks, but he handled it with ease, like he did everything else.

Of course, he's not the one suffering. All he has to do is tell me *what to do.*

I entered the dining room to witness the colorful menagerie of girls at their master's feet, crawling as I descended down into the kinky rabbit hole.

Curiouser and curiouser.

CHAPTER 27

I T WAS DURING the pet play that I started to feel a breakdown of the rules. Too much alcohol and familiarity leading to hands straying where hands shouldn't stray. To subs that didn't belong to a particular Dom.

The men talked, sipped whiskey, smoked cigars. The submissives remained dutifully on their hands and knees, parading in costume, preening. Almost every girl had a tail, similar to mine, and that made me feel a little better. Graham chatted away, asking pointed questions, trying to suss out our culprit. Only once that evening did I bite back a smile, chuffed to find he continued to work as we'd decided–isolating and targeting one person from each "clique." The plug rubbing at my insides made it difficult to pay attention to the dialogue. The evening felt like it went on and on. I particularly hated the public nature of it all.

Graham sensed whenever my humiliation grew too much to bear and reached down to run a hand under my hair, stroking my neck, assuring me. I nuzzled into his leg, both to look more submissive and to stop myself from crying tears of frustration. Whether I liked it or not, Graham was the anchor I clung to amidst a sea of dark trousers. Especially when he sat proudly in an armchair in the parlor's center and a man passed by, reaching out his hand. Blatantly against rules, the man pet my head, condescendingly. I turned my cheek away and into Graham's thigh, twining my arms around his leg for protection as if I were a frightened submissive and not an irate one.

It was just my *head,* but these minor infractions made my blood boil. The casual invading of my personal space. All the more because, under normal circumstances, I suspected Graham would break the arm of any man interfering in his business. But we had to grit our teeth and smile. Make nice, make *friends.*

Still, Graham said something I didn't hear and the man quickly scurried off. *Could he sense my tension?* Once more he thread his hands through my hair.

Why can't you just be numb, be an agent? I scolded myself.

Surprisingly, an answer came. There, on the floor, in the middle of some kind of pet party, I understood what Graham knew that I did not.

This was harder for me than it would have been for any other agent at ODX… because it hit too close to home; smacked up against what I *did* enjoy. This event took my secret fantasies and stretched them beyond my comfort zone. Left me with mixed-up feelings between pleasure and pain, desire and distaste.

Another girl, a girl who found *none* of this arousing, would have kept her head straight. Would have played the role, like any other. But for me, it was puzzling as hell.

How did Graham know?

More men walked by, increasingly intoxicated, some now *accidentally* brushing past me. I pressed tighter into Graham's legs. A lump formed in my throat and I didn't know if I was going to cry from the forced humiliation of being displayed for a party of men, or from the confusing anger-arousal washing over me at seeking Graham's protection.

A staff member I didn't recognize entered the room, carrying a little wooden dais. It looked like it might have been the same kind the girls were tied upon when auctioned—only a few inches high. I looked around, unsure what was happening, but sure it couldn't be good. Couples crowded the small parlor, but only about half could comfortably fit. The other half crammed into either of the two doorways leading into the room.

My heart picked up speed and I tightened my grip on Graham's leg as I watched a girl dressed like a kitten crawl onto the makeshift stage. Another girl, dressed like a puppy, came up behind her.

I knew where the scene headed when they began kissing and fondling one another. I could see the rest of the evening unfold.

Oh, dear god. This was a show; a pet show. The girls were performing for entertainment. These two would probably end up bringing one other to climax by way of their mouths before their act was done. Who could say what the next performer might do?

And me... I thought, gulping. Would Graham want *me* to be on stage? I didn't even want to watch. I enjoyed porn and I didn't begrudge anyone their exhibitionist pleasure, but it was just *too much* for me—a live show, three feet from my eyes, and the looming threat that at any moment someone might ask, might *challenge,* to see me perform.

Had I gone stiff? Clenched my fingers around Graham's thigh?

Graham knew. Somehow, I bet he knew all of it when he asked, rhetorically, "Tired, pet?"

He rose before I even nodded, giving me the break I needed, removing me from the threat.

I followed Graham, crawling out the room. People gave us curious glances, but they were only too happy to fill the empty space we left, closer to the action.

Once we reached the castle's rear patio, Graham helped me stand. As soon as he did, my knees buckled and he seized my waist, hands firmly pressing into my sides and pulling me toward him with authority. I buried my head against his chest, ready to burst into tears.

"Shh…" he soothed, stroking my hair as I clung to him.

I don't understand, I wanted to scream. What I was feeling. Sorting out the truth from the lies. What I hated about the night and what I… may have found arousing. Terrified that… things I wanted to be real, to rely on, were just a part of the game.

I couldn't consider that the comfort of Graham's presence might be amongst what I enjoyed.

Let alone, that I might be aroused by the man himself.

CHAPTER 28

"I'VE GOT A surprise," Graham announced, safely ensconced back in our cottage.

"It better be alcoholic," I quipped.

"It is."

Graham crossed into the small kitchenette and opened the refrigerator. To my delight, he withdrew a bottle of Veuve and two old-fashioned coupes. I arched an eyebrow, knowing the kitchen only stocked sad-looking juice glasses.

"I borrowed them from downstairs. Why don't you get changed and I'll pour?"

"You aren't going to dress me?" I asked, suspicious.

"After today's events I think you've earned the night off."

I refused to budge. *I smell a trick.*

"But what should I wear? Sir."

His eyes glinted, amused. "Why don't you decide? After I remove the plug, of course."

My body deflated knowing I had one final humiliation in store, even if I'd been granted permission to choose my own outfit.

"Bend over the table, please," he said.

Reluctantly, I trudged over to the dining room table I'd come to associate more with punishment than actual dining. Come to think of it, all the objects in this room were hateful. Chairs to drape over for spankings, coffee tables to display oneself upon.

"Legs spread."

Groaning softly, I obeyed.

When Graham's hands met my legs, I jolted as if I'd been shocked. His touch, gently caressing my thighs so close to my core, was unexpected and frustratingly pleasurable. It brought back reminders of when he'd stroked me to orgasm in competition with Randson. Only at that moment did I realize that I'd wet my strange minx costume. *Had the party turned me on, in spite of my discomfort?*

Graham's fingers edged closer to my aching slit. I chewed my lip, terrified he'd slip his fingers inside me and that I'd like it too much to stop him—humiliating myself in a way from which there'd be no return. Because what was the point of it now, without an audience to justify pretending?

Just when I felt I was losing the battle with my swollen pussy, when my hips made unwanted rocking motions, Graham moved to my ass and grasped the end of the plug.

Of course, you idiot. He'd only been relaxing you to make it easier to do what he needed to do. Like an animal trainer easing a horse or a dog into an uncomfortable act. And you allowed yourself to be manipulated. Fool.

That's all I was. The undesirable horse Graham had been saddled with. He'd admitted as much our first night together.

Although, I argued, trying to make myself feel better, *he did tell Randson that he wanted to bid on you to deter the cruel man. So he doesn't hate you completely.*

Or maybe he lied and he just did it because he thought Randson would hurt you enough that you'd blow your cover.

I cringed when the widest part of the plug passed through me. After, it emerged easily enough. I'd worn it so long, I almost felt strange without its presence inside me. Almost… not bereft, but, as if I were missing some…

The word *connection* came to mind.

To Graham? That couldn't be right. I shook my head to dislodge the thought.

"You may rise and get changed."

I scurried into my room at his order.

"THESE OLD-TIMEY CHAMPAGNE FLUTES, THIS outdated kitchen, these records!" I cried. I was giddy and half-sloshed on champagne. "What is the point? I don't understand the vibe they're going for here. I get the antiques, of course. But it's not like record players existed in the medieval ages. And if we're reaching back into a time period, why not cylinders and gramophones, like when these champagne glasses were en vogue?" I held up my glass and a bit of champagne spilled over the lip and onto the floor. "I can't put my finger on all the disparate periods of history. It's a hodgepodge of eras. Everything acceptable, as long as it's not modern, not now. I don't get it."

Biting his lip, Graham gave an easy chuckle as he listened to my rant. He looked… kind of adorable, when he did that, I had to admit. When he let himself relax, when he wasn't scowling, *when he was half-sloshed as well.* Graham had a boyish grin set in a sharp, masculine face. His lips were just slightly asymmetrical, I noticed up close, and when he cocked a crooked grin it was positively wicked.

I also felt half-drunk on the freedom of speaking easily in front of him. Graham never let me let down my guard like this. *He* never let down his guard.

I smoothed the skirt of the feminine, lavender dress I wore—my own choice. The silky top, held up by delicate spaghetti straps, hugged my lean torso and the bias-cut skirt flowed prettily to an inch or two above my knees. I wasn't wearing it to look nice for Graham, but to just *feel* ladylike after an evening in a minx costume and butt plug. When I emerged from the bedroom, Graham's eyes lingered over me a second too long, I think, and that muscle feathered in his cheek. I *may* have taken extra time to fluff my hair and pull one section back with a dainty purple bow. But only because I wanted to reassert my… my… *cleanliness*… after being forced to crawl like a dog around the castle.

"I like Bowie, don't get me wrong," I said, flipping through the album covers. "And ABBA is fun. But that's not really sexy music to put anyone in the mood, which is why we're all here! And the rest of it… I haven't even heard of most of this stuff."

Pulling out another album I threw my head back and cried, "Wayne Newton? Really? Is this all a deterrent because they want us socializing? I'd kill for a modern playlist on an iPhone right now. Netflix. Anything."

Graham snapped the record from my hands, still grinning. I momentarily stiffened, worried he might roll his eyes or chide me for complaining, but he looked to be enjoying himself. Gently, he lowered the record onto the dusty player.

"Give me your hand," he said, turning to me.

"What? Why?"

"Must you question every order, Klara?" His voice was sharp. He kept his hand level. An offering gleamed in his eyes, *not* an order. Something... unsure in his gaze.

Tentatively, I put my hand in his as *Danke Schoen* began playing. The gravelly strain of the record contrasted the feminine, high-pitched voice of a young Wayne Newton in a way that was rather enchanting. But before I could think on it, Graham began to dance.

"I don't know the steps!" I cried, nearly stumbling.

"I'll lead."

And he did.

But it was still work for me. My clumsy feet scurried in their effort to follow his, and he didn't count out or tell me where to go. I had to *feel* it to follow. *A box step? Fox trot? Rumba?* I had no idea what to call the pattern, but after a while I was able to get it down.

And it became *fun*.

The music swelled and Graham spun me. Again and again. He twirled me out and back to him and I couldn't contain the huge grin on my face, laughter bubbling from my lips. Graham smiled one of his rare kinds of smiles that touched his eyes. He was such a suave dancer, of course. Or maybe he wasn't. I was no expert capable of judging, after all, but he was good enough to lead me.

The music came to a sixties, lounge-style crescendo and the intensity and speed of our spins matched the tempo.

My head rolled along with our turns; my laughter grew, fueled by bubbly and the beats. Graham caught me firmly on my last spin and slowed us down to match the final, softer strains of the last few bars of music, swaying gently.

I looked up at Graham's blue-gray eyes and my heart stopped.

The moment was… unprofessionally intimate.

Which made no sense.

Why was it easier, at times, to have him spank me, than to share something casual, fun? I blushed, suddenly wondering if Graham pictured the intimate parts of my body. He'd seen them so often he could conjure them to mind at his leisure.

He'd taken that from me. It belonged to him now. And I could never take it back.

I ripped my hands from his so fast, I covered up the rudeness by saying, "Thank you. You're a good dancer."

For a moment, he didn't say anything, and it became increasingly awkward as the record spun without music, just a soft *thwump, thwump* as it went around.

Abruptly, Graham walked over to lift the needle.

"Have you ever been to Las Vegas?" he asked.

"No. I can't imagine you there either. Why?"

"Listening to Wayne Newton made me think on it. Just curious." He retrieved our champagne glasses from the table and handed one to me.

"Claire used to perform gymnastic stunts on The Strip," I said. "She misses it. I think she misses the applause. You don't have an audience undercover."

"Mhm," Graham mused in agreement. "Do you want to get some air?" He walked to the back door, which opened onto our private patio. I followed him out and took a seat in one of the lounge chairs. The nighttime sounds of the country greeted my ears and I thought it would be a lovely spot in the fall, with firepits and wine.

"So where do you like to travel?" Graham asked, from the seat opposite me.

"I haven't traveled much," I admitted. "This is my first time out of the country."

"Where do you want to go?"

"Um… to be honest, I'd be happy to go anywhere. The Mediterranean Sea would be nice. Italy or Greece. When we were talking about myths before, I was thinking it would be interesting to visit the places I'd only read about. You know. To walk in history."

"I have been a few times," Graham said.

"Lucky."

"It's not so far to travel from here," he pointed out.

"That's true."

"What about the beach?"

I shrugged. "Love it. I could swim all day. Well, not here. If your beaches are anything like that stream, I want no part. Too cold."

"I think they're refreshing."

"That's because you're inhuman. You don't seem affected by the cold or the heat, I swear. It's unnatural."

Graham only smirked. "A *Mediterranean* beach," he clarified his earlier statement.

"Oh. Well, yes. If we're playing the dream vacation game, I'd want to mix historical sites with beach time. Sure."

"I have a friend in the rental business. Private islands and beaches and the like."

"Of course you do," I said, this time rolling my eyes.

"I didn't tell you for boasting."

Something genuine–almost earnest in Graham's voice–caught my attention. I cocked my head, remembering how he once told me about positions within EI6, and how I mistook him for bragging... when he *might* have been hinting at opportunities.

Was it possible Graham was being helpful?

Did he maybe feel guilty about everything he'd done to me, for the mission?

"Are you saying you can hook me up with a discount rate for a vacation when this is over?" I didn't imagine he meant *for free.* "I have a friend who likes to travel... she's been asking me to go on a trip for years. Maybe if she chipped in, we could work it out together."

Graham's lips twitched, almost in displeasure.

Had I presumed too much? The bubbly had gone to my head.

"I'm sorry. I just thought that... since you know someone... it was an offer to get me a better rate."

"You can rent a stay at full price with the money you earned here, no discount needed," Graham said, dismissively, placing his champagne glass on the small table between us.

"What money?"

He stood. "The club gives you half of your winning bid, at the end. Why else do you think the girls flock to participate? They just don't like to openly discuss it."

"They... do?" I furrowed my brow, recalling how Adriana had suggested as much when we prepped. Was I naïve?

"Yes."

"Oh." I looked down at my hands, twisting the hem of my dress between them. "What—what was the uh… the um… price you paid… for me?"

"Enough." Graham opened the door to the cottage, turning his back to me. "Regrettably, I need to take a shower and I don't want you out here alone. I think it's past your bedtime anyway. Wait for me in your room and I'll come change you after I'm done."

What had I done wrong?

Graham gave the commands gently, formally, but abruptly. I slipped back inside the bungalow, confused by the unexpected end to our conversation and his stonewalling about my price.

Still carrying my champagne, I sat on my bed and Graham disappeared into his room.

He couldn't have meant… for me to use a rental *with him.*

You're just projecting your own friendlier feelings, I told myself, rubbing my face and smearing my makeup. I'd grown suddenly tired. *Graham can't wait to complete this mission. Or maybe… maybe he meant it to fool you somehow.*

I couldn't see the ploy, but Graham was clever. Who knew what he was really capable of, underneath his chameleon-like persona?

CHAPTER 29

I T WAS LATE when I awoke; Graham had let me sleep in. When I opened my door, I saw him shuffling through papers on the dining room table.

"Have a soak in the tub this morning. I have work to do." His tone was business-like, immediately reasserting the tension from the night before.

Where was he getting all this work? I didn't see any laptop or cell phone he'd smuggled in, but he combed through a small stack of papers he must have brought in his suitcase. Or perhaps he'd printed it all in some business center while I'd been ordered to my room at night? Paper trails were dangerous and I wanted to ask questions or maybe peek over his shoulder, but I knew where that would get me.

Wait. Why hadn't he mentioned my morning spanking yet? Odd.

"O—kay. I'm going to take a bath." I said it like a question, but Graham only nodded slightly, without bothering to turn from his work.

An inexplicable disappointment nagged at me while I filled the tub. I poured the same jasmine-scented bath gel into the water that I'd used two days ago, and idly wondered if Graham's tub was bigger. He hadn't allowed me into his room.

It is strange that he keeps telling me to take a bath, I thought, lowering myself into the hot water. Long soaks were something I enjoyed, and I wondered if Graham somehow knew, the way he seemed to know everything. Maybe this was his little way of rewarding me, like the massage. Maybe he was trying to make it up to me, all the humiliation he put me through.

When I got out, I decided to press my luck.

"Sir," I asked, clutching my robe across my chest. "Would you tell me what it cost to… secure my participation for the week?"

"You mean what it cost to buy you?"

"Uh–yes."

Graham didn't turn around, but he paused in his work. "I told you, enough to win. We'll debrief on mission specs when this is over, but don't trouble yourself about anything out-of-pocket. I'd already had a line of credit for expenses through EI6 and they don't pay attention to such bills."

"Oh."

Graham's tone–cold, detached–hit me harder than I expected. And he still didn't tell me my price. Oh god. Was that a bad thing? So low, accounting wouldn't bat an eye?

Chewing my lip, I scurried into my room, wondering if he still planned on dressing me.

GRAHAM *DID* DRESS ME, BUT he skipped my morning over-the-knee spanking. Throughout the day, the tension between us grew. Sometimes Graham's answers were even shorter, more impatient than usual. Other times, he looked at me just a second too long, rubbing his thumb and forefinger over his lower lip as his gaze lingered. It gave me the notion that he volleyed between wanting to kiss me and kill me, but then I worried I'd imagined it, that I'd projected some of my own pestering desire. Because, *damn,* when he ran his fingers over his lips like that, my tongue darted out in response, licking my own. *You hate him,* I'd have to remind myself. *He's an arrogant ass. Underneath the necessary act, he hates you too.*

All day I felt jumpy, self-conscious. Sometimes, I'd open my mouth to say something about the night before, maybe even to apologize. *Had I misinterpreted his offer about the house in Greece?* But then I'd remember my place and close my lips tightly, pursing them as if to prevent foolishness from spilling forth.

Our stiff, awkward behavior gave off a chill I began to worry could be picked up on by the other couples. Most of them were laughing, flirting, teasing. Or, at the very least, seemingly more in sync than we were.

Now that I thought about it, we had a certain rigidness that might have been perceived from the beginning. But I brushed off the idea that it might be hurting our cover. Surely, pairs in the past must have been mismatched and seemed to dislike one another?

Things relaxed a bit at cocktail hour as Graham sipped an old-fashioned and allowed me a glass of Zinfandel. The alcohol worked its magic to loosen us, at least a little. Regardless, it was difficult to remain stiff or distant when I'd been ordered to sit in Graham's lap and his hand rested against my waist. We chatted with the other couples or quietly observed. With only three days left, we still had no clear lead on our suspect.

After, we walked the back halls of the castle, heading to our cottage to change for dinner. The first night of our stay had been white-tie themed to celebrate our arrival, and the night before Graham and I had attended the pet party. Tonight's theme apparently had something to do with Rome, judging by the togas I'd spotted on a few of the couples making an early appearance. I assumed at least one person—if not both—would be going commando beneath their white shift, allowing for quick and easy access to forbidden regions. I just hoped the partying didn't devolve into some master/slave Bacchanalian orgy. Not that there was anything wrong with that; I just didn't fancy getting groped by strangers and I didn't know how often Graham could excuse us if the party norm tended toward sharing.

I'd been preoccupied with the thought, stirring a resurgence in nerves as I walked next to—but not touching—Graham. I must have borne a look of consternation, but it was only because these worries swam in my head.

I barely paid attention to Randson and Allison walking toward us.

"My, this girl, always so petulant," Randson said, in passing. I could smell the liquor on him wafting through the air. "Makes you want to hear her neighs as you ride this filly right into the ground."

To my shock, on the word *ground,* he smacked his hand on my ass and squeezed—much too hard.

My nerves were frayed, my temper at being touched at its limit, and new instincts took over as I yelped. Too late, it occurred to me that the incident might not have happened if I'd been walking closer to Graham. Too late, it occurred to me to let him handle it.

Before I could think, I turned and grabbed Randson's arm, twisting it behind his back and shoving him to his knees in one of the moves Margot taught me.

Randson grunted, Allison gasped, Graham's eyes widened… then closed, pained.

Holy shit, I did it!

I blinked, startled at my own speed and success. I'd never used any of the defenses she'd taught me; I didn't know I had it in me.

Half a second later, I realized the error of my actions. How dangerous it was to push Randson to his knees. Even if he deserved it, even if–deep down–it delighted me. That momentary feeling of triumph faded, quickly replaced by utter panic. The men weren't supposed to touch women who didn't belong to them. But instead of letting Graham handle it as my Dom, I'd gone and made a mess in less than two seconds. I'd not only attacked a Dom–something a submissive would never do–I threatened our cover.

Everyone was deathly quiet. I caught Graham's eyes and threw myself to my knees.

Oh, fuck.

"I'm sorry, sir," I said. "I–I don't know what came over me."

Cold fear crept up my spine, spread throughout my veins, and roiled like ice floes in my stomach.

What had I done?

I placed my hands on the floor in front of me, bowing my head, supplicant.

Fuck, fuck, fuck.

"How dare you touch me," Randson spat, rising to his feet and dusting his trousers. "Graham, she needs a lesson in manners. I think the crop is just the tool."

"She does." Graham walked over and I kept my gaze affixed to his shiny shoes. His voice was hard, cruel. "But I think something more severe is in order."

"What do you have in mind?" Randson asked, much too eager. "A visit to the dungeon right now is in order, don't you think? The bite of my crop across her breasts will serve as a reminder of her place."

My heart sank. *Please don't let him punish me.* Unlike the other girls here, I didn't have the freedom to protest, I couldn't complain or refuse to participate. Undercover missions didn't have safe words. *Please don't let him, Graham. I thought, heart pounding. Please.*

"Worse. I have something in mind back in our room. She needs to be thoroughly broken, once and for all." Graham's reply caused tears of relief to prick my eyes at the same time fear clutched my heart. *What did that mean?*

"However, Randson, you should not have touched my belongings in the first place."

"Well I, I only gave her a playful squeeze and she acted like some... some... ruffian, some street fighter."

I hated the sound of Randson's pathetic protests. I couldn't look up, but I imagined him like a caricature, wiping the sweat from his brow with a handkerchief as he stammered.

"If I overstepped my boundaries, I apologize," Randson added, unctuous, barely repentant at all. "Allison will of course be at your service this evening to make amends."

Allison? I thought, confused. *Why was he offering Allison in apology?*

My stomach knotted.

Oh god. Was it a ploy to have Graham offer me in exchange? In pleasure, if not in pain?

I scrunched my fingers and toes, nervous at the silence above. *Had Graham nodded, accepting? What was happening?*

Finally, Graham's fingers found my chin, giving it his familiar lift. I didn't have to fake my quivering lip as I met his pitiless expression. *My anchor. Don't let me drown. Don't toss me adrift in this sea of danger and depravity.*

I shifted my eyes to Allison and Randson, then anxiously back to Graham. *I'm so sorry.* I tried to will the words through my wide eyes.

"We're returning to our room immediately," Graham said, coldly. "Another Dom should not have touched you, but the proper course of action would be to alert your master."

"Yes, sir," I whispered.

"It certainly is not to raise a hand to your superiors."

"No, sir."

"You will be punished more severely than you ever have in your life. Tomorrow, you will bear the marks for all to see."

I gulped, terror washing over me. I blinked back tears and shivered visibly before whispering, "Yes, sir."

Graham was right—it was good that I was afraid of him. I'd never have been able to fake any of these reactions this convincingly.

"I don't like sharing my toys, Klara. But if you don't take your punishment with total obedience, if I don't believe you've completely changed your behavior, I will allow Randson to try his methods of correction. Is that clear?" Graham's heartless tone made it clear that's exactly what would happen if I didn't properly submit.

"Yes, sir."

CHAPTER 30

"SIR, *PLEASE*," MY arms seemed to move of their own accord, unsure whether to clasp in prayer, indicate *stop,* or to grab the lapels on Graham's blazer as I begged. "I'm so sorry. I don't know what came over me. I shouldn't have done that."

"No, you shouldn't have. You should have let me handle it." Graham tossed his room key onto the side table and ran his hands through his hair. "Now instead of Randson being in my debt, I'm in his."

Graham folded his arms, glowering at me with that stone-cold stare. "This is exactly what I suspected would happen if I didn't rein you in."

Just his words caused my stomach to flip. Towering over me, everything about Graham in that moment screamed *dominant.* The firm set to his jaw, the steel in his eyes, his rigid posture. I bit my lip and awaited his verdict. Whatever it was, I wouldn't make it worse by protesting.

"I'm going to belt you harder than you've ever been spanked before. Until you're covered in angry weals from the top of your backside to halfway down your thighs. You'll bear the stripes tomorrow for *everyone* to see."

Despite pursing my lips, a squeak escaped. Terror didn't begin to cover the feeling seizing my heart, gripping my gut. The wall between us was up again. I didn't know the man before me; the dealer of punishments, the administer of discipline. He was something beyond human, a demon or deity that couldn't be reasoned with.

I covered my face, trying not to weep.

"I'm going to tie you down to the table. You won't be able to hold position for this."

Without removing my hands from my eyes, I nodded.

"Take off all your clothes, Klara."

I gulped and obeyed, slowly. I wasn't trying to rile him further, but I was too afraid to make my hands move quickly. There was no point in begging, I'd brought this on myself and I understood the necessity. I'd made a fucking mess. Raised questions as to why I knew moves like that, roused suspicions about my submissiveness. Whatever Graham thought about me, I thought worse of myself at that moment. Some part of me even welcomed the punishment, knew I deserved it. Yet I couldn't stop myself from pleading.

"Please, please, sir. Not too hard."

"Bend over the table, Klara."

This was it. Everything I'd most feared when I'd been purchased by Graham. A punishment that exceeded my limits of play and passed into harsh reality. The first time Graham spanked me had turned my world upside-down, but this was something else altogether. There was always a troubling realism to our intimacies, but never anything this honest.

My mouth was parched, so I swallowed a few times and licked my lips. I stretched my arms across the table and without being instructed, I spread my legs. Knowing I faced the belt didn't lesson the shame of presenting all of my womanly areas to Graham's view. The blush came, as it always did, and I squeezed my eyes shut in a child's attempt at hiding.

Graham left the room, then re-entered. I quickly learned he'd retrieved rope, as he tied my wrists and wound the rope down, knotting it to each leg on the far side of the table.

"Lift up."

I raised my head, confused, to see Graham held a pillow. At his coaxing, I raised my hips and he slid it beneath my midsection, bracing me from the table's sharp edge.

The least of my worries.

Greater panic than ever raced through me when Graham tied my ankles, spread, to opposite legs of the dining table. My breath fell in frantic puffs against the polished tabletop.

"Klara," Graham lectured, emphasizing the name as if to remind me to keep cover. "You've behaved woefully. You're undisciplined, disobedient, and disrespectful. You've given me no choice but to apply the belt until a lesson is learned. This will hurt, considerably. You will cry. When the lesson is complete, I expect a contrite, obedient little girl to come out the other side. You will do as you're told. Do you understand me?"

"Yes, sir," I whispered. That strange aroused-terror coiled deep inside me, heating me. But when I heard Graham unbuckle his belt, I lost my battle to remain composed.

"Don't... wait..."

Graham tapped my unprotected rear with his belt and I groaned.

The air thickened with tension when the cool leather disappeared; silent, unbearable.

I heard the *snap* against my bottom before I felt it.

Jesus.

I yelped, pulling at the ropes. I knew it wasn't the worst, wasn't the hardest he could hit. But he'd given me no warm-up and it hurt worse than I expected. *How long would that mark last? An hour? Two? Oh god.*

Graham needed a bigger display. For marks to show everyone at the party that I'd been properly brought to heel–Randson in particular–how much would *they* hurt?

Yet, still… the smack seemed to reverberate in my pussy.

My head snapped back on the second hit–harder and lower. I groaned on the third–again harder and right on my sit-spot.

No, no, no. Please, I'll be good.

I didn't know how many lashes to expect. Graham hadn't announced a number and I knew the answer to the question in my mind, regardless. *How many strokes would I take?*

However many were necessary to do the job.

I curled my toes and danced on them; wiggling as much as the ropes would allow in vain attempts to evade the blows. Graham was right; I'd never be able to hold myself down for this. Every inch of me screamed for escape–save my pulsing core, which refused to acknowledge the panic and pain the rest of my body endured and seemed to have a different agenda entirely.

Smack, smack, smack.

"Ow! No…"

I started sobbing, little whimpers at first. But as the cruel leather mercilessly seared my backside, I broke down into tears. Senseless moans and wails tumbled like prayers from my lips.

"Please, please, I'll be a good girl!" I cried. "No more, I'm begging you!"

Smack.

I bucked and pulled, but Graham had tied me too tightly. I shrieked and pled, uncaring if anyone outside our cottage could hear my pitiful cries or if I put on a show for Graham.

All of it fell on deaf ears. He became that otherworldly creature, something beyond human that couldn't be reasoned with. I lost count of the strokes. The belt swung, hitting my helpless bottom, my sensitive thighs… snapping around to the vulnerable flesh in between my legs. Biting that private flesh, marking it. Marking it *his.*

Tamed, every stripe on my bottom declared. *Owned. Chastened.*

Confusing words bubbled to the surface of my mind as well, rising from some primordial subconscious I didn't want to examine.

Protected. Possessed. Cherished.

I was descending into that primeval place, a dark forest of base passions. Or else I was floating, flying. I wasn't sure how two contradictory sensations could seize me at once, but I couldn't sort out which was happening.

Smack—and no! But… oh god, yes. And now another cruel hit crossing both cheeks, right at the base, ensuring I'd never sit comfortably again. *God, this pain couldn't be endured.*

Tears fell down my cheeks and hysteria seized me. It grew larger and larger, expanding like a bubble. Then, suddenly, when the weight of it could no longer be borne… it unexpectedly burst.

I shattered along with it.

I became very aware of the wetness pooling in my core, the ache in my pussy. A hunger like I'd never known, a raw desire, grew in tandem with the pain–if not eclipsing it, then matching it.

My breathing grew labored and my hips rocked, desperately seeking touch. *Graham's* talented touch. Oh god, oh yes. What he did with his fingers that day; I ached for *that*. No! I wanted more. I wanted his *cock*. He had to be erect, he always was when he spanked me. I wanted him to strip naked and bury himself deep inside me. Drive into me, to the hilt. Filling me, riding me, until we both exploded in ecstasy.

I felt like I floated above the Earth, carried by Graham. So high I couldn't *see* anything but him, *feel* anything but him; holding every part of my being within his embrace. Or else we danced together in that strange, dark wood, and the rest of the world blurred, but for his visage before me. Holding me, twirling me, leading me. The steps of this strange dance were ancient, but my soul knew them, sought them.

The pain didn't matter, the cruel bite of leather. I dripped slippery wetness down my legs, ready for him, eager. *Take me.* My clit ached, swollen. *Use me.* I arched, writhing, begging.

Fuck me. Now, Graham. Please.

Holy shit, I wanted Graham. I wanted Graham, and more than I'd ever desired anyone.

Moments before, my mouth ran dry, hoarse from screaming. But I couldn't feel the same pain anymore; it had changed. I knew my rear was inflamed, striped with welts. Yet I felt weightless but for one feeling connecting me to the earth–every molecule of my being screamed for Graham. Every nerve ending on my skin was alive, anticipating. Nothing else in the world mattered. If we failed to find the suspect, if I died tomorrow, if the world exploded, I didn't care. I saw nothing, knew nothing–past my need for Graham to unsheathe his massive erection and thrust it deep inside me.

I'd been reduced to nothing but a vessel for his cock.

And I never felt more alive.

I didn't notice the belting had stopped.

Not until Graham rubbed a finger over my clit and I nearly cried as I saw stars. Inhuman sounds fell from my lips. He dipped two fingers inside my sopping pussy and I groaned, nearly ready to come already.

Yes, please, this is what I want.

I heard his zipper fall.

Oh god, yes. He wanted it too.

"Graham…" I moaned.

He pressed his groin against me, hard.

Yes, oh yes.

"Fuck me, sir," I whimpered, wiggling to indicate my desire. "Fuck me, please."

Why didn't he thrust?

"Graham, I–I want you so badly. I want you, Graham. Please, sir. Fuck me."

Why wasn't he moving?

Graham's body stiffened behind me. Suddenly still as a rock. Not only could I *feel* the tension in his muscles, I could almost *feel* it rolling off his body and permeating the air.

What just happened? What was wrong?

"Fuck," Graham swore. Confused, I felt the comfort of his weight disappear. The air shifted as he moved away from me. Did he... zip up his pants?

He backed away further. *Why? What had I done wrong?*

The realization that Graham might not fuck me slowly dawned on me. With it, a whole host of emotions took over. Humiliation, hurt, despair. Utter confusion.

A knock struck our door and I jumped.

"Fuck," Graham growled. *"Not now."*

"Graham?" I heard someone call from the other side. "I'm waiting for you."

It was a girl's voice. Allison's. *What the fuck?*

I heard Graham move to answer the door and I gave no thought to my exposure. Perhaps he shielded me. Perhaps he wanted her to witness my humiliation. I didn't even care. Graham whispered something to Allison my muddled brain tried to guess. Promises to be in her room shortly? Was this the offering or apology Randson had promised?

A funny feeling crept over me. It took me a second to identify it.

Jealousy.

I added that to the mess of confusion weighing me down, bringing me back to Earth too fast, too painfully.

I was going to crash. I started to feel sick.

I heard Graham close the door and cross into the kitchen. Still sluggish, I listened as he rummaged through his bags, and then, I caught the sound of water splashing in a glass.

Why did he leave? What had happened? Why weren't we fucking?

"Drink this," Graham said, standing above me and pressing what looked like a glass of water to my lips.

I lifted my head as much as I could from my prostrate angle and did as I was bid, perplexed as hell.

I want you, Graham. Please. What's happening? Did he want to make sure I was properly hydrated before… before what? Would we continue?

"All of it," Graham insisted.

I put my lips to the glass once more and drank, spilling a little as it was difficult from that angle.

My eyes focused on Graham's waist. He'd rezipped his pants, but his erection bulged beneath, clearly ready for action. So why wasn't he using it?

Nothing made sense. I looked back up at Graham's face for understanding, but he was unreadable.

"Graham," I begged. "Please…"

I couldn't say the word again. *Fuck. Fuck me.* Something had changed and now I felt too ashamed.

Graham reached for my arms and untied them.

I blinked. *Don't,* I thought. *Don't.*

Crouching down, he did the same for my legs.

Why? What was happening?

Suddenly, I felt like I was going to cry.

Rejection. That's what was happening.

Graham picked me up off the table and swept me into his arms. I didn't understand his intentions; it was as if someone scrambled my brain, preventing the formation of logical, cohesive thought.

Graham carried me to my bedroom and gently laid me down on the bed.

Oh… right. This was better.

He intended to take me there, on the soft sheets. My hurt ebbed and hope flowed. I felt half-drunk as I reached up to hold Graham, to bring his body down to mine. I gazed at his gorgeous face through half-lidded eyes: his sharp nose, kissable lips, perpetual five o'clock shadow.

Graham stepped back.

Away.

From my embrace.

I didn't understand and, like a goddamn fool, reached harder.

I blinked rapidly, trying to make sense of what was happening. I saw Graham's hands fist. He stared at me, hard. Hungry? I saw it in his eyes, he wanted to fuck me. Didn't he?

Slowly, Graham unclenched his fists. The crease that furrowed his brow smoothed.

"You're in subspace, Klara. It's not right to leave you like this, but I must."

Leave me? What was he talking about?

"This… isn't how it's done. But Randson is expecting me to see to Allison."

Allison? Why were we talking about her?

"This isn't fair to you. To… either of us. But I can't jeopardize the mission."

That muscle in Graham's cheek twitched as he clenched his jaw.

"Fuck, Klara, you're deep in subspace. I'm sorry. I gave you a fast-acting sleeping pill. Something we've been working on at EI6. It's the best way. You'll sleep this off and I'll be back before you wake up."

I licked my lips, *finally* finding my voice. "W–what are you saying, Graham? You're… leaving?"

I felt so… abandoned.

"I have to go."

"You drugged me?"

My thoughts began to gather, pooling together to form reason.

I tried to fuck Graham. *Begged* him to fuck me. And instead… he drugged me. And was leaving to… what? Spank Allison? Fuck her?

"Klara…"

The shame of rejection made me throw my next words.

"If you didn't want to fuck me, Graham, you only had to say so. You didn't have to fucking drug me."

Shit. I could feel the drowsiness already. He wasn't kidding. I'd only just begun to climb up into coherent thinking and he'd pushed me back under.

"You son of a bitch." It came out slow, slurred. "You had no right."

"Fuck, Poppy," he growled between clenched teeth. "You don't understand now, but you will. It would be dangerous to leave you like this and I can't stay. This is the best way."

"So you fucking drugged me…" My words trailed off as my eyes closed.

I suddenly felt my nudity. I wanted to cover myself, as if covering my body would cover the exposure of my lust for Graham. But when I felt him pull the downy comforter up my legs, I wanted to kick it back off, just because he had done it.

He saw too much.

My body. My desire.

A thought popped into my mind, so shocking it nearly jarred me back to fully awake.

My… *love?* Unrequited. Rebuffed. Was this more than lust? Had I fallen in love with Graham just now? Sometime on this trip? Had I loved him before and simply refused to accept it? Or maybe this was all just some strange emotion brought on by subspace?

Liar, a voice inside me accused. *Coward.*

It didn't matter. Graham certainly didn't love me. He didn't even want to fuck me.

Could he see the worst of my truths before sleep claimed me? Or did my stillness cover the shattering of my heart? Did it only happen inside, hidden from his ever-perceptive gaze?

My last thought before I fell asleep wasn't a thought at all. It was a total-body tremor running through me, the reverberation of my breaking heart.

CHAPTER 31

I AWOKE WITH A jolt at the sound of the cottage door opening.

For a moment, I forgot where I was, what had happened. Then it all came rushing back, crushing me.

I scrambled out of bed, bolting to the shared door between our bedrooms, intent on fleeing the goddamn bungalow. I pulled fruitlessly on the knob, forgetting it locked from *his* side, trapping a sub inside.

When I heard the door to my room open, I tried pulling even harder, as if I could rip off the knob.

"Poppy," Graham ordered, from the other side of the room, *"stop."*

I kept pulling at the door like a madwoman, pounding it with my fists when it refused to budge.

"Poppy, what are you doing?"

Fearful that he might spank me again, I slammed against the door with my full body, like I'd seen in movies. It made no sense because the door opened in the reverse direction, but that didn't stop me. My mind was groggy with the effects of the sleeping pill, and I couldn't bear another punishment session under his hands. My heart couldn't take it.

"Let me out, Graham! I can't do this anymore. Just let me out!"

He didn't listen, of course. Instead, I felt his arms around my waist, yanking me away from the door. I shrieked, clawing at him.

"Poppy, listen, stop. This is my fault. I shouldn't have left you like that, your first time, your emotions had nowhere to go…"

"Stop condescending, Graham!"

I kicked and punched the air, volleying between anger and heartache. Graham's arms tightened around me, nearly squeezing the life out of me.

"For god's sake, Poppy, listen. You never listen."

"Why should I listen you to you? You drugged me! That's *crazy*. And you're a liar!"

Not just because you're trained to deceive enemies. Because you misled me. Because there was a promise in what you did to me. What I let you do. A promise to care for me after. And it was a lie. You left and left me broken.

Pathetic, I thought. *I was pathetic.* I took a deep breath, forcing myself to stop struggling so hard, but only because I was making a fool of myself. In response, Graham loosened his hold on me and stepped back.

"Get this thing off me!" I demanded, switching direction and pulling at my metal collar.

"No, Poppy, you must wear it at all times."

I squared my shoulders and lifted my chin, still facing away from Graham. As calmly as I could, I said, "I want out of here. Let me out. I need air."

"No, you need to listen to me. Just pause for a minute. Close your eyes. That's an order."

"No."

I heard Graham sigh though his nose. "Do what I say and if you still want to leave, I'll let you out. That's a promise. *Please.*"

I folded my arms. "Fine."

"Close your eyes."

Huffing, I deliberated for a moment, then obeyed, figuring I had nothing to lose and freedom to gain. Graham had a funny tone to his voice. Softer, more melodic. He came close behind me and I jumped when his hands touched my shoulders.

"Shh…" he soothed, speaking so close to my ear I could feel his breath. "I won't hurt you. I won't do anything you don't like. Just listen to me. Keep your eyes closed and listen."

Gritting my teeth, I kept my eyes shut. My arms were crossed in front, covering my naked breasts. Why were we always so imbalanced? Once again, Graham was fully dressed, blazer and all, while I had not a stich of clothing to protect myself from his gaze, his hands.

"This was pretty much the worst-case scenario that could have happened after I punished you. I should have been here to provide aftercare. You're right, Poppy." From behind, Graham's hands ran gently down my arms, stroking. It felt good, I hated to admit. "But I couldn't blow our cover. And I couldn't leave you like that… it would have been worse to leave you alone, awake. We can talk about it in the morning if you like. But for now, you need to relax."

Such a condescending ass. We fucking better.

But that's not what really bothered me. A pesky lump formed in my throat.

"But why did you… stop? Leave?"

"Allison knocked on the door and I had to go."

Liar. That's not what I mean. You stopped before she knocked. We were going to fuck and… you changed your mind. Why? Why didn't you want to fuck me, Graham?

I *was* a coward. It was too humiliating to say out loud. Instead, I asked the other question that burned.

"What did you do with Allison?"

Graham stiffened, then sighed. "I spanked her for Randson's inappropriate actions towards you."

"What the fuck? Is she some kind of whipping girl? That's messed up, Graham. This place is messed up."

But what I wanted to say was, *we're* messed up. What are we *doing?*

How could you do that to me and then to her?

Why did it feel like a betrayal?

Why was I such a goddamn coward?

"I know." Graham's fingertips lightly traced my back, almost tickling. They traced upwards, drawing circles on my neck. "Put your arms down, Klara. Relax, please."

Cautiously, I did as I was told, almost surprising myself. "What are you doing?"

"I'm calming your mind."

"You're commanding it."

"I know."

I wanted to roll my eyes, but all I did was murmur *"mhm,"* in dazed agreement. Maybe I would have rolled my eyes if what he was doing didn't feel so good.

"Back away from the door. Keep your eyes closed. Relax into me."

I didn't even realize I shook my head until Graham warned, "Klara. This is for your own good. Listen to me. If you disobey me, I will have to punish you. I'd much rather give you pleasure, than pain."

He spoke in melodic tones, not harshly. While I deliberated, Graham gently-but-firmly tugged me backwards.

"Good," he praised, when I allowed myself to be led, "very good, Klara. Keep your eyes closed until I say to open them. Do not speak."

His mouth pressed against my ear, whispering, and the husky timbre in his voice had a strange effect on my body. Graham reached around, caressing the skin on my chest as he spoke.

"Shh… back up… lie down…"

I followed his orders in such a trance-like state, it didn't even hurt much to lay on my backside, at least not on the plush carpet. His tone was soft, bu tfirm, as if he prodded me along with a sheathed sword. I knew the threat of the blade rested beneath, but he wouldn't draw it; only guide me with the stiff-leather casing.

"Shh… Klara… let me touch you."

Without opening my eyes, I let Graham adjust me on the rug. Goosebumps rose all over my skin as he stroked. The urge to look, to run, to think, faded as time passed. My world narrowed, containing only Graham—his soothing voice, his gentle touch. I relaxed into his power, letting myself get swept up in it, never knowing what he would say or where his fingers would next graze. My stomach? My breasts? Some part of me, hypnotized, was barely conscious of what was happening.

I spread my legs when ordered, and Graham's warm fingers traced swirling patterns inside my thighs, but he never dipped any digits inside me. I couldn't tell how much time passed when I flipped onto my front and he repeated the caresses between my legs from behind, being extra-gentle over my welted rear.

"Shh… Klara, my pet, my dear. Let me touch you, let me care for you…"

I felt like I descended, lower and deeper, spellbound by his words, his touch. In a reversal of earlier that evening… without spanking, without pain… he brought me to a state of eroticism that made me boneless, weak. It felt like I'd had the best massage of my life, a killer cocktail on an isolated beach, and bathed in post-orgasmic bliss, all at the same time.

"Keep your eyes closed, Klara," he murmured. "I'm going to pick you up and carry you to your bed."

I must have been dead weight, limp and lolling, but his arms reached beneath me and he carried me like a feather. If I had any thoughts in my head, I might had mused that we were done.

We weren't.

Graham started again, using his mouth where he'd previously used his fingertips. Planting soft kisses along my ankles, shins, thighs. Teasing with wet ones the closer he neared my entrance, but never going so far as to actually turn overtly sexual. It felt caring, it felt… a lot like love. *What the hell was he doing? If he didn't want to fuck me, why this?*

I sighed as he reached my stomach, moaned softly when he rounded my breasts—mouth warm and wet on my hardened nipples. In another state, a more awake state, I might have gasped that Graham did that–that I allowed it. But as I was, I only felt dreamy bliss.

The simple pleasure of his hot mouth on my neck may have been the best of all. I'd never been so relaxed in my life. I don't know the exact moment I fell asleep.

I only know I woke up in Graham's arms.

CHAPTER 32

IN THE LIGHT of day, I was even less inclined to discuss what happened or to examine my feelings.

"You're awake," Graham whispered.

How did he know? I hadn't stirred, I'd only opened my eyes. *Had he been up? Waiting? Watching?*

I was facing away from him, curled on my side. He was sort of spooning me, sort of stretching away, I think. It was hard to tell.

"Yes," I said.

"Klara. I want you to know how sorry I am for last night. And… how important it is that you show submissiveness today. I hope… my actions don't cause a setback."

I froze. The wheels in my head started turning.

"Are you implying that you might have to punish me more, because of *your* actions? To ensure I'm in line?"

"No, *no, Klara.* That's not what I meant at all."

I flipped over, hugging the bedspread up to my neck. I wanted to look Graham in the eye. Once again, we were so close I could see the finest of lines around the edges of his blue-gray eyes. His dark hair was tousled from sleep.

"That's not," Graham paused, scratching his morning stubble, "how I wanted you to experience it."

What did that mean? I felt the blush heat my face. His words were too intimate, implying… he wanted me to experience it? Another way?

Then why didn't you fuck me, Graham? half of me wanted to shout. The other half wanted to forget the whole embarrassing incident. Which was difficult to do, being naked in bed beside him. He'd removed his shirt before sleeping and I got a good look at his broad chest, covered with only a small smattering of chest hair.

"It's fine, sir," I lied. "You don't need to apologize. But you didn't need to drug me. I'm a big girl. We have a job to do. This is work, not play. You don't need to coddle me. The mission comes first."

I forced myself not to look away as Graham stared intensely at me. I kept my face firm and stared back.

"I'm going to examine you today, examine the bruises. I'll put cream on. It will help. You did so well," Graham said, reaching out and tucking my hair behind my ear. "I'm proud of you."

I sighed. Did he mean as an asset or a sub? And if the latter, what a fucked-up thing to say. Or was it just me being fucked up for liking it? What was *wrong* with me, that a compliment for taking a belting well gave me a fluttery feeling in my heart? That, deep down, I was secretly happy to have pleased him? A man I hated. Or used to hate. Or still hated, yet wanted to fuck.

Or… loved?

Shit. Don't think it, don't think it. The remembrance of those illicit feelings rose once more, criminal emotions I'd locked away having escaped when I turned my back. *No.* Mentally, I chased them down, caught them, and shoved them back into the dungeon where they belonged, where I'd forget about them.

I noticed Graham still staring too deeply. As if he saw through me, could read all my thoughts on my face.

Eager to put him on the defense, I asked, "So, is drugging your ally something that's sanctioned at EI6? Is that appropriate behavior between colleagues?"

What a stupid remark, I thought. *As if stripping, spanking, and probing each other was appropriate behavior between colleagues.*

"No, it's not," Graham said. "But I don't think you realize how deep in subspace you were last night. I could never leave you like that, and we'd already jeopardized our cover too much for me to stay."

My comment backfired; I didn't want to talk about the strange and unfamiliar state of my mind the night before. I didn't want to go anywhere near memories of my feelings.

I wondered what Graham was thinking, when he suddenly said, "I worked for MI6 once."

Whatever I would have guessed, it wouldn't have been that.

My mouth fell. "What? Why… why are you telling me this?" I frowned, searching Graham's face for the lie.

He rolled his eyes. Obviously, a gesture he was permitted.

"I'm indebted to you for last night. You wanted to know more. I'm telling you. Lie down."

I hadn't even realized I'd propped myself up on my elbows. I let myself fall back onto the pillow and listened to Graham, slightly bothered by his business-like reasoning, but enraptured nonetheless.

"I knew I wanted to serve in Intelligence since I was fifteen. Earlier, I suppose, but that's when I started taking it seriously. I began learning German and several Arabian dialects, off the record. Back then such skills were even more in demand than today."

"And mummy and daddy indulged your ambitions? Provided the requisite tutors, I suppose?"

Graham chuckled. "Worse extracurricular activities could have been indulged. I had French and Spanish classes at school already. I did not begin Mandarin until university."

"What, no Korean?"

"That came later."

I half-rolled my eyes before I stopped myself. Graham was quiet for a moment.

"So what happened?" I asked.

"I completed my graduate degree and was offered a place in their training program." He spoke carefully, choosing his words. "We used to run through drills, practice scenarios. Timed set-ups, made to be as realistic as possible. Though such contrived brawls never really happen in the field, nor anywhere outside of a Bond movie. But it does prepare one for remaining calm under pressure. Not to mention, it was fun for the trainees. A bit like starring in a video game. We'd have to pick a lock or two, sneak into a building without being detected, engage in hand-to-hand combat or shoot-outs with special training weapons, similar to paintball guns."

Graham trailed off, took a deep breath. Then his voice deepened. "Or sometimes, we'd use actual guns, with blanks. Usually, at the end of the scenario, we'd need to disarm the target and carry out the assassination. Often, they'd use men and women from administrative branches of MI6 to play a role. Folks loved it, doing something exciting outside of their normal day. To make it as realistic as possible, to ensure we'd pull the trigger when the time came, they'd work off a changing script. Begging for their lives. Talking about their children. Professing innocence. Some of the actors were good, shrieking and crying while tied up to a chair, pleading for me not to pull the trigger."

"And you always did?"

"Always. That was never a problem. It was my attitude outside of training that troubled my supervisor."

Graham paused. *"Unable to relinquish control,* they'd flagged my file. *Difficulty heeding authority."* He scratched his beard again. "So they set up a test. To see what I would do when control had been wrested from me. How I'd react."

I scarcely breathed, so wrapped up in Graham's story. I could tell he was going to reveal something critical.

"I ran through a drill like any other. There'd been a few bare-knuckled fights against men bigger than me and I was running high on adrenaline by the time I found my target. He'd been locked in what was once an office for a now-dilapidated, old factory. Like so many others, he begged for his life. I made him kneel. And I shot him, point-blank, in the face."

I held my breath, waiting for him to continue.

"Only it wasn't a blank."

Graham's finger stroked his lips, his eyes gazed into the distance, unfocused. "The bullet pierced the man's skull and blood wept from the wound while I staggered backwards. I killed him without knowing beforehand. My first kill."

I let out a puff of air only to gasp a shaky breath once more.

"But… why?"

"They wanted to see how I'd handle it. Having decisions made for me. Not being in control."

"How did you… handle it?"

"I went to the source of the control experiment and I handled *him*. After that, I realized MI6 and I weren't compatible."

"And EI6 recruited you?" I asked.

"Something like that," Graham replied. I could tell from his tone that was all the explanation I'd be getting. For now.

"I could see why you wouldn't want to talk about it," I whispered.

"Well, I couldn't if I wanted to, now could I?"

"No. I suppose not. Why did you tell me now? Does anyone else know?"

"Though I had no better choice, I wronged you last night. I wanted to even the score."

The matter-of-fact way Graham explained it disappointed me; a business-sounding *quid pro quo* for me having bared a part of myself, or as payment to make up for his transgression.

But then he added, "I've never told another soul."

The room felt suddenly very still, very quiet.

"God, so many secrets," I whispered. "Do you ever get tired of them? Of this life?"

"Not in the least. I rather enjoy it. If I didn't like it, I'd do something else."

"Right. Endless funds. You can do whatever you want."

"So can she."

A funny feeling pinched my heart at the word *she*.

"Who?"

"The one who wants to do it with me. Anything or nothing. The world is open to us."

I bit my lip, hard. Once again, Graham's words crept close to what felt like an offer. Only this time, not for a job or a vacation but for a… *romantic* partnership?

That couldn't be right, that had to be my own foolishness hearing what it wanted to hear. Graham didn't even want to fuck me when he had the chance. When I *begged* him.

Anxious to change the subject, I asked softly, "Graham, what price did EI6 pay for you to buy… for you to work with me?"

In his pause, I knew he weighed whether or not to answer.

"What translates to about one hundred thousand U.S. dollars."

Was he being serious? One hundred thousand dollars? For a week? Of which Wistlock would offer me half?

I looked down in disbelief, hand pressed to my forehead. "Are you saying… Wistlock is going to give me fifty thousand dollars?"

Graham nodded, curtly.

What I could do with that. Pay off the last of my school loans. Take a vacation. Put a down payment on a house. I didn't even know where to start.

Then another thought occurred to me.

"I can't… can't take that money. I have to donate it. Maybe I can find a charity that works with trafficking victims. I can't accept it."

"Why is that?" Graham's voice was hard. "The money belongs to you."

"But I… I don't want it. I didn't earn it." *It's more than a year's salary,* I thought, *but I didn't earn it.*

"What do you mean?"

What *did* I mean? I'd been stripped, spanked, subjugated, and still I didn't feel like I'd earned it because... why? Because I didn't *feel* like it was work or I didn't *want* it to be work? This was all so fucking confusing. I couldn't sort out my reasoning, only... I knew somehow, Graham being here with me, Graham being the one to dominate me... made me unable to accept it.

I couldn't explain it to him. I just repeated, my voice a whisper, "I don't... want it."

CHAPTER 33

SOMETHING WAS DIFFERENT about Graham, and not for the better. It took me a long time to figure out.

I'd been so focused on what he did *to* me, I didn't fully appreciate what he did *for* me; what *I* did to *him*.

He protected me the only way he could. But there were consequences.

Jesus, was any of this real? It *felt* real, the night before, when he'd caressed and kissed me all over. It felt like he wanted to fuck me until… something stopped him.

Whenever he spanked me, Graham's erection stood out, visible. Sometimes even when he simply saw me naked. But maybe… he was just naturally dominant and I was only there filling a gap, a need. Maybe he didn't desire *me;* he just got turned on by disciplining a girl, any girl. Maybe he hated me and it shamed him to be aroused by me.

…Much like I had felt all this time.

Until last night, when my passion far exceeded my pride.

But then Graham turned right around and shamed me for that desire by denying me.

Or, fuck. Were those *feelings even real?* Or, deep down, was I ashamed that I *didn't* hate him? That, despite how he'd treated me in the office, I desperately wanted him. That I was… falling in love with him? Only, I couldn't acknowledge it, couldn't accept it before. And now, having been dammed back for so long, it came rushing forward through the holes and cracks in a current I wasn't strong enough to swim against.

God, I couldn't sort the games from the reality. Even in my own head.

The tall girl standing beside me bumped into my hip as she told a story, gesturing wildly, nearly spilling my drink. Ingrid, the blonde I'd met the first day. I hadn't spent much time talking to her since the night of the auction. A group of submissives, myself included, had gathered to one side of the room for cocktail hour, chatting idly. Ingrid must have told a funny story because everyone laughed. I smiled, as if I heard. But I kept stealing glances at Graham, across the room and talking to a group of men.

The theme for the night was a leatherpalooza of some kind. Graham had dressed me in a very strappy bondage bra, a leather-and-metal harness for my midriff, and a super short black skirt that did not cover the lower curve of my rear. The purpose, we both knew, was to intentionally show off my belting. True to his word, Graham had rubbed an ointment on me that morning which served both to lessen the bruising and confuse the hell out of me with the intimacy of his gentle hands. From my rear to halfway down my thighs, I bore the marks of his work. They were highlighted by the fact that I wore black, thigh-high stockings, so that all the exposed flesh showed as freshly strapped.

I'd been keeping my backside toward the wall as much as possible and sipping a strong vodka cocktail.

I stole another furtive glance in Graham's direction.

I could see the nuances now; I'd figured it out. The way he held himself stiffer than usual, more calculating as he conversed.

I'd undermined him, embarrassed him. And despite that, he hadn't traversed my hard limits, a limit we hadn't even discussed; he just somehow always *knew*. He hadn't spanked me in front of everyone, when it would have been good for not only his position, but our mission itself. He hadn't allowed Randson to touch me. When either scenario would have better kept our cover, he chose protecting me over both.

Who was this man, capable of so much more than anyone else? Not a man at all, I thought, *something more.*

The contours of Graham's face were so gorgeous, it almost hurt to look at him. It *did* hurt. Seeing his beautiful face made something twist inside my… gut? Heart? Yet I couldn't tear my eyes away, I was riveted. Everything about him made him larger than life; no mere mortal, but a god. To me, at least. That's what I saw chatting with the group of gentlemen, more guarded than usual. A god.

It moved me, *he* moved me, without even looking in my direction. *Physically.* As if possessed, my hand found the table without looking down. I discarded my drink, never removing my eyes from Graham. I barely knew what I was doing as I sank to my knees.

Immediately, the gesture attracted attention. Curious eyes followed me as I crawled slowly across the floor, willfully subjugating myself. My skirt hiked up even further in the back as I swung my hips languidly, letting the welts on my bottom and thighs display themselves. It wasn't that I didn't care—I did. It was just that I cared about something *else* more. *Someone* else more. As the night before Graham had cared more for my well-being, in his own twisted way.

Get a good look, I thought. Ignoring the heat in my cheeks, the race of my pulse. *See how he wields a belt.*

Halfway across the red-and-black oriental rug, the men by Graham had turned, causing him to turn curiously in my direction as well.

The whole room stared at me but I saw only Graham.

He *almost* concealed the astonishment in his eyes, but I caught it. I was getting good at reading him now. If the room held its breath watching me, if there were whispers, I didn't know. I focused only on the towering, dark-haired god before me.

When I reached his feet, I bent my head and kissed his shoes. One at a time, adoringly, willfully displaying my subservience. I swallowed back any displeasure at the public nature of my humbling; making a spectacle of my subjugation was the *point.*

Not to even the score between us or for the good of the mission. Because I wanted to. *For him.*

You're in charge. I'll obey.

My skin was hot, feverish. My heart pounded. Rising only to my knees, I held Graham's eyes as I kissed his pants, directly over his cock, slowly. Placing my hands lightly against his legs, I kissed again and again in total submission.

You make the rules. I belong to you.

Graham's fingers found my chin, lifting my head, coaxing me to rise.

I saw the heat, the hunger in his wild gaze. Before I knew what I was doing, I jumped *up;* into his lap, forcing him to place his hands beneath my well-spanked bottom to hold me. I wrapped my legs around his waist and kissed him deeply. This god of a man… *my* god. I kissed his mouth with all the contrition I could convey, with all the desire I couldn't deny.

It felt so good to kiss Graham. Heavenly. Wicked.

Sliding my tongue deeply around his, it was only after a few rapturous moments that I remembered anyone else existed in the room. Good-natured applause and amusement broke out, hitting my ears as we broke apart.

Graham studied me intensely, still holding me up, when a man entered the room to announce dinner. People began to funnel out of the parlor and into the dining hall.

Graham and I didn't leave. He continued to stare as he released me slowly back to the ground. My heart was still pounding. We were no longer touching, but I didn't back up.

"You've become quite the player, Poppy," Graham whispered. "I almost thought that was real."

The compliment should have elated me.

My heart sank.

WHEN WE ENTERED THE DINING room, I quickly understood why guests had already self-sorted along gender lines at cocktail hour. Tonight's dinner was separated—the men sat together at their own two circular tables, the women at another two. I didn't know if it was just for variety's sake or some other reason, but I crossed the room and took the only open chair, next to Allison.

Part of me was eager to escape Graham's scrutiny. I wanted to hide, to cover my face. What did I think I was doing? *Showing the party how Graham had put me in my place? Or showing Graham… something so much more?*

"Klara, how are you finding England?" I nearly jumped as Angus Ainsworth came up behind me. He was neither a lithe man, nor gentle on his feet; I must have been deep in thought.

"I uh–I haven't seen much beyond the estate, but you have a lovely place here."

"You're too kind. I'm sure you've spotted so many updates we need to make here in our humble home. I bet everything is so fresh and modern where you live. You're from New York City, aren't you?"

I couldn't place Angus's throaty accent; I didn't know enough about the regional nuances. It wasn't quite Scottish, but it wasn't a posh or polished accent, either–the kind that frequently traveled across the pond through Hollywood movies.

Like Graham's, I thought. *You're just thinking of Graham.*

"Yes," I agreed.

"Must be so exciting. I can't even imagine it. All the hustle and bustle, full of movers and shakers."

"Um… I suppose. I mean, a lot's going on at any one time, but it's not any more exciting than London, I'd think."

"You're too kind. Truly. Our American guests are always so friendly, so gregarious."

I smiled, weakly. Sure, we might be known for our outgoing behavior, but I'd been anything but chatty during these events. Perhaps he was thinking of Graham's socializing on our behalf. Or maybe it was just more of Angus's over-the-top flattery.

He's definitely hiding something, I thought. To *look* at Angus didn't raise the hair on the back of my neck. With his shock of red hair and ready-grin, he seemed rather jolly–almost reminding me of Santa Claus. But I couldn't shake the notion that all was not as it seemed beneath that laughing exterior, and I shifted away from the man who might be our trafficker. If he noticed, he didn't say anything, and we were saved from further conversation by the first course arriving.

"YOU CAN'T SEE FROM YOUR angle, but your master keeps looking at you," Allison whispered.

My wha–oh. Graham. I didn't know what to do, so I offered a shy smile.

"I have to be honest. At first, we all thought you didn't get along. But I always knew there was something more to it. There he goes again! It's like he's afraid you'll escape or someone will steal you away."

The information made my heart flutter a little and my smile grew naturally this time. *Was he watching over me?*

"He's very possessive," I explained.

"Very dramatic. Like a secret love affair," Allison said, casting me a conspiring look, as if *we* shared a secret.

"What?"

Allison bent her head, whispering, "Graham told Randson that's what you're into. Why you're always so tense, so hot and cold, like a… like a real-life couple fighting all the time."

"What do you mean?"

"Graham said you two like to play dramatic games," Allison whispered, cupping her hand over her mouth in a manner that was not at all subtle. "Like, pretend to be having a forbidden, torrid affair, to add to the excitement. That you like it if he pretends to be in love with you."

I felt like I'd been smacked. A sudden lump formed in my throat. So many thoughts collided in my head, it was like a pile-up on the highway. I didn't know where to look first amongst all the screams and destruction.

"He... told you that?"

All this time... was I right to have thought Graham showed signs of desire... even love... but all this time, had it only been an act for my benefit?

"Mm-hm. I don't judge. I mean, look at me," she exclaimed, holding up one bruised wrist and grinning. I tried to smile in return but I felt tears coming.

Was it all just calculated manipulation to subdue me?

"Honey, are you okay?" Allison asked, looking concerned.

Get a hold of yourself, Poppy.

I blinked back my tears and squared my shoulders. "I'm sorry. It's the kiwi in this dessert. I had a–a tickle in my throat and thought I was having an allergic reaction. I was about to panic and make a fool of myself. Would you mind if I had a sip of your water?"

"Here, here," she offered helpfully, pressing the glass into my hands.

Pretending to love me? I took long gulps, buying time to get my emotions under control. *That's fucking enough,* I thought.

One way or another, I was putting an end to these games, tonight. No more cowardice.

CHAPTER 34

I DIDN'T WANT TO confront Graham, to have this talk, in bondage gear. For *once,* I wanted to face him as an equal. Or at the very least, not while being chafed.

The contraption harnessing my midriff was complex enough that I nearly had to call him into my room to help me get it off. But I was so surprised and relieved he let me undress myself in the first place, I wasn't going to ruin it. I wasn't sure what caused the generosity but I'd been instructed to put on whatever I liked for the evening and to wait in my room. Which suited me just fine; I was not up for having a humiliating talk while wearing leather fetish gear, to boot.

My fingers were clumsy with angry haste. I broke one of the buckles in my urgency to get the damn thing off me. I went to work on the bondage bra, barely paying attention to the pink marks the outfit crisscrossed on my stomach wherever it rubbed. They were nothing compared to the welts on my backside.

Or the ones I bore inside. *The lashes that whipped my heart bloody.*

I squeezed my eyes shut. *Don't think about it. Don't be dramatic. You don't love Graham. You can't.*

I heard the noise just as I'd stripped myself bare. I froze, chills creeping up my spine.

It sounded like whispering from the other side of my bedroom door. Had someone come to our cottage without me hearing? Was Graham speaking with them?

There it was again! Graham's hushed tones… he was definitely talking to someone.

So distracted by my pounding heart, I forgot about my nudity. I needed to know what was going on *now*. I ignored Graham's command for me to stay put and quietly pushed my door ajar, sliding through the small opening.

Graham's back was turned and his arm bent, hand pressed to his ear… *oh my god. He was holding a cell phone.*

By the tensing in his shoulders, I knew he heard my gasp of surprise—even though it was no more than a small intake of breath.

I glowered at him, eyes blazing, teeth clenched. *So we had access to a cell phone but he never felt the need to share that knowledge, despite the danger of this mission? I* wasn't permitted a phone, but the rules didn't apply to *him?*

I knew I was growing irrationally, disproportionally angry. But it was just one more slap in the face, one more inequality between us. One more way he held all the cards and left me in the dark.

And it was easier to focus on than what really upset me.

Without saying goodbye to whoever was on the line, Graham ended the call. He pocketed the phone inside his blazer and turned.

"Is that why you keep telling me to take a bath and to stay in my room?" I grit out, before he could speak. "Were you keeping me contained while you secretly made phone calls? Why? To get an edge over me in this mission? To report our findings to EI6 before I got any word back to The States? Or just to keep me dependent on you?"

Graham worked his jaw but his tone was frustratingly calm. "Klara, you might not like me having tools you don't have access to, but I'm in charge of this mission and I'm in charge of you."

"Only because you butted in! I was fine here on my own, this was a *solo* mission! Who were you speaking to on your cell? And don't lie."

"I don't like your tone," Graham said, folding his arms. "I will answer your question if you ask it respectfully. After you are punished."

I hated that, even now, the threat gave me a hot feeling deep in my belly.

"You can't just punish me when you decide you want to!" I roared. It came out enraged, partially because I was angry at my body's own traitorous reaction.

"Klara, not only am I superior in the field, but if this were a real power exchange, you'd have to accept punishment not just on *your* terms, when *you* want it for play. I don't know what the girls had you read or watch to prepare you, but that's not how it works, my dear. If this were real, I'd punish you when I felt you needed it. End of story."

Even after a pause, my voice was weak. "If this were real?"

Graham paused in return, bringing his thumb to his lip, rubbing softly. *Could he see me struggling to hold back tears?* "That's not what I meant," he said.

I smiled, but there was no mirth in it. I was *humiliated.* "Right. Right, Graham. That's exactly what you told Allison, isn't it?"

I stalked out of the living area and into my bedroom. *Everything she said was true, wasn't it? God, I knew it. I knew he was playing me somehow. Making a fool of me.*

"Klara, come back here," Graham called, chasing after me. He caught my bicep and held it in his iron grip.

"Let me go!" I yanked my arm, but of course I couldn't free myself.

"Will you stop and listen to me?"

"I know what you told Randson, Graham!" I couldn't say it, though. My face burned hot, mortified.

"Stop, Klara," Graham grabbed both my arms now, pushing me over and onto the bed. Suddenly, I couldn't hold back the tears any longer.

"No. You lied to me Graham. You lie about everything." God, I was pathetic, blubbering like a baby, struggling against Graham's hold. The tears streamed down my cheeks and the words came tumbling out. "Every time you touched me, every look. You made me believe…" I broke off in a sob.

Made me believe you loved me.

I couldn't say it. It was worse than any punishment he'd given me, any display he'd ordered me to present. I'd rather have bared all of my body, spread every secret part for his view, than to show him how he'd hurt me.

To show him how I loved him.

Fuck. *I love Graham.* Madly. All this time.

I couldn't say more. Especially not when I fought to catch my breath and free my arms against Graham's efforts to pin them down on the bed.

"Poppy, I don't know what Allison told you but anything I said to Randson was to cover for us. We've been… strained and erratic since the beginning. I had to come up with an explanation."

My heart thumped against my ribcage when I realized Graham was reaching for the leather cuffs. Not because I worried what he would do to me physically–because I didn't want him to *look* at me. Because I'd have nowhere to hide my shame.

It was no use. I might as well have been fighting a robot or a machine–as hard as steel both inside and out. Graham straddled my waist and clasped my wrists one at a time into the leather cuffs.

What right *did he have? What right did he have to treat me this way, to manhandle me?* I yanked at the restraints, intent on breaking the bedposts if I could.

Unsuccessful, I began shrieking.

Graham reached into the nightstand and withdrew duct tape I didn't even know was there. For a moment, I wondered what other toys he'd hidden nearby.

"I just need you to listen," he said, tearing a section and securing it over my lips. To do so, he had to clamp my mouth shut with his free hand because I kept trying to scream.

Graham took a deep breath when he'd totally secured me, running his hand down his face. Without the use of my arms, legs, or mouth, I accepted defeat and I closed my eyes, hoping that would stop the mortifying tears from leaking. It didn't.

I flinched when Graham slowly brushed them away with the pad of his thumb. The gentle act only made me snivel and whimper and I hated myself for it.

"This isn't how I wanted this to happen," he said, cupping my face. I turned away.

Of course. My disobedience in not heeding Graham's every word annoyed him. He hated the lack of total control.

Graham pulled back, running his hand through his hair. "And I wanted this to happen. For so long, Poppy."

Those raw words seemed to reach out and seize my heart. Wanted *what? What was he saying?*

"You never listen to me, Poppy. I shouldn't be surprised that the only way I can tell you this is with you tied to a bed, your mouth taped shut."

I narrowed my eyes disdainfully, helpless to do anything else. I don't think it had the effect I wanted because I was still crying.

Breathing heavy, Graham's gaze raked over my bare breasts, slowly. I hated that I felt the heat. I longed to turn it off, to stop my body and *my heart* from responding to him the way it did, even now.

What did you want, Graham?

Then why didn't you fuck me?

I wanted to scream the question. *Why, Graham?*

He cupped my cheek again and my heart picked up speed. Once more, he brushed away my tears.

It was as if he could read my mind.

"I couldn't do anything about it before. You don't see yourself after I spank you, Poppy. You're like putty. I couldn't fuck you like that, not our first time. I'd never know if it was because you wanted me or if you were just too aroused, too submissive to know your own mind. You're in such an altered state, it's beyond consent. Like being drunk. You might hate me for it in the morning. I couldn't... it would be like rape."

Oh. My breath caught. *Oh.*

"Our first day here, when I spanked you in the morning, I took it further than I planned. Jesus, Poppy, you were naked and squirming on my lap…you were fucking soaked, Poppy, and I grabbed you between your legs. But after, you were so cold I thought I'd violated you, scarred you. Thought you hated me even more. My vow not to touch you again lasted mere hours. That afternoon, you were strapped to the table and I… probably could have gotten you out of the predicament. But I didn't try. I wanted you tied to the table. I wanted the excuse to touch you, to make you accept pleasure from me. I told you. I'm not the good guy."

I couldn't believe what Graham was telling me. *Had he felt the same all this time?* Unsure whether I desired *him,* or if I was just so aroused, any man would do?

"I wanted you that night I belted you, Poppy. God, I wanted you so badly I couldn't see straight. Do you think it was easy for me? If I had to do it over again, I don't know if I could stop myself. But that night… it was so much more than just my fingers and you were so deep, so far under. I didn't want to take something from you I wasn't sure you wanted to give."

He grabbed my shoulders, holding them tightly, forcing me to meet his gaze. I blinked, hard. Everything felt surreal.

"And to make it all so much worse, I had to leave. Even if I wasn't crazy about you, I wouldn't have wanted to leave after punishing you like that. But we have a job and at that moment, there was something more important at stake."

If you weren't crazy about me?

My heart seemed to do a somersault. It wasn't a slip. Graham Kellum didn't make slips. He knew exactly what he said. I didn't dare breathe. I searched Graham's face.

Goddammit, his beautifully sculpted face that hurt just to look at.

"If you don't feel the same, just tell me Poppy. I won't lay a hand on you again, at least not in this room or for any reason other than to maintain our cover. But if you do have feelings, don't let that night be a reason to doubt them. If you don't desire me because you don't like the way I look or the way I touch you or the way I chew my food, so be it. But don't let it be because of the lies I told Randson or because you think for one moment that I didn't want to fuck you. I've wanted you since the day I saw you, Poppy. And if you don't feel the same, then I won't... I won't push."

My heart pounded. *Feel the same? God, yes! Yes, I felt the same.* Graham squeezed my shoulders as he said it, as if he could hold on, could *push,* despite his vow.

"If you still want to fuck me, tell me now. Because seeing you —" his eyes raked my naked body up and down, "–like this all the time is fucking killing me. You don't even have to *move,* to lift a finger, and you'll be the death of me, Poppy."

Graham spoke like a man possessed; white-knuckled as he clutched my shoulders, trying to still his hands from moving lower. He lost the battle... or won, depending on how you looked at it.

Graham's hands trailed down and cupped my breasts. My eyelids fluttered shut and I moaned beneath my gag, hips bucking up in need.

Yes, Graham, yes, please! Was that the answer he sought? Was that enough?

No more was said. His hands pulled at my hips and my legs spread, inviting him inside. *Oh yes, please. I've wanted this for so long.*

I felt Graham reach for the tape on my mouth and my eyes flew open. I shook my head and he froze, knitting his brow.

I didn't want him to remove it. I didn't want to speak; I just wanted to *feel*. I couldn't explain it, but I wanted him, the moment, exactly as it was. The burden of speech or even the responsibility of moving my arms felt like more than I could handle.

Take me, I thought, crying it in my mind, trying to convey it with my eyes. *Just take me.*

I didn't know how much of my desire Graham understood from studying me. But he must have gleaned something because he removed his hand and placed a dry kiss against my mouth, still taped.

Yes. Please. Now.

Graham rose, unbuttoning his shirt and revealing his muscled chest to me. I watched, completely captivated, breathing hard. When he slid his trousers and briefs to his ankles, I moaned, wanton. His cock sprang free, erect, *intimidating*. I knew my eyes rounded and he didn't fail to notice. The hint of a pleased, smug smirk ghosted his lips.

I'd felt his size beneath me before, but seeing it unsheathed was something else. I guessed him to be a thick eight inches. Even the way he stood—proud, bold—screamed masculine confidence and turned me on. It was so different to how I felt naked—shy, nervous.

Graham climbed onto the bed between my legs, pushing my knees wider to accommodate himself.

Please. Now. But oh, gentle with that thing.

My hips canted in anticipation though I blushed as he held my thighs apart, freely examining everything that lay between them. The ever-present instinct to cover myself ran through me, but with my wrists cuffed I had no choice but to accept the inspection.

Graham brushed his thumb over my clit, making me gasp and shiver. He rubbed, insistent, forcing me to give myself over to the sensation before dipping two fingers inside me.

Oh god, yes, but more, fuck me, but oh, yes.

Bending down, he took my clit in his hot mouth. If the cuffs and his hands didn't hold me down, I would have bucked right off the bed. Under his muscular arms, my thrashing was forced to mere wiggles.

Fucking fuck. Of course Graham knew exactly how to torture a girl with his tongue.

I felt my orgasm build so quickly I knew he'd be gratified. But I could no more stop myself from coming in his mouth than I could stop the world from turning. Being tied down and unable to speak only heightened the pleasure. I ground myself against his lips, curled my toes and threw my head back–

–And then my cry of pleasure turned to one of pain.

Before I climaxed, Graham pulled his head back, denying me. I looked down at him, shocked and confused.

"Wait for me," he said, voice filled with lust, panting. It wasn't an order; it was a plea. "Wait for me. Together."

I understood what Graham meant as he moved to line up his erection between my legs. I nodded furiously, still bucking and writhing, desperate.

God, yes, fuck, yes.

I cried into the duct tape as he thrust inside me.

It hurt deliciously.

Graham hadn't untied my arms; I couldn't embrace him. I could only arch up into him, pressing my breasts to his chest and wrapping my legs around his trim waist. I struggled for some way to control our sex, to affect him as much as he was affecting me. Either it drove him into a frenzy or he wanted to assert his own dominance in return–or both–because he pushed deeper, fucking me faster and harder. Graham growled, wrapping his hands around my wrists and pinning them further despite the cuffs.

God, he was so big. I was going to come. Every thrust hit just the right spot deep inside me, every snap of his hips rubbed my clit exactly as it needed to be stroked. It was just like when he'd fingered me on the table–I was going to come, and, for the first time ever during sex, I didn't have to *do* anything to bring myself to orgasm. I didn't need to help my partner; I didn't need to concentrate and chase my climax. Graham *took* it from me, brought me to the edge whether I wanted to go there or not. With my wrists tied, I couldn't stop him, couldn't stop the pleasure washing over me.

I shuddered, feeling it build. There were things I would have shouted if I had the use of my lips, but all I could do was *feel*. Focus on the sensation of his massive hardness filling me, thrilling me, bringing me to the height of pleasure. I groaned into the tape as I climaxed, convulsing.

Yes, oh god, yes, Graham!

"Fuck, Poppy," Graham breathed in my ear, stretching me as I squeezed my orgasm against his erection. *"Fuck,"* he swore again, as his own climax rose. He bottomed out as he came with a growl. I was on the pill, but something base, something primal, *wanted* him to spend his hot seed deep within my womb. It turned me on beyond words.

Breathless, Graham collapsed on top of me, limp–save for where he held my wrists tighter than ever. I loved the feeling of his strong hands, his elegant fingers, wrapped around me.

My overwhelming emotion as I came down was gratitude. Thanking whatever forces of fate brought Graham's gorgeous erection to drive into me for an orgasm I'd never forget. I might have cried tears of joy. My heart beat so fast I gave another little prayer of thanks that it hadn't burst. And still I couldn't help but writhe, greedy for another orgasm, even as Graham had softened inside my walls.

My eyelids fluttered open to find Graham staring darkly at me, face etched with raw desire. He reached for my tape and this time I didn't protest when he ripped it off. The momentary pain was forgotten when he claimed my mouth in a deep kiss.

My heart soared, my pussy clenched again, hungry.

"Don't worry," Graham whispered, breaking our kiss. He nuzzled my cheek with his own, the scrape of rough stubble against tender skin. "Give me two minutes and I'll be ready to take you again." Graham slid his body downward. Still restrained in leather cuffs, I couldn't stop him. Not that I had any desire to.

"But first, I want to give you what I denied you. Now I can hear you plead and scream." Grinning wickedly, he stared at my swollen pussy, now level with his eyes. "I want to feel you come in my mouth, my love."

My love?

Jesus, I was going to swoon.

PART V
The Devil You Know

CHAPTER 35

WAS THIS REAL? *Did we really just do this?* I came in *Graham fucking Kellum's* mouth. The British Bastard. The man I hated.

And it was maybe the best experience of my life.

I couldn't say for sure–it tied with the glorious sensation of his big, hard cock pounding into me.

Fuck.

Could we have been doing this for days instead of fighting with each other? Could we do this… forever?

Graham straightened, moving up on the bed. He wasn't done with me.

I felt his massive girth poking my entrance and I moaned, deep and guttural, as he pressed himself into me once more.

I would be sore.

It would be worth it.

GRAHAM UNHOOKED MY CUFFS, THOUGHT-
FULLY rubbing my wrists before flipping onto his back and
pulling me into the circle of his arms. I sighed contentedly, burying my head between his neck and chest, inhaling his masculine
scent. I fought to still the canting of my hips against his thigh,
eager for more. I couldn't get enough of him. Graham reached
down, cupping my rear, telling me the feeling was mutual.

I breathed a soft laugh, almost unable to believe what had
just happened, what was *still* happening.

Did Graham Kellum and I really just fuck? Multiple times?

"Tell me something real," I whispered. "Something true.
Did you really want to fuck me when you belted me?"

It should have been obvious, considering. But we'd been
playing games for so long that I needed to hear it.

He paused for a long moment, then began caressing my
sides absent-mindedly as he spoke.

"I've wanted to fuck you since we met, Poppy. Since before.
I saw you in the hallway at ODX. Your cascade of red hair
bouncing softly as you walked. You were wearing a blue skirt
and a white blouse. You wore skirts occasionally, back then.
I don't know why you stopped."

I furrowed my brow. He was right. I did wear skirts when
I first started at ODX. But then... I started to feel more
self-conscious, less sure of myself. That shouldn't be the case,
should it? After college, I should have grown in my confidence.
Did other girls ever feel that way? I wondered if it meant I
was on the wrong path or if it was just a consequence of being
constantly bombarded with the unnatural concentration of
perfection surrounding me in the office.

"Carter dropped a folder on the floor and his meeting notes
scattered. You immediately bent down to pick them up. I saw

your skirt rise, revealing more of your long legs. I saw more than that. Kindness. Submission. Both. I wasn't sure, but I… hoped. I caught a glimpse of your porcelain thighs and I wanted to run my hands up along their smooth paleness. In that moment, even without knowing you, I wanted to hike up your skirt and push aside your panties and dip my fingers into your cunt and feel you squeeze around them. I wanted to make you moan. To make those pouty lips cry my name."

My eyes rounded. I had no recollection of the event Graham discussed.

"Desire at first sight, I thought," Graham revealed, letting out a soft breath. "I was riveted, I'd never felt such raw wanting before, simply by looking at someone. And fate, as if to spite me, made the object of my desire take no notice of me in return."

I swallowed thickly. Was Graham telling the truth? He lied so easily, how would I know?

"You walked past me. That day, and the next."

Had I? Had I failed to notice Graham Kellum? *Impossible.* But… I'd been so nervous when I first started, perhaps I'd been too distracted to pay attention. I followed Carter around with my head down, jumping at his commands like a puppy. At least I didn't do *that* anymore. My professional confidence grew, if nothing else.

"I wasn't deterred," Graham said, and I could hear the smile in his voice. "Perhaps I acted bolder to attract your attention."

Bolder was a nice way to put it. Cockier, I'd say. The first time I noticed Graham, and each time thereafter, he'd been insufferably cocksure. If I were honest, I *did* find his confidence intriguing… but for the fact that he quickly turned antagonistic as well.

"I asked you out to dinner and you declined. On the pretense of having to work. And then right after, that wanker Riley walked in the room and asked you out that same night, and you accepted."

Hold on, I thought. My mind flashed back to that day. I couldn't remember exactly how it went down. *You asked me to do something… something having to do with work, I thought. And I couldn't because I already had a pressing project. The same one Riley approached me about when he suggested getting coffee while reviewing the data. It was all just work, to me. Nothing more. Certainly not a date with Riley, of all people.*

But then I remembered what Margot had said at *Off the Record.* It was a date to everyone *but* me.

"It all happened right in front of me, while I was still standing there," Graham continued. "And I wondered how such a sweet-seeming creature could be so cruel."

Had I done that? Seemingly humiliated him on purpose?

Chuckling, he remarked, "You may have bruised my ego, more than a little."

Graham's fingers found my hair, threading it, stroking it. Turning serious, he said, "I know you now. You're not the girl I thought you were. I hope… I'm not the man you thought I was."

I closed my eyes, shaking my head. *All this time,* Graham believed I intentionally humiliated him. And so he'd returned my disdain? Jesus… had we done this all by ourselves? Needling one another, pushing, raising the bar, egging on the other's scorn?

Except… there was *also truth behind it.*

Graham *could* be a bastard and a snob, at times, and it drove me *fucking* crazy. And I could be reckless, and a brat, at times… and he probably found it frustrating. Especially in our line of work.

"You're not what I thought you were, Graham," I whispered. "And I'm sorry for all the times I acted up… especially here."

"You shouldn't be here, Poppy. If you were mine, I'd never allow it."

If you were mine.

Was he saying he wanted me to be?

"Carter is using you. He knows how dangerous this mission is. He shouldn't have sent you here; he sees you as expendable."

I frowned, defensive for my boss, who I knew to be a good man, deep down. "Well, yes. He didn't do anything wrong. That's what being an agent means. We're assets, expendable assets for the good of the country."

"Not to me," Graham said, voice husky. "You weren't expendable to me."

My heart did flip-flops as his fingers clenched my bicep, as if to emphasize his meaning.

Graham took a deep breath then said, "We'd all been monitoring this case for months, waiting for a lead. Our offices were playing nice. When we finally found a way to infiltrate the ring, it worked out that U.S. had both the girl we needed to impersonate *and* just the girl to replace her. We had the opportunity in the form of this event, on English soil. In the spirit of cooperation, no one wanted to step on anyone's toes. Carter tried to cut a deal–EI6 steps aside, we let you in as the asset, and eventually, he'd release you."

"Release me? What does that mean? Where? *Wait…* what deal? EI6 didn't step aside. You tried to put Agent Brooks on the mission. It was only because she was injured that I replaced her."

"I didn't take the deal."

"What *deal?*"

"If we agreed to let ODX run the mission, Carter would let you go," Graham explained. "To London. Permanently."

"London? What are you talking about? Why?"

"Because I asked him to. ODX would never allow the intelligence transfer. Even for a process manager."

"But why would I go to London?"

Graham was quiet, still.

"You wouldn't. But I hoped… just in case… one day you would."

My world spun; I could scarcely believe what he was implying. *That one day I'd go, for him. Because he wanted me to.* I didn't know whether to be flattered that he thought I might, or angry that he'd made plans behind my back. At the very least, I was impressed by such a long game.

"I'm confused," I said. "I'm here. But you're here, too. EI6 never stepped aside."

Graham stiffened. I could feel the rise and fall of his chest when he began breathing again.

"This mission isn't sanctioned by EI6. I came for you."

My mouth fell. Since the night of the auction, I believed Intelligence forced him to be here, that work was making him do it and that he hated every minute of it. And yet… *he'd come for me.*

Oh my god, it was *always* his plan to buy me.

"But… but, wait. How did you win the auction?"

"I bought you," Graham rasped, slowly.

I sucked in a breath, hearing the unspoken end to that sentence. *With my money.* I bought you, *with my own money.* That meant… he'd spent one hundred thousand dollars on *me.* Money he'd never see again. For a week with *me.*

Wide-eyed, covering my mouth in shock, I pushed myself up to look at Graham.

"When Carter assigned you the mission, I flew back to London. There was no way in hell I was going to let you within ten kilometers of this place alone on a *good* day, and especially not with our suspect here. It wasn't easy to change places that late in the process. I called in every favor I had to get into the party, to take Archie's place. But *Jesus Christ,* the idea of some other man touching you, commanding you, *let alone* while someone lurked about to possibly kidnap you. Once you agreed to come here Poppy–that afternoon out there in the parking lot–that was it." Graham clenched his jaw, shaking his head. "From that moment on, it was never going to be any other man. No one was ever going to buy you. No one but me."

Tears welled in my eyes. I should have been mad, shouldn't I? But I didn't feel angry. I felt the opposite. I felt love swell within me, rise from the core of my being and expand, floating up to my head and making me dizzy.

"I didn't know if you'd hate me even more, seeing me win you," Graham said. The room was so quiet, I could hear our synced breathing. "Do you? Hate me?"

"How can you ask a question like that?" I whispered.

"For everything I've done to you. For everything I *want* to do to you."

My heart skipped *several* beats. I looked down, shyly.

"No, Graham. I… I want that too."

"Poppy, you can't possibly know. I see your porcelain skin and I want to mark it. I watch your mouth as it moves and I want to wring screams of pain from it. I catch your brattish little wiggle as you walk and I want to fist your hair and bring you to your knees before me. I want to make you crawl around my house and forbid you from wearing clothing. I want nights where you forget everything but pleasing me; exist only for my pleasure."

My mouth ran dry as he spoke and I licked my lips to wet them. He wasn't even done.

"I want to tie you down and make you beg for permission to come, and then give you so many orgasms you beg me to stop. I want to wake up in the morning with your mouth around my cock, obediently, as I've instructed. I want you to wait for me to come home from work, naked, spread, bent over my desk. I want to do terrible things to you, Poppy. And I want you to thank me for them."

My pussy was soaked, *again.*

"Graham…" I whispered hoarsely, clutching him. "I… I want all that, too. From you. Only you." I climbed on top of him, straddling him so that I could lean down and kiss him.

When I straightened, Graham's hands found my collar, stroking it. "I don't want to own just your body, Poppy. I want to possess your mind as well," he slid his hands down and cupped my breasts. I moaned, arching into his touch. "I want you to come to me with a paddle and ask me to discipline you hard, because you know you need it. I want the deepest parts of you, *your soul,* to crave my hand, my control."

My mouth hung, slack. He'd stolen my breath. Graham spoke, *and his words alone stole my ability to breathe.* It was just as erotic, if not more, than the sex we'd had.

"I don't want it like this," Graham said, working his thumb into my open mouth. Willfully, dutifully, I sucked it. "Public. Play. I want a power exchange behind closed doors. And I don't want it with someone unwilling. At least, not initially. Once there's a transfer of control you wouldn't like everything I'd do to you. Some things you'd hate. But I'd do them anyway."

"Graham…" I croaked, tearing my head back, away from his probing thumb. "I… I'm not a submissive. You said it yourself, I'm a brat. Even if I consented to a power exchange, I know myself. I couldn't stop from pushing back, from holding my ground. At least, not every time. I think… no, I *know*… there would be times I'd fight you. Like when you first tried to spank me here. So I'd… I'd only let you down."

"I *did* say you're a brat, Poppy," Graham decreed, seizing my waist and suddenly flipping me onto my back. "You are. But it was only you who said that's not what I wanted, you who decided—in total brat fashion—that you know better than I do."

Graham took both my wrists between one of his hands and gently held them above my head. "I'm well-aware of what I want. I know myself better than you. And I know what you want—and need—better than you as well."

With his free hand, Graham slid his fingers down to tease my slit, gently stroking up and down.

"So how about we let me decide whether I want you or not. Do you think you can do that, little girl?"

"O—kay…" I whimpered, rocking my hips as he rubbed my clitoris. "You're not—not playing fair."

"I told you," he said, thrusting two fingers hard inside me and curling them, "I'm not the good guy."

CHAPTER 36

DAY SIX–MORNING

THERE WAS NOTHING unique about the depth of my love, I knew that. It was a story as old as time, setting aflame the hearts of countless men and women throughout history.

But it had never happened to *me*.

I'd never felt that magnetic pull. Locked in orbit around another human being, inescapably drawn, to the point where one person could feel, could *sense* the other. Not with eyes or ears, but as if the object of your desire entered a room, and the hair on the back of your neck stood on end. As if some part of your heart or your soul called out in silent cry to the other's.

You, my entire being commanded. *Graham. His* name branded upon my heart. His voice racing through my blood. He burrowed so deep, I could no more separate him from my body and live, than I could cleave my own heart or slash and drain the blood from my veins.

Graham stood behind me, pulling my hair into a ponytail with an oversized, azure bow.

"Matches your eyes," he told me, hooking the back of a modest, white bra. He tucked the white, collared shirt into my blue and green plaid skirt. Leaning down, he slid two white knee-high socks onto my legs, and completed the schoolgirl look by buckling two patent-leather shoes onto my feet. As always, I wore the locked, silver collar that he never removed.

Today's theme was Doms and dolls, which I was pretty sure meant lots of subs in baby girl attire.

"Stay here. I'm going to get dressed," Graham commanded, eyes boring into mine.

I smiled, pleased. He liked my little schoolgirl outfit, I could tell. Besides the throbbing erection beneath his boxer briefs, he couldn't take his eyes off me. For once, I felt I *did* look cute; it suited me. Perhaps it reminded Graham of the day he first saw me.

It made me feel very brattish.

Graham hadn't finished getting dressed when I peeked into his bedroom. Patience was never my strong suit.

I'd finally seen the inside of Graham's room the night before and realized I'd *definitely* gotten the short end of the stick. He had a massive, king-sized poster bed and dark, sexy decor. We could have gotten into a lot of trouble with that bed, but by the time we made it to his room, we'd had no energy to do anything but collapse.

As I curled into his arms that night, I asked, "Why did you make me sleep in a separate room? We'd done so much else, why not just sleep together? Were you hiding to work in here?"

"No, I… wasn't keeping you from me," Graham had replied, running his hands down my sides. "I was keeping *me* from *you.*"

His words sent a thrill through me, and I remembered them as I crept into his doorway that morning. Graham cocked his head, hearing, but not seeing me enter.

God, he looks so fucking handsome. Crisp, white shirt showing off his muscles. Pressed, black pants hugging his trim waist. I licked my lips. Every masculine, towering inch of him radiated dominance.

"Why is it that you don't stay where I put you?" he asked, turning around with a stern expression.

"Guess I'm just good on my feet," I shrugged.

"Perhaps I'll use rope to hobble them."

I cocked a one-sided grin. "But *daddy,*" I teased, "I thought you liked watching my little wiggle-walk?" Underscoring my words, I crossed the room, swaying my hips with a slight exaggeration.

When I reached Graham, he fisted my ponytail roughly, tugging my head back. With his free hand, he grabbed my face, cupping it. He brushed his thumb over my lips.

"And this naughty little mouth," he said. "What should we do with this?"

I kept my eyes locked on his and he kept his fist clenched around my hair as I slid to my knees. I couldn't say if he guided me there or if I'd done it myself.

I unbuckled Graham's pants, *hungrily.* That was the strange part, new. It's not that I didn't enjoy fellatio, but I never salivated for it the way I did at the delightful prospect of feeling Graham's cock in my mouth. I freed his erection, panting. When I licked my lips, his cock twitched.

I wanted to tease him. God, he spent so much time teasing me. But I wanted to please him more. *Later,* I told myself. *There would be plenty of time later to play games.*

I closed my mouth over his tip, working my way up to suck all of his massive erection. *This will take practice,* I thought, *an enjoyable effort, but definitely a skill to acquire nonetheless.*

I must have been doing well enough, because Graham groaned as my head bobbed. Relaxing my throat as best I could, I took all of his manhood in my mouth and heard him swear. I worked a steady rhythm, sliding my tongue up and down his shaft, licking and sucking like I was in a contest–like when Graham had worked me to orgasm in competition with Randson… or as if I competed against all the girls who may have wrapped their lips around Graham in the past, and I sought to wipe out the memory.

He gripped harder on my hair, pumping into my mouth with short thrusts.

"Poppy," he groaned my name through gritted teeth, spilling hot seed into my mouth. *"Fuck, Poppy."* Dutifully, I swallowed all of it. I held his eyes and slowly licked my lips as I finished, just to give him one last saucy memory.

Graham stroked my cheek. "Such a good girl," he said, with a wicked gleam in his eyes.

"WHO WAS ON THE PHONE earlier?" I asked, as we quickly re-assembled our clothing and hurried to leave the cottage. We'd idled away too much of the day as it was. The weeklong party ended the following morning, and we still hadn't nailed down the suspect. We needed to get out and mingle.

"My mother."

I paused in the adjustment of my knee-high socks and looked up. "Are you serious?"

"Only-child responsibilities," he said with a boyish grin, despite rubbing his head as if fending off a headache. "I adore her, but if I don't take the call, she'll just keep calling. I keep a burner phone for a variety of purposes, though not usually familial. But since we haven't left the country and have the security of the room, I let her have the number. She knows what I do for a living, though she doesn't approve, seeing as how we…"

"Don't need the money?" I asked.

Graham shrugged. "You'd think we never see each other, but she visits every month or two. She's in a community for seniors down in Devon. She gets around alright but prefers the company of people her own age and she has a few friends in that area. My father passed away several years ago. It's just the two of us now."

I scrunched my lips, digesting all the information. "What else do you have that I don't know about?"

"You've already seen it all, except my gun. The anti-bugging equipment, one burner, one gun, for safety. And, of course, I smuggled in a bag of tricks to keep you in line. I couldn't rely on the toys they'd provide here. Not with a girl as wild as you."

"Well, you are just full of surprises, Graham Kellum. *Cian* Kellum," I corrected, standing.

"Call me that in the future and I'll address you as Ms. Volkov. You won't like what I intend when we use that name."

"Is that so?" I asked, grinning. Teasing, I reached under my skirt and slid my panties down. *The party could wait a few more minutes.* When my underwear hit the floor, I stepped out, shaking my ass and biting my lip. Graham raised his eyebrows, eyes dancing with mischief, heat.

The power I had over this man. He knew we were late and he'd already been sated. But one hint at an offering and he abandoned any plans other than devouring *me.*

"Just one of many games I intend to play," he said, crossing the room to grab my hips forcefully. He spun me around and bent me over the bed.

I turned my head to the side, gasping as he lifted my skirt. "And why do I think all the games are going to end with my backside sore?"

"Amongst other places…" he rasped, touching between my legs to imply a more intimate punishment.

"You… wouldn't…" I breathed, eyes wide.

"You have no idea what I plan to do to this little pussy, Ms. Volkov."

Graham grabbed my mound as he said it and I cried out, whimpering with shameless lust. The next thing I knew, he'd removed his pants and positioned himself at my entrance.

"Would you like me to fuck you, Ms. Volkov?" Graham asked, grasping my hips tightly.

"*Yes, sir, yes,*" I panted. *Jesus,* we were going at each other like bunnies.

"What a naughty little girl you are. You'll have to be punished later tonight for your disgraceful behavior. I think the cane is in order."

I groaned, half with displeasure, half with desire.

Thrusting into me, Graham said, "Or perhaps I'll get the strap to give your pussy just a taste of what's in store for the future."

I practically came right then.

AFTER DINNER, GRAHAM AND I watched the guests from one side of the room, pausing in our heavy mingling and conversing over the grand finale meal. Our last dinner was a knock-out, showcasing a potato-leek soup topped with goat cheese, medium rare filets, more side dishes than I could sample, and a summer pudding with fresh berries and cream. My appetite had returned in full. In fact, I was ravenous from all the fucking we'd done over the last twenty-four hours.

"I don't want you alone with Victor," Graham ordered, keeping his eyes on the man from across the dining room.

I rolled my eyes. "I know you don't trust him, but–"

"I don't trust anyone," Graham cut me off. "But especially not him."

"I'm telling you," I whispered. "Angus is hiding something. No one is naturally that nice."

As we sipped after-dinner cordials, Angus stood by the door, nervously telling a story to a group of submissives dressed as little girls. It was like he was trying too hard to impress. Someone suggested a nighttime stroll and several guests decided to join in. The weather was lovely and the sky, clear and bright. It was a new moon. *Perfect for stargazing,* someone had mentioned.

We should join them, we really *should,* I thought. But Graham's hand squeezing my bottom underneath my plaid skirt told me he had plans that couldn't wait. *We'd be quick. Just a short diversion and then, back to work.*

CHAPTER 37

QUICK MEANT SWEATY. Graham's muscles glistened with a pleasing sheen, having done most of the work as we coupled.

"I need a shower," he said. "Just a rinse and we'll get back to it."

It meant work, but I couldn't help but fast-forward to imagining other things, later. In the worst-case scenario, if we didn't determine with certainty our suspect by the last day, we'd at least eliminate some of the party's attendees. Through days and nights of clever questioning, Graham and I were positive there was no guest involvement and that narrowed the field considerably. EI6 could tail Victor and Angus for the next few weeks; even a junior agent could do it.

"Okay," I sighed, contented from my place on the couch. We never made it to the bedroom, which was fine by me. I wanted Graham in every room of the bungalow, and later that night, maybe outside on the patio.

I heard the shower start from his bathroom and I imagined water dripping down Graham's hard, slick body. I wasn't planning on joining him, but I couldn't help it that my feet carried me into his bedroom, hungry just to *look* at him.

In the near-darkness, a muted, eerie light emanated from the top of his dresser. Cocking my head, I realized it was Graham's burner phone, half buried in his black bag. The light went out… then abruptly went back on.

I paused as the light faded once more. Then, for a third time, it flashed again.

I moved before I even realized I'd made the decision, fishing through Graham's bag to grab the phone. Some otherworldly force pushed my legs, an intuition raised my arms.

A message slid down from the top of his phone. There was just a long string of numbers, no name.

> A redhead? This one better be hot!

> Don't worry about the last leg of the journey, we're too remote. I'll arrange transport.

An uneasy feeling bloomed in my gut. I stared, wide-eyed at the phone. For a moment, nothing happened, and then a third text flashed on the screen.

> And what you've already paid is more than enough for me to attract additional attention. The new pics will have parties with deep pockets lining up for a go.

My hands began to shake.

Paid? For a go at a redhead?

Oh god. Oh god. No. *No, please, no.*

I covered my mouth, horrified.

It's Graham.

The pain in my stomach was so harsh and sudden that I doubled-over, ready to be sick. It was as if I'd received a swift kick; I couldn't breathe.

Graham is the trafficker.

And he is going to sell me.

Oh god.

Do something! Do something, Poppy!

I tried to unlock his phone to call ODX, but I didn't know the passcode and my hands shook so much I could barely press any numbers.

911, I thought. That would work even if the phone was locked, wouldn't it? But no! We weren't in America and British phones weren't programmed for 911. *Shit, shit, shit. What was I supposed to dial?*

I covered my mouth to hide the whimper.

Please, don't let this be real. Please tell me this isn't happening. Not Graham.

I needed to escape. To find a phone, another person, *something.* As if in a trance, I dropped the burner into his bag. I jerked my head toward the shower, listening, making sure I could still hear water run.

Back away slowly, Poppy. Remember your training. Just keep breathing. Don't make any sudden—

From behind the bathroom door, the water shut off and fear shot up my spine.

Not now, please no.

Involuntarily, I squealed.

The gun, I remembered. Digging through Graham's bag, my hands clasped around the weapon he'd mentioned. A Glock, I realized, recalling my training.

I heard the shower door swing shut.

Not yet. Please.

Once more I dug through Graham's bag, tossing aside rope and strange plastic toys, until I found a pair of handcuffs just as he opened the bathroom door, towel tied around his waist.

I swung the gun, leveling it at his chest.

"Don't move."

Shit. It didn't come out at all as fierce, as I'd intended. I was crying. I hadn't even realized I was crying, hard.

"Poppy," Graham exclaimed, voice thick with worry, brow furrowed.

How dare he? How dare he act like he cared?

"Don't you *dare* try to talk your way out of this." I tossed the handcuffs onto the bed. My hands shook so badly, they barely made it.

"P—put these on. *Now.* Attach them to the bed. Just because… because I'm crying doesn't mean I won't shoot."

Graham didn't move. He studied me, head cocked, licking his lips.

Don't think I'll do it? I will. I will.

Would I?

My heart hammered too loudly; my blood rushed in my ears.

Finally, Graham scooped up the handcuffs, eyes on me. He sat on the bed and put one wrist through the cuff, hooking the other onto the canopy's post. That's not what I meant and he knew it. I wanted both hands cuffed. But it would have to do.

"Now can we talk?" he asked cautiously. As if he worried about *me* when he should be worrying about himself, when *I* held the gun.

"I saw your texts. I know what you're planning." My declaration fell upon the room like a bomb, leaving deep, unnatural silence in its wake.

Graham's mouth twitched; his eyes searched my face.

"I see that you're angry. I can explain."

I whimpered, squeezing my eyes shut.

It was true. I didn't know what I expected but… some miracle, some explanation. Something to make this all not be real.

Oh god, I need to get out of here. My whole body shook. *That won't do. Stay calm. Remember your training.*

But nothing in my training prepared me for this.

For my own partner to be the trafficker.

The partner I fell in love with.

Who planned to traffic *me.*

I gulped, fighting back more tears.

"I should have told you. I planned to tell you. I thought, when we left here… I thought you might want to. That you'd be interested…"

I gagged, audibly. "Are you serious? Are you fucking serious?"

What the fuck was he saying? Did Graham really believe that… *what?* Because I enjoyed submitting to him, I'd want to… become a sex slave? Join a ring of trafficked women?

I was definitely going to be sick. My heart thumped so fast I thought it would burst. I held one hand over it as if that would steady its beat. God, I *believed* him. That stupid story about talking to his *mother?*

"I should have known," I spat. "You *told* me. You said *'I'm not the good guy.'* Maybe… maybe I should just shoot you now."

"Poppy. There are no bullets in that gun."

"Liar!"

"Check the magazine."

Why would he say that? Obviously, there were, or else he wouldn't have agreed to handcuff himself.

"You're just… trying to distract me so you can escape!"

"Where am I going to go? I can get out of these handcuffs, yes, but it will take some time."

Fumbling, hands shaking, I tried to release the magazine to check for ammunition.

"Ah, no, not like that–"

"Shut up, shut up!" I cried.

Finally, the release clicked and I pulled down the magazine to see emptiness. Narrowing my eyes, confused, I pushed it back into place, as if it would do some good.

"You're… tricking me somehow…" I mumbled.

"Well, you haven't checked the chamber yet. But I assure you, you'll find it empty as well."

Right. Dammit. How did I open that up again?

"Poppy. Please. Talk to me. No, not the base, pull the frame–"

"Shut up!" I cried, sliding the top of the gun back to reveal…

…no bullet in the ejection port.

"This is a trick! Some kind of augmented EI6 weaponry that hides the round, until it… it… reads a special fingerprint," I babbled, "and releases a bullet from a secret compartment…"

"That's a feasible design," Graham said, matter-of-fact. "But not on a weapon of this size."

What the fuck was happening? Graham was right. The gun wasn't loaded. I didn't understand any of this and it hurt *so much*. My wretched sob cut across the room as I started bawling. I wasn't even pointing the gun at Graham, I'd covered my face instead.

"Why, Graham? Why?" I cried. With effort, I yanked my hands away and forced myself to look at him.

He said nothing, just stared at me, looking pained. *What right did* he *have to look pained?*

"Poppy…" he finally croaked.

I couldn't take it.

With another sob, I threw the gun and ran out of the room.

CHAPTER 38

DAY SIX–EVENING

I NEEDED A PHONE. If I could just make it to a phone somewhere inside the castle, I could call ODX. *Fuck,* not that I even remembered how to dial out of the country.

First, I needed to clean up my face. I couldn't blow our cover. *My* cover. Graham was the enemy. Roughly, I swiped at my cheeks with the back of my hand. Maybe I just looked like any other chastised sub. *Yes, that's it, that's what I'd pretend if I ran into anyone.* I'd just been punished, that's all.

Calm down, Poppy. Breathe. Remember to breathe…

Goddammit! It was Graham's voice in my head, reminding me to breathe. He was in too deep. I clutched at the flesh over my heart. It burned as if hell itself blazed within. My fingers curled, clenching, nails digging, as if I could reach inside and rip out my heart, rip away the pain.

Pain later, Poppy. Save it for later. Get through the next few minutes and then you can cry.

I inhaled a long, deep breath, blinking away the last of my tears. Straightening my back, I forced my wobbly legs to carry me forward and across the wide lawn. I slipped through the back doors of the castle, hoping everyone was still strolling about the gardens.

"Klara," I heard a voice call, and I spun in its direction.

Natalie stood at the end of the hall. *Oh, thank god.* I stumbled toward her.

"Natalie, I–can I use your phone?"

"Sure, it's in my room. I've got to tell you something anyway!" she said, waving me to follow her deeper into the wing of the castle set aside for management. I scurried to keep up with her long strides.

"Natalie, I–I need to use your phone."

"Hmm? Yes, it's in my room. I've got something to tell you that you're not going to *believe.* Where's your Dom, by the way?"

Get the cell, get the cell, I repeated in my head, barely processing her words.

"Klara. Where's Graham?"

"Oh, he's…" *Why was I out without my Dom in the first place?*

"We had a fight," I said, mixing truth in with the lie. "He went to sleep and I snuck out. I… needed air."

There. That would explain any obvious distress on my face.

We walked down corridors of the castle previously off-limits, until we reached a tiny room at the end of a long hall. When she opened the door, I realized it was Natalie's bedroom.

"Klara," she whispered, gushing with excitement. "I've got something to tell you!" Bending her head to mine, Natalie said, "I've been invited to a secret party. And you're not going to believe this–I have to pack tonight!"

The hair on my arms stood on end.

"Me! Out of all these girls. It's finally happening. I'm going to meet someone Klara, I just know it. No more being stuck in this dreary castle, catering to rich people. I'm going to meet someone wealthy and it's bye-bye rain and hello sunshine!"

My stomach began to knot. "Natalie, where is this secret party?"

"It's on a yacht!"

"But *where?*"

"Oh, um… I think Morocco? I can't remember, the port of departure hasn't been finalized because they're waiting for all the RSVPs or something like that. To make travel easiest for everyone. Plus, I can't reveal the location to anyone anyway, it's a very secretive, exclusive party. Isn't it exciting, Klara?"

Oh god.

My stomach dropped and my vision swam, making the room spin.

Natalie was being recruited as a sex slave.

"Natalie," I began, then stopped, folding my lips between my teeth. What could I safely say? What *should* I say?

"Who invited you to this party?"

"A friend of Angus's. Why?"

I blinked. *Angus? Was I right all along and Angus was the suspect? So how was Graham involved? Was Graham working with Angus? Was that why he always defended him—to throw me off the trail?* But no… I'd never seen them share so much as a sidelong glance, and Graham had been with me all day and night. Plus Natalie wasn't a redhead. Something wasn't adding up.

Natalie scurried about the room, tossing her hairbrush, a scarf, and a makeup kit into her bag. Why was she moving so quickly? This didn't make any sense. My mind felt slow, sluggish, as if I waded through a river of mud to reach clarity on the other side.

"Who… who's hosting this party?" I asked, standing between Natalie and her bag, trying to slow her down. "I mean, do you know them? Do you really think you should go?"

"Why ever *not?*"

"To be… safe."

Natalie barked a laugh, smoothing back her dark, glossy hair. "It's plenty safe. I love Morocco and if not there, I know I'll adore a fancy yacht in any port. Plus, they've already said there's going to be other girls there as well. All the girls are going to meet on the yacht first."

Oh god, oh god.

"Stop, Natalie, listen to me. Don't go," I begged.

"Klara? What's gotten into you? It's just a party. Are you xenophobic or something?"

"No, not at all." My hands clamped around her wrists, but she yanked them away.

Natalie narrowed her eyes. "Are you jealous? Because I've been asked? That's it, isn't it? All the beautiful girls here and it's plain old Natalie that's been invited to the party."

"No, no!" I insisted.

Natalie folded her arms, scowling. "Well I'm going. I only wanted to tell you because I thought you'd be happy for me. I thought we were friends. I can see that I was mistaken." Natalie zipped up her bag. Was she leaving *this instant?* Didn't it seem suspicious to her that she had to abandon everything suddenly? Was she so desperate to escape her life that she didn't care?

What should I do?

"Wait!" I cried, grasping her hands again, but she pulled away once more.

"I don't have time. I have to leave tonight. I'm sure Victor and Angus can get along fine without me."

No, no, no. I couldn't let her go. I'd never live with myself.

"Natalie, stop, please, listen," I pled, blocking the door. I took a deep breath. "You can't go to this party. It's not what you think."

Natalie folded her arms again, giving me a half eye roll.

"Please," I whispered, reaching out to hold her shoulders. *I was going to blow my cover. But only to save her. Saving lives was what brought me here in the first place.*

"Please listen to me but don't say a word to anyone."

Natalie frowned. "Klara, you're scaring me."

"I'm sorry. But I need you to know. That party isn't what you think it is. They're not just going to give you champagne and sail around the sea. Whoever is hosting this is planning on kidnapping you. For human trafficking. *Sex* trafficking. I'm so sorry."

Natalie made a face somewhere between a grimace and disbelief. "Sex… trafficking?"

"But… you can help us. I work with the U.S. Government. You can trust me. If you can help me find the traffickers, we can shut down this ring and save hundreds, maybe thousands of girls. Please, Natalie. Can you point me to the man who invited you to this party?"

Natalie backed away. "You're lying," she said.

I licked my lips, shaking my head. "I'm not. I'm so sorry. But you're safe now. As long as you don't run off to wherever and get on that boat, you're safe."

Natalie kept backing up. When she neared her nightstand, she reached underneath and pulled out something that had been secured below.

She raised her hands and it took me a horrible half-second to realize she held a gun.

A Beretta. Abnormally extended by the silencer screwed onto the muzzle. I recognized it from my training.

"What are you doing?" I asked, freezing, gut clenching.

"Saving my future."

"Stop." I was confused as to why she had a gun, why she thought she needed it to stop me from stopping her. *What could I say to make her understand?* "Natalie, you can't mean to get on that boat. They're going to hurt you. Steal you. Make you do terrible things."

"No. They won't."

"Natalie, you have to trust me. Please. I'm with the U.S. Government and I'm here to help you."

"How can I trust you, Klara, when you've been lying to me?"

"Only because I'm here to help," I argued. "You can help too. Please."

"Oh, I intend to help. Myself. My business. As usual, it's up to me."

"Your what? What are you talking about?"

"Klara, you're so naïve, I don't understand how you managed to make it this far, but I intend to find out. Because you're going to tell me everything. *Everything.* And then we'll decide your fate."

I *was* naïve, willfully naïve. Because the words she spoke started to make sense enough that horror crept up my spine, but part of me refused to accept what they meant.

"Natalie, are you… working for the traffickers? Are they blackmailing you or something?"

It happened in cases sometimes, I thought. Loved ones were used as leverage. We had an incident last year where a son and a daughter had been kidnapped in order to force a high-ranking official to disclose classified information, and he'd given up everything he knew. My mind raced; I clung to the desperate idea that Natalie had a secret daughter somewhere, and if she didn't help the traffickers, they'd hurt her child. That she *had* to do what she was doing.

"No, I'm not *helping* anyone," she said it with such anger that I breathed a sigh of relief. "God, you're daft. I'm not working *for* anyone. Well, not here anyway."

"No..." I whispered, not wanting it to be true. Natalie looked indignant, as if I'd insulted her.

And what the hell did Graham have to do with any of this?

Oh god, oh god, oh fucking fuck. Everything Graham had said was right. My concern for trying to save Natalie had been the very reason I compromised my cover. *Shit, I was a fool.*

"But... why?"

Natalie ignored my question. She narrowed her eyes. "Raise your right hand. Do it. Now."

I gulped, slowly raising my hand. Natalie pointed the gun at it. "I'm going to ask you some questions. If you lie to me, you lose a hand, got it?"

I nodded, fighting back tears.

"Are you here alone? Think carefully about how much you value your hand before answering."

I *didn't* think before answering. That was the most incredible part.

"Yes," I whispered, nodding—before I even realized what her asking the question meant.

Graham isn't working with her.

She doesn't know he's with me.

Graham can't *be involved.*

…Then what was he confessing for?

I didn't understand what it all meant, or why. But deep down, my instinct was to protect him, despite not comprehending. From that point on, protecting Graham was the only thing that mattered.

"Your Dom isn't aware of what you're doing here?"

I affected a scowl, remembering Graham's advice to distract, to provide a false lead. "No, I don't like him very much. He… he hurts me in ways I'd rather forget. I wanted a new Dom, someone easier. But I couldn't draw attention to myself."

Natalie cocked her head, considering. "Yes, you did seem very reluctant to obey him. What is your real name and how did you find out about us in the first place? Are you CIA or something else? You don't seem like an agent."

"I–I'm not. I don't know who recruited me." The lie fell easily off my tongue. I told the story as I made it up, mixing truth with lies. "My name is Poppy. I work as an admin for a healthcare company. Someone approached me. They'd searched private databases and records to find a girl who was a match for Klara. I was mad, I *am* mad, that our government illegally violated privacy laws like that. But… I wanted the money they offered for the job."

I looked down, as if ashamed, trying not to cringe as I half-expected a bullet to shatter my hand at any moment. I didn't even know where the story came from, maybe all the years voraciously tearing through books made it easy to tell a tale.

I looked up, letting my fear show freely, honestly. "Why are you doing this? It's… evil. Don't you feel bad for the women you're condemning to this, this horrible fate? Think about it."

Natalie huffed. "I *have* thought about it. I'm not *doing* anything, anything everyone else doesn't already do. If you don't think greatness is consistently built on anything *but* the backs of the unfortunate, then you're more naïve than I thought. *You* think about it. Who sews the very clothes on your back? Assembles the plastic gadgets you use daily in your car or your kitchen or your phone? Do you even *know?"* she laughed, once, throaty. "Is it child labor? Modern indentured servitude? Others suffer for your benefit every day and you don't call it evil. It's just the way it's been done since the dawn of time. Every empire from the Romans to the British."

Holy shit, she'd justified her actions so profoundly in her own mind, I could tell there was no empathizing.

Natalie shook her head, stepping closer. "Every great endeavor achieved its greatness through the misery of others and it's still going on and we all look the other way. Why is that okay on a grand scale? But I find a smaller-scale, personal way to do it for my own benefit and *that's* evil? *Why?* Seems fucking hypocritical to me. Seems like what I'm doing isn't nearly as bad."

I didn't know what to say. There was no point. She'd worked herself into intractable rationalization, going so far as to not only see her actions as *not evil,* but almost *good,* compared to other injustices in the world. I *wasn't* so naïve to think I could change her mind. The only thing I could do was protect Graham and maybe… maybe save myself if the opportunity came.

"So you sell women for the money?" I whispered, wanting to keep her talking.

"It's the way of the world, Poppy, and you know it. Just like you said. Why did you come here in the first place? For the money."

I blinked. *Holy shit.* That wasn't true at all but what a lucky lie I'd picked. It was something she could relate to.

"Now you have two choices, Poppy. I can kill you. Or *you* can get on that boat."

Kill me now, I thought. *I'd rather die than surrender to that hideous fate.*

But another voice spoke in my head. It was Graham's voice, from that day on the mat when he'd pinned me.

Live to fight another day.

The lump in my throat made it difficult to speak. I swallowed.

"I–I…" A choked sob cut me off before I whispered, "I'll get on the boat."

"Good girl," Natalie said, turning my stomach sour at her use of the phrase I'd heard so often on Graham's lips. "I knew you could be an obedient slave. And you look so young. How old are you really?"

"Twenty-four," I croaked.

"From now on you're nineteen, just like Klara. Turn around," Natalie commanded.

Slowly, I did as she bid.

"Hands behind your back. Don't try anything stupid unless you want to die."

With my heart pounding in my ears, I put my hands behind me and felt Natalie secure them in some leather bondage device I couldn't see. I knew she struggled to hold the gun while binding me, but I didn't have enough training to trust that I could make a quick and clean attack against her. It was as if I heard Graham again in my head.

Don't do anything unwise. Live to fight another day.

Roughly, she spun me back around.

"Please," I begged, tears pricking my eyes.

"Open your mouth," she said, unmoved.

I parted my lips just slightly and she yanked my mouth wider. Natalie shoved a ball gag into it and secured it around the back of my head. The tears I struggled to hold flowed freely.

"There's an empty cottage in the woods, about two or three kilometers from here. I've got a car on at the far end of the grounds. You'll walk there *quietly.*" She said it as if I could shout with a gag in my mouth. "If you try to run, I'll shoot your kneecaps. Damaged goods meet even less kind fates where you're going, I can promise you that. Now, move."

CHAPTER 39

I DON'T KNOW HOW I made my feet move; bound, gagged, through the darkness of a night blacker than any night I knew under the continuous lights of D.C. The new moon, perfect for stargazing, also made the perfect cover for Natalie. No glimmer of light, of hope, shining down that someone would see us. I had no way to brace myself if I fell, and every errant rock and tree root became a threat.

Less so than the one pointed at me, the gun Natalie held as she bid me deeper into that strange wood.

At least my lies protected Graham.

That was my only consolation. I'd hold onto it forever if I had to. It was all I had now, but it was everything. If Natalie suspected Graham… if she'd burst into our room and found him handcuffed… would she have shot him?

I was a *fool* to suspect him. That was something else I'd hold onto forever—my regret. I had no *idea* what he was talking about with his text messages. But I should have listened. He was right. I never listened. And when it mattered, I couldn't say that *he* didn't listen to *me.*

God, Graham, if I make it out of this somehow, I swear I won't make the same mistakes.

At least you're safe, handcuffed back in our room.

When Natalie and I reached the edge of the woods encircling the castle, we came upon her battered, old Ford, parked beside a weathered shed. She forced me in through the driver's side and over, so that she could keep the gun pointed on me. It was unnecessary; I couldn't get very far if I tried to run. When the engine turned, it was so loud and out-of-tune that my heart leapt, thinking someone might hear. But then, I hadn't seen anything or anyone else in the area.

Natalie drove slowly, with one hand on the wheel and the other on the gun, but it didn't take long to reach our destination. I spied the abandoned cottage and started shaking. *Was someone waiting in there already?* The structure rose two stories above the ground. All of the windows were missing and either open to the air or hastily boarded up. On one side, the ground worked to reclaim the building; ivy and other vines climbed up the stone, burying a quarter of it. The back of the house faced the forest and the front was partially obscured by a small hill with tall bushes and weeds.

At Natalie's prodding, I stumbled forward, crossing the threshold. She entered behind me and moved about the room, lighting candles she must have intentionally scattered beforehand. As a soft glow filled the space I realized the interior of the cottage had been maintained a bit more than the exterior. Not so much as to be called clean or modern, but enough that it was obvious she utilized the building from time to time.

I was going to be sick.

How many girls had she forced here? To begin a journey into horror?

"GET COMFORTABLE, IT'S GOING TO be awhile. We've got an hour before your transport arrives. If you have to pee..." Natalie trailed off, shrugging. She'd deposited me into a pitiful pile in the corner, while she sat on the chair, casually aiming the gun in my direction.

There was a noise at the door and I screamed beneath the ball gag, but it only came out like a muted grunt. Natalie jumped to her feet.

Victor. Standing in the doorway, eyes scanning the room.

"What are you two playing at?" he asked with suspicion.

Help, I thought. *Help me.*

Natalie was quiet for a moment. "How did you find us?" she asked.

"I saw you taking her to the car, tied up, and I followed you. What game is this? Is her Dom here?"

Please stop asking questions and help me!

"Listen, Victor, I need you to understand something and I need you to keep an open mind," Natalie spoke cautiously, like she was afraid he'd react badly and that made *me* start to panic more. "There are places that pay a premium for girls like this. Someone... someone is coming to collect her. She's going to disappear; she won't be a problem anymore. In return, we'll receive some money. Money we can use to help keep Wistlock. Or we can use it to disappear ourselves. Just you and me. I've been saving it. A few more girls, a few more years, and we can do whatever we want with it. Do you really want to cater to these rich assholes for the rest of your life or do you want to take the next step up? This is it, this is the way up. *Together.*"

Holy shit. It dawned on me that Natalie might be in love with Victor.

Victor's tongue ran along the base of his teeth, his eyes narrowed. "Are you saying you're going to sell her?"

"Yes," Natalie said, breathing a hopeful sigh. "But only so that we can make a better life for ourselves."

Please! I thought, wildly. *Help me!*

"Where is she headed?"

"Does it matter?" Natalie asked, softly.

Victor smushed his lips, pursing them out in thought. For a moment, he wore that distorted expression, before finally concluding, "I suppose not."

My stomach sank and I started to cry again. I didn't realize Victor's eyes on me until a few seconds passed.

"You know… there's no reason not to have fun with her before she goes… wherever she goes. It's probably best to break her in anyway."

Natalie struggled to keep her face even. The corners of her lips turned down into a hard frown, but she said, "Go right ahead."

No. I shot to my feet.

"Bend over the table, girl." Victor's voice crooned seductively, as if offering me a good time.

No, no, no. I shook my head rapidly and pressed myself into the corner, fighting the panic that threatened to take over, to cause me to swoon.

Natalie raised her gun to my head, smiling, though it didn't touch her eyes.

"Victor's in charge and we want to have a little fun with you first. Someday you might be grateful he broke you in. I doubt many men like him will fuck you where you're going. Show some appreciation."

Victor charged and I tried shrinking into myself as if I could disappear, feeling the tears leak from my eyes and onto the gag. Roughly, he grabbed my shoulder and yanked me forward. Pushing me ahead, Victor forced me over the splintered, old table in the center of the room, while I screamed beneath my gag.

"Don't, no!" I begged, but my words were lost, muffled. Not that he'd heed them anyway.

"Do you have rope?" he asked. "Toss me the rope."

I heard the shuffle behind me as Natalie located rope, and Victor worked the rough cord around my neck, pinning my head down onto the table. It choked my throat, making me gasp and sputter and even that wasn't enough. I felt Victor's hands on my thighs, spreading them and tying them to opposite table legs. My heart *screamed* in agony. It was a horror, a grotesque inversion of everything Graham had done to me, everything that I wanted him to do that night he belted me. I struggled not to vomit into my gag.

Victor paused, as if savoring his erotic conquest. Just the thought of him touching me made bile rise in my throat again. I swallowed it back, fearing that with the rope so tight around my neck and gag in my mouth, I'd choke on it.

Victor lifted my skirt and tore off my panties. I didn't want to give him the pleasure of my cries, but I couldn't stop them when I felt the air on my exposed sex, defenseless against him. There were no words to describe the height of my fear. Victor paused, savoring the moment again, I assumed. I screwed my eyes shut and waited for the worst.

Natalie came forward and stroked my hair. I didn't think she did it to soothe me, but out of jealousy to be a part of the act with the man she desired.

I felt Victor's calloused hand caress my rear. "Shh…" he whispered. "You shake like a scared little animal. Don't worry. I'm going to mount you and you're going to like it. You'll see."

God, please, no.

I heard a zipper fall.

Victor pressed closer.

I couldn't stop the violent shaking. I squeezed my eyes shut tighter, trying to prevent myself from crying–

Bang!

I jumped and screamed at the unmistakable sound of a gunshot ringing through the cottage. I immediately cried harder as my muddled mind thought I'd been shot and braced for the pain, or death. At the same time I realized agony wasn't forthcoming, my brain registered the sound of Victor's grunt.

"No!" Natalie screamed.

I couldn't comprehend what was happening. My fear was like an ocean churning over my head, making me struggle to hear or see, as if the voices, the light, filtered through dark, rushing waters. But Natalie moved quickly, pushing the hard muzzle of the gun against my temple.

Graham? My heart leapt at the prospect. *Was he here?*

My head faced away from the door and I didn't dare turn it with the barrel of a gun so close.

"Shoot me and I shoot her," Natalie ground out, before a whimper tore through her whole body, causing her hand to shake, once, and making me wonder if she would accidentally pull the trigger.

"I didn't shoot to kill. He's alive." It was Graham's voice. Low, steady.

Graham! My heart leapt again. *I'm so sorry.*

"He will die, though, if you don't get him to a hospital quickly. If you shoot her, I shoot you, and then he won't make it on time."

Oh god. Hope and despair warred within me. *Please help me,* I thought, at the same time as: *Please go! Run! Far away from here.*

I couldn't stand the thought of having dragged Graham into danger.

"And if I don't? You'll send me to prison for the rest of my life. I should have known you were working with her." She shoved the barrel of the gun harder against my head. I tried to focus on their voices, but I was distracted by that hard metal threatening to end my life at any second.

"No. I can make you a deal."

"MI6 will be all over this place in no time, I know how you work. You're all so fucking self-righteous, so—"

"I'm not MI6. Neither is she. You let her go, I let you go."

"Ha!" Natalie spat, sounding maniacal. I squealed, tensing against the shot I feared at any moment. "I just walk away, you think I'll believe that?"

"No, I can't let you just walk away. I shut you down. You tell me the people you work with and we go after them. Your information in exchange for your life."

"You mean *her* life in exchange for my life."

"Both."

"And his? You'll call an ambulance? Say it was… what? Some drive-by attempted murder?"

"Whatever story you want to go with. Just put the gun down. I can get you out of the country. Him as well. You can't stay here; the authorities were already looking for you anyway. If whoever you're working with suspects you've been compromised, I'm guessing they'll likely kill you themselves. I'm your only way out. This can end in bloodshed, or this can end with your toes in the sand on the Bahamian hideaway of your choice. Think carefully. But think quickly. He doesn't have much time."

I wished I could turn my head. I wanted to *see* Graham. If my life ended now, I wanted to at least see him first.

"Who are you then, that you'd let me go?"

"An agency that's comfortable operating in the gray zone. An agency that understands that you have to make compromises to get what you want. An agency willing to bend the rules. Just like you, Natalie."

"*Shit,*" Natalie swore. I could hear her anxious breathing. In the heavy silence filling the room, it felt like the very walls of the cottage itself sucked in a deep, bated breath, waiting to see what would happen. I blinked and more tears fell onto the rickety, old table.

After a torturous, infinite pause, Natalie demanded, "You get me out tonight. In exchange for her life and my information. I want enough money to live like royalty. He goes to the hospital and you send him to me as soon as he's well."

Graham replied with a voice low and firm, "Done."

The blunt press of the gun's barrel disappeared from my head. With a *clunk,* I heard Natalie discard the weapon on the table next to me.

Unbelievably, a gunshot rang through the air again and I screamed beneath my gag, certain it meant my demise. When I realized I was still alive, I couldn't stop screaming. Because instead, Natalie slumped to the ground underneath me—with a bullet in her head. Her eyes stared up, frozen in death.

"Poppy!"

Graham called my name but the sound came from faraway again, like my head had been plunged back under the ocean. I felt him cut at the ropes and untie my gag, freeing me. Shaking and crying, I collapsed limply into Graham's arms.

"Poppy, are you hurt? Are you hurt?"

I shook my head. *"No!"* I cried so pitifully it might as well have been *"yes."*

My mind lost control of my limbs, as if I were drunk. My head lolled back, trying to look at Graham, to ensure he was really there. All the fear that built up through the course of the night had nowhere to go. The untapped fight-or-flight response, needing direction, seemed to course through my veins, weakening me, like I'd been injected with a drug.

Is this shock? I wondered.

Then I blacked out.

I AWOKE IN GRAHAM'S ARMS and all the horror came rushing back, making me gasp. I couldn't have been out for more than a minute. We were still alone in the cottage. I curled into Graham, throwing my arms around his neck, crying.

"I'm sorry," I sobbed.

"Shh…" he said, holding me tighter, rocking me. We were both on the floor and he had me half in his lap. Graham's strong, safe arms wrapped around my torso. "I've called EI6, they'll be here soon. I need you to think, Poppy. Is someone coming for you? Was Natalie to meet anyone here?"

"I, um, yes. But, oh god, not for a while. An hour, maybe?"

I felt Graham nod. "Good, that's good. EI6 will be here first. We'll set up a sting."

"How—how did you find me?"

"There's a locator in your collar. I told you never to take it off."

Instinctively, my hands flew to the metal ring around my neck. *All this time I thought Graham was being extra-dominant. And, in a way, he was.* But he'd done it to protect me. Of course, without telling me.

"It took me a bit of time to get out of those handcuffs," Graham explained. "By the time I turned on the tracker, you were moving. Too fast to be walking. I borrowed Angus's car and followed you here."

"You… You killed her. Is he dead too? Are they dead? Oh god, oh god."

"Shh… you're in shock."

Was I? Is that why I couldn't stop shaking? I felt very funny, both chilled and feverish at the same time. My head pounded with an all-over ache.

"He'll be fine, better than he deserves. Take this," Graham said, holding up something small.

"What is it?"

"Just a light sedative. I grabbed the entire medical kit, not knowing what I'd find. It will help calm you down."

"I don't want to calm down, I have questions, I–I–"

"For once in your life, Poppy, listen to me. Open your mouth."

It was his dominant tone. I obeyed, parting my lips and swallowing the little white pill with difficulty. I didn't have any water and my mouth was a desert; it took several attempts for me to even gather enough saliva to get it down.

"Victor... he's–he's... alive?" I whispered, hoarsely. "But y–you killed her. She put down her gun but you killed her."

I gazed at up Graham's pitiless blue-gray eyes, unsure what to feel.

"The only reason Victor is still alive is because I needed him for leverage in the moment, and the only reason he continues his tenuous hold on life is because I think he'll be more miserable spending several long years in prison on a host of charges we can and will add to those of which he's already guilty."

Graham's voice dropped an octave, cold. "I didn't need her as leverage."

"But she... has the information, the contacts."

Graham stroked my hair and planted a soft kiss on my sweaty brow. "Feinberg's back at EI6 headquarters, he's a technology wiz. We're working on her electronic trail and we've already got people headed to her room to comb her things. We'll find out who she was working with. The next man up the chain will be a lot more valuable than she'll ever be."

"But you, you made a deal and you *killed* her."

"I wasn't taking any chances with you in the room and the gun within her reach." I felt the rise-and-fall of Graham's chest as he took one heavy breath. The hand cradling my head clutched harder. "I told you. I'm not the good guy."

CHAPTER 40

GOOD, BAD, WHATEVER *he was, Graham was mine. And I was his.* By some miracle, I found the man I loved. In the very man I hated. Or thought I hated.

We were in a nondescript, brick safe house somewhere in Devizes, a small village in Wiltshire. Graham refused to leave my side for debriefing, so we rode along with several other members of EI6, whose names I couldn't remember and whose faces I was sure I'd forget.

They'd quickly whisked us away from the abandoned cottage so that British Intelligence could quietly set up their sting operation. They planned on capturing alive whoever Natalie had contacted to collect the newly-promised girl.

Despite my insistence on being fine, once we made it to the safe house, men and women kept examining me, and I was shocked to discover I suffered physical marks I didn't even feel. My chest was crisscrossed with deep scratches from the table, my wrists and neck were bruised, and my legs had been cut from god-only-knew-what on my forest hike. Thankfully, it didn't look like anything would scar. Thankfully, Graham arrived before anything worse happened.

In the modest upstairs bathroom, Graham helped me wash up and change into a t-shirt and sweatpants someone had brought. He changed as well—somewhere along the line the blood from my cuts seeped through my shirt and onto his crisp, white one.

Only after tucking me under a quilt did Graham sit for questioning, on the bed where I lay, dozing in and out of sleep at random intervals and for irregular periods of time. Between my exhaustion and the sedative, I completely ignored the three men crowded into the room with us.

It remained dark when I woke once more, and Graham and I were finally alone.

It was only then that I remembered the metal collar still ringing my neck. *My protection, my lifeline.* Graham had either forgotten to unlock it or felt safer leaving it on, for the time being. Stroking it, I felt the circle emblazoned with the initials *AR*.

"You—you said this was your friend Archie's collar." I spoke suddenly into the darkness and felt Graham's hands begin to move, to caress me in response. Sometime during my sleep, he'd wrapped himself behind me. "The man whose place you took. You said you didn't have time to change the letters, but you had time to embed a tracking device?"

"I had to make it look realistic," Graham said.

I wondered what he meant. "Realistic to me, that you'd made an unplanned, last-minute entry? Or realistic to the event organizers?"

"Both," he replied. "I'm sorry I didn't tell you. I'll try to be better about telling you things like that in the future."

I practically snorted. "No, you won't."

"Well. I'll *try.*"

"Then what the hell were you talking about when I hand-cuffed you? It doesn't make any sense. Why did you pretend to be the trafficker? You confessed!"

"I didn't."

"I saw your text messages Graham. About bringing a redhead to some remote location and pictures and money you paid!"

Graham nuzzled his beard against my cheek as he spoke into my ear. "I overpaid my friend in Greece for a priority stay at his place. The one you and I discussed on the patio. Then I set him up with better marketing for the rental. It's on a remote island, as I mentioned, so he needs more professional shots to attract attention. I put him in touch with a company that records drone footage, produces videos from the air, that sort of thing. I had hoped you'd accompany me when the mission was complete. I might have... intended to... persuade you, one way or another."

"You mean manipulate me."

"Let's just say, with your increasingly unnerving ability to guess my intentions, I could understand your anger. You do have a temper, my dear. The gun was a bit much, I thought. But you were so obviously upset beyond anything I'd seen, I decided it best to play along and decrease the odds that you'd hurt one or both of us."

A potent cocktail of shame and regret roiled within me. I covered my face, speaking through my hands. "I'm sorry. I'm so sorry, Graham. I–I made everything worse."

Gently, Graham lowered my hands, holding them firmly by my chest.

"If you hadn't done what you did, we wouldn't have found our suspect. Your empathy *is* a liability, I stand by that claim. I promise you won't be seeing field work ever again. But in this case, it worked like a double-edged sword. Natalie already suspected you. I'm guessing that just as Intelligence had been tipped off about the party, someone may have alerted her to the potential attention she'd attracted. She used your compassion to entrap you; it worked to make you unknowing bait."

I groaned. "Great. So by my foolishness, I stumbled backwards into trouble and landed our man. Or in this case, woman."

"You can see why you need me to manage you," Graham mock-scolded, his breath hot against my ear. Even now, even in a situation like *this,* it made goosebumps rise down my neck.

"We were both wrong about Victor and Angus, though," I pointed out.

"Yes and no. Victor certainly was up for going along with the activity, once he was made aware of it, so I was right to think he had it in him. And Angus was hiding something, you were right about that."

"What do you mean?"

"It appears Wistlock is massively in debt. It's a costly endeavor, keeping a property of that size afloat. And I have a feeling we'll find out Natalie was helping herself to some of the funds. Angus understood the direness of their situation and was anxiously working to find new investors. Likely, he also wanted to make up for Victor's off-putting nature with the guests. Victor, it seems, didn't care much about Wistlock *or* Natalie."

For one ridiculous second, I almost felt bad for Natalie, who was probably in love with Victor all this time. But then I remembered everything she'd done to god-only-knew how many women. And what she'd almost done to me.

"What will happen to Wistlock?" I asked.

"The authorities will shut them down for what Victor and Natalie tried to do to you."

"But Angus is innocent. He doesn't deserve to lose his castle. Couldn't you help him, Graham? Couldn't you partner with him? Be the investor he's looking for and help transform the castle back to its full glory? Oh! You could use it for a good cause… to help the victims of trafficking somehow…"

"I'll look into their financials," Graham said, slowly. "But if I help, it will be for business, *not* charity."

"Well," I protested. "It *is* where we got together. You don't want to see such an important historic site like that mismanaged, do you?"

His words were harsh, but I could hear the smile in his voice when he asked, "Why do I have the feeling you're going to push me on this forever if I don't help save that castle?"

Forever? *Would we have forever now?*

"Thank you," I whispered, turning serious. "Thank you, Graham, for saving my life."

"Show me," he teased.

I let out a soft laugh. "How?"

"I can think of many ways. For now, come to Greece with me. We'll have a week to recover here, back at my house. You can debrief Carter virtually. The least he can do is give you time off. We'll fly out the following week."

My heart thudded against my chest. I almost couldn't believe any of this was true.

"Graham," I whispered. "I want to tell you something and I want you to just listen. Okay? Don't–don't laugh or anything. There's a quote by Edith Wharton and I want to share it with you."

I took a deep breath and recited the words I'd committed to heart.

"I have sometimes thought that a woman's nature is like a great house full of rooms: there is the hall, through which everyone passes in going in and out; the drawing-room, where one receives formal visits; the sitting-room, where the members of the family come and go as they list; but beyond that, far beyond, are other rooms, the handles of whose doors perhaps are never turned; no one knows the way to them, no one knows whither they lead; and in the innermost room, the holy of holies, the soul sits alone and waits for a footstep that never comes."

I licked my lips, steeling myself.

"All my life, I've been waiting in that room, alone. Waiting to hear a footstep. And I finally have. And it's yours. It's you, Graham."

My voice cracked as I tried not to cry. "I've been so, so *untouched*. Not physically, of course, but I mean… my soul. I began to think no one would ever set foot inside that room. That no one would ever knock, or even find the door. And then you came along."

Despite my efforts, I started sniffling. "You just sauntered right into my innermost room and made yourself comfortable, I–I couldn't remove you if I wanted to."

I licked the tear that reached my lips, tasting salt. "You're what I want, Graham. You've made a home in the room of my soul. You *own* it. It's mine but… it's yours too. To, to… adorn as you see fit. I want you to. I want us to share it, to share everything. I want everything with you. Everything or nothing. Whatever you decide."

The rough brush of Graham's stubble pressed against the side of my face once more.

"May I speak?" he asked.

I nodded.

"Poppy, I could never put it as you just did. But if you think you own anything less than my soul, you don't understand the power you've had over me since…" Graham broke off, sucking in a breath, "almost since I first saw you."

"When you watched me bend down in that skirt and wanted to dominate me, first thing?" I teased.

"Lucky me. Little did I even know at the time how much you needed it. I told you. I've never met anyone who needed a good, hard strapping more than you, Poppy."

"And you're just the man to give it to me?"

"You bet your ass I am," he growled into my ear.

EPILOGUE

GRAHAM

GOD, SHE WAS beautiful. I couldn't take my eyes off her.

Poppy splashed in the surf, bottle of rum in one hand. The *entire* bottle. Flavored with peach or mango or some other horrendous infusion, sure to give her a hangover if she drank too much.

I wouldn't let that happen. Not just because she'd regret it in the morning, but I didn't want her too intoxicated for what was to come.

Poppy danced and twirled like she listened to music I couldn't hear.

At the moment, I was grinning at what she couldn't see.

What she didn't know.

"Poppy," I called, letting my voice drip with warning and relishing the way all of her being instantly responded, halting and turning to me cautiously.

"Come here."

She came. Sandy and dripping and curious.

WE'D ONLY JUST ARRIVED AT the house the night before and had done nothing more than fuck —hasty, rough. Poppy fell asleep and I read until midnight, watching her chest peacefully rise and fall.

She didn't do that before—sleep easily, tranquilly. In the week between the Wistlock mission and our trip, her body relaxed more each night. She fell asleep faster, and her small hands always found me—either the neck of my shirt, if I wore one to sleep, or the muscles of my bicep. She'd curl her fingers around whatever hold came readily and drift off.

I arranged for her to start at EI6 next month. After our holiday, we'd fly to D.C. together and pack up her things. Carter wasn't happy about her sudden departure, to an agency outside the country no less, but I'd negotiated our dual-consultancy without strings for the next six months, as well as more transparency between our operations, indefinitely. Which was the direction we were headed anyway, but I could have made things more difficult.

Negotiating Poppy into the manse proved the trickier task. She had notions of running around London with all the independence of the young and newly emigrated. Sharing a flat with other girls, bar hopping until midnight.

I thought she'd be swayed when she saw the estate.

"I never even set foot outside the country and now you want to whisk me away and cage me? To hide me from… what? City boys with dirty minds?" she teased.

I was going to have to do it the way I would have to do everything with Poppy.

I grabbed her waist hard enough to command her

attention, reached under her skirt, and pushed my fingers into her without waiting to see if she was ready.

Poppy moaned before I even spoke.

"I'm sorry, my love," I growled in her ear, continuing to probe in and out. "Did you say you wanted to *defy* me?"

"I... I...not fair..." she moaned, head rolling back.

"What happens to naughty little girls who disobey commands?"

Poppy began rocking forward as I moved my fingers faster. I could feel the win, literally, within my grasp.

"Do you want me to stop? Or are you going to live here like a good little girl?"

"O...kay," she breathed, before she lost the ability to speak—other than to cry out *oh, sir, don't stop, don't stop.*

After she shuddered the last of her orgasm into my hands, Poppy spun around alarmingly fast.

"I resent being manipulated," she scowled.

"Best get accustomed," I replied.

"REMOVE YOUR TOP, PLEASE," I instructed as she approached my chair.

Her eyes rounded and she bit her lip, looking nervously to the left and right, down the long expanse of secluded beach.

There'd be no one here. I'd bought out the island, but I didn't let her know that just yet. The hint of the threat, that someone might have rented the house on the other side, was just enough to make her squirm, make her quick to obey. After the public nature of that party, I didn't want to share her with anyone ever again.

"Here?" she asked.

She knew better.

I raised my eyebrows and watched her reach for the strings of her bikini. I was already hard, but it would have to wait. Her two pert breasts spilled forth when she dropped the white bikini top onto the sand beside my chair. Poppy shifted her weight from foot-to-foot. She knew what was coming next, but dare not mention it, hoping I'd be merciful.

She should know better.

"Your bottoms, too, Poppy."

She groaned at the command even as she wiggled, telling me everything I needed to know.

She loved the battle of wills. Even if she almost always lost—*because* she almost always lost.

Testing my patience, as usual, Poppy slowly brought her bikini bottoms down to her feet and stepped out of them. Like a child, she closed her eyes to hide.

"Look at me, Poppy."

So many times I'd commanded it and she still needed the reminder.

"Or do you need a spanking here on the beach?"

Not only did her eyes open, she shook her head vigorously.

I crooked my finger, beckoning her closer. She moved, as if on strings, sending a rush to my head with her obedience.

Her nipples danced hard before me, so I pulled her lower and took one salty tip in my mouth. I heard Poppy gasp, felt her arch into the pleasure of my slightly-hard bite. After a moment, I released her with a *popping* sound, watching her face for the disappointment I knew would cross her features.

But I had something *much* better in mind.

"Take a swim," I said, patting her sexy bottom in that authoritative manner I knew she hated-but-loved. "I'll watch.

And then, we should have another cocktail. I'll mix up something special for when you're done."

My little minx flashed a seductive smile and sauntered to the water completely naked. I wasn't sure who I tortured more—my cock strained against the denial. *God, she was beautiful.* But I liked to think patience was one of my best assets. Without a long game, I'd have never won Poppy in the first place.

Fuck, though. It would be delectable to take her now. Not to mention, her bottom was entirely too pale, a blank canvas just begging to be reddened with the paddle I packed. If I hadn't left it up in our bedroom, I might not be able to resist.

There was always tomorrow for a nice beach spanking.

From the house, we'd brought down a little cooler with wine, vodka, several mixers, and Poppy's hideously flavored rum. I'd planned for afternoon drinks on the beach, and later, we'd cook together. Maybe the tuna already stocked in the refrigerator or something else from the week's supply.

I wouldn't be allowing Poppy to wear much today. Likely nothing at all.

Except for one item, of course.

From the sea, Poppy looked back to me and I beckoned her once more with the crook of my finger. She emerged from the water like Aphrodite, long copper waves dripping down her bare breasts, sparse hair between her legs slick, wet, inviting.

From my pocket, I withdrew the only other item she'd be wearing. I hoped.

The Mediterranean sun caught the diamond as it moved, igniting a light within and shining it back out in shimmering beams.

I watched Poppy's face as she approached. This was how I wanted her at this moment.

Bare to me. Glistening. Obedient.

Rapturous when she saw it.

God, she was fucking stunning. Clever. Kind. And mine. She didn't seem to understand that *I* was the lucky one.

Her mouth dropped.

If her heart thudded even half as much as mine, we were going to be very happy together.

THE END

ABOUT THE AUTHOR

Una spends her free time reveling in fantasy. Nothing snaps her attention like a dominant male in single-minded pursuit of a headstrong female—except when those same lovers initially despise one another. She reads and writes these angst-filled pairings (and their happy endings) from the East Coast of the U.S.

Romance? Dark. Characters? Gray. Cheeks? Flushed pink as you read, I hope.

Didn't Austen say something like, "It is a truth universally acknowledged, that a dominant man in possession of a powerful will, must be in want of a brat." (Or did I get that wrong? ;)